TERI TERRY

BLACK NIGHT FALLING

Book 3 of The Circle Trilogy

Hodder
Children's
Books

HODDER CHILDREN'S BOOKS

First published in Great Britain in 2022 by Hodder & Stoughton

1 3 5 7 9 10 8 6 4 2

A CIP catalogue record for this book
is available from the British Library.

ISBN 978 1 444 95509 5

Typeset in Bembo Schoolbook by Avon DataSet Ltd,
Alcester, Warwickshire

Printed and bound in Great Britain by Clays Ltd, Elcograf S.p.A

The paper and board used in this book
are made from wood from responsible sources.

Hodder Children's Books
An imprint of Hachette Children's Group
Part of Hodder & Stoughton Limited
Carmelite House
50 Victoria Embankment
London, EC4Y 0DZ

An Hachette UK Company
www.hachette.co.uk

www.hachettechildrens.co.uk

For all those who chase the fish:

resistance is never futile

I had a dream, which was not all a dream.
The bright sun was extinguish'd, and the stars
Did wander darkling in the eternal space,
Rayless, and pathless, and the icy earth
Swung blind and blackening in the moonless air . . .

Lord Byron, July 1816
The year without a summer

Prologue

London 1941

'It's too soon, she's not ready,' Mam says, but they ignore her and push me into the sickroom. My nose wrinkles at the smell – a mix of sickly sweet and foul, like something dead and rotting.

But Alicia's eyes are still open. 'It is what it is, and what it must be,' she says, her voice a bare whisper. 'Come closer, child,' she says, and when I don't move, one of the aunties pushes me forwards.

Her cold hand – a circle of bone – grasps my wrist.

'Leave us now,' Alicia says and they go, even my mam. When the door shuts I want to run after her, but I'm so scared I can't move.

'Cassandra, don't be afraid. The Circle must be complete before it is too late. Now you have to concentrate. On the four: say the words with me.'

She starts and I join in, my voice faltering at first, then stronger as I focus on each word and what it represents in turn:

Sun . . . Sea . . . Earth . . . Sky . . .

Sun . . . Sea . . . Earth . . . Sky . . .

As we say the words again and again, the others begin to join us – past, present, future – voices that I've learned are different to my own, but that I can sometimes hear, whispering inside me. Today they are louder than whispers and somehow fill me with calm, acceptance. This is what must be.

'Good. Now take the circle.' Alicia gestures to a table next to her, something wrapped in red velvet. I unfold it and inside is a ring of shiny metal bigger than my hand. I pick it up and cry out as the sharp edges cut my fingers, but I can't let go – I mustn't, the voices say, and the pain dims. Alicia grasps the other side of the circle in her hand and her hand is cut, too. Then she holds it up to her throat, taking my hand with it, and when I see what she means to do it is too late to try to stop it. She slides it across her neck and *red, red* gushes from the wound, pulsing with her heart. Warm and wet, it runs down my hand and arm.

Her blood, my blood, the blood of all our sisters back in time.

Everything they have been, lost and suffered is flooding from her to me with her blood. The *pain*, the *terror*, of so many lives slamming inside me, all at once – they push and shove to get to me before her blood drains away.

She slumps back. She's gone from her body but whispering inside me now with the others. I focus on her words – **Sun** . . . **Sea** . . . **Earth** . . . **Sky** – to still their shouts and cries, and gradually I steady inside. I'm as surprised as if I'd somehow brought a bucking stallion under control.

All that has been, is now and will be is spinning around, with me at the centre of all the circles. Different paths lead to different circles, but there is sureness within me as to which will follow, one to another.

Don't, Alicia whispers inside me. **Time is spinning, in flux. Don't follow the thread, lest by looking you influence what will be.** She tries to hold me back, but mesmerised, I follow them: this circle, then that, and another. This war – with its bombs, like the one that ruined Alicia's legs – will end. More will follow.

2

So much pain and sorrow men inflict and will inflict on themselves and each other; it's overwhelming. I could be lost in it and not return. I try to draw back but it's too late. I can't unsee what is before me. Before all of us.

How can this be? The future – it goes silent? I panic and trace back and forth, all possible ways, not just the one I see, but all circles lead to this:

Nature – *screaming* – in the throes of dying. Humanity will do this to the earth and themselves, and then the voices will go silent for ever.

It's *wrong*, and the wrongness is pulling and twisting inside me so, and the fear, the panic, this can't be what must come, it can't, it can't – and then I'm screaming too.

Some small part of me is aware when the aunties return, tend to my hand and carry me away from this place. Where Alicia died and I wish I had done so.

Much later, I revive enough to eat, to splash water on my face. When I look in the mirror, my hair has gone pure white, like Alicia's was.

But what does it matter?

The end has begun.

Part 1
Undersea

Tabby

@HaydenNoPlanetB

When Industria United injected chemicals into the atmosphere to shield the earth from the sun, they said this would reduce global warming – that it would stop the sixth mass extinction, without having to radically change our energy production and use. This is madness. Consider the oceans: more and more carbon is being absorbed into the seas. The acidification that results prevents formation of shells and corals, and if it continues will begin to dissolve existing reefs. A quarter of all marine life is dependent on coral – they will be gone for ever if we don't act now.

#NatureIsScreaming

1

The wild sea is so close, tantalising me, offering a way out. How easy it would be to let everything end *now*, a time and place of my own choosing.

I'm half-dead from their drugs already, and the temptation to finish the job and rob them of their prize is there. But there are too many of them and only one of me; even if I could bring myself to do it – to jump from this ship into the unknown, the howling storm and darkness – there is no real choice.

One of them opens the door of a small craft fixed to some sort of crane on the deck. They call it a submersible and, from what Malina said earlier, it's like a two-person submarine. It doesn't look like any I've seen on TV – it's small, mostly round. With the door held open now, I see the walls are so thick it is even smaller inside. They steady it and I climb in after Malina as directed, and she shows me how to pull straps down from the top of my seat to cross over on both sides to buckle myself in.

The door is sealed. There are no windows, but external cameras project on a screen. The view shifts wildly as we are lowered from the ship to huge waves that surge and crash around us, throwing us side to side, and I fight against the memory that would take reason with it: the hurricane. Simone – my mother, even though I didn't know her for long – trapped in our car next to me, drowning . . .

Somehow I manage to push it away, to stay here, now.

Once the sea swallows us whole, and we descend from the wind and rain, the maelstrom of the surface is hidden. The currents below are strong enough to make the submersible shudder and shake, but there is still a kind of peace.

After a while, an increasing sense of pressure builds, both outside and in. It's as if the sea and my blood are equal, and the air inside this vessel too thin; either my blood must explode out of my body or the sea will crush the walls. I hold my hands, fingers splayed, against the metal that encloses us – both pressing and being pressed – and my blood thrums, hot, as if it wants to join the sea on the other side. I'm not scared, not even in denial: it's more that the sheer power of the sea we are descending through makes fear or not-fear irrelevant.

'All right, Tabby?' Malina says.

I ignore her, focusing on the power throbbing through my veins and the wall, but then the sound and shape of her voice, beyond the words, penetrates.

Is something wrong?

Keeping my hands on the wall, I turn towards her. She's strapped in next to me, the controls – our lives – in her hands. Her eyes meet mine and I study her. As if that makes her uncomfortable, she soon looks away.

Unflappable Malina – the queen of calm – is nervous. Why?

'You've come this way before?'

'Many times.'

'Is it different now?'

'It's close. The pressure rating of this vessel: we are close and getting closer to its limits.' She shrugs. 'Rising seas give rising

8

pressure, but I'm assured it is still within tolerance.' I'm listening to her words and they give a reasonable cause for her disquiet – but that isn't why she is nervous. It's something else.

What's that? A low sound – eerie – almost outside hearing. Then it increases just a little, then a little more. It's our submersible – it's alive and in pain. We've been swallowed by a beast and are giving it indigestion. It wraps its arms around us tight and protests, groaning.

'You see now why we couldn't bring Isha.'

Isha was one of us at swim school, but in tank training – when we had to hold our breath underwater as long as we could, encased by glass and steel – she flipped out, lost it completely. She was claustrophobic. Imagine what this would have been like for her, inside a small toy tossed and crushed by the currents, the weight of water above increasing every moment?

So they didn't bring Isha, but what about the rest of us? Did anyone survive when the school was destroyed by storm surge? Or are there any others, like Isha, who weren't there when it happened?

Like me.

And Denzi.

I ran; I left him behind, lying still and motionless on the beach. The anguish of not knowing if he is alive or dead is tearing me apart. And what did I achieve? Nothing. They caught me anyhow. But there is no use asking Malina what happened to Denzi. I have already, many times, and she always refuses to answer.

Thrum.

The pressure increases inside me and outside the ship until, surely, we will implode and explode – both at once.

Throb.

It's like being born, or so I imagine it must be – *blood, pressure, pain.* Just when I might scream from it, I sense rather than see that we have reached the end.

Malina steers us towards what looks like a gaping black mouth – a nothingness, only distinguishable by being even darker than its barely-seen surrounds. We go through it and after a few moments she puts on lights – like the front headlights of a car, but weak in the dark water. Further in we go, and then the water moves; we sway. The opening we came through is closing behind us.

Malina explained this before our descent. We go through a succession of locks – like canal boats go through to get to higher or lower water levels – but here it is the water pressure that changes. Pumps in each chamber make the pressure step down with each stage. The pounding in my head eases with each one.

We stop in the last chamber, wait as water is pumped out of it and replaced by air. Then lights come on above.

Malina opens the doors of our vessel.

Instead of death, we are reborn.

2

We step out on a rocky platform, to a space not much bigger than our submersible. Rough rock walls drip with seawater; the air tastes of rotting seaweed. The ceiling above is too regular to be a natural cave – was it carved out of living rock? It's damp and cold.

'This way,' Malina says and gestures to a sort of hatch in the wall. There's a wheel on it; it's tight to turn so she gets me to help her. It finally gives, turns around and around. She pulls on the wheel and a door swings out towards us. It's heavy: must be almost a foot thick, to withstand the pressure when this space is full of water?

We step through the hatch into a short hall and Malina pulls the door shut behind us, turns the wheel on this side to close it tight. We pass through the hall and into a square room at the end. Two women wait for us. One is Elodie, Simone's mother, my grandmother. Even though I'd been almost sure she was in The Circle, there is still a stab of disappointment to see her here, as one of them. She'd been pretending to care for me when all along she was hiding who and what she really was. When I meet her eyes, she must see the accusations in mine; she flinches a little, looks away.

The other woman is tiny – maybe five foot – with pure white hair and keen, sharp eyes. I'm sure I've never seen her before, but there is something about her that is familiar without me being able to say just what it is.

She smiles. 'Tabby, child. At last.' There is emotion in her voice. 'I've longed to meet you for so long. I'm Cassandra Penn; Catelyn, who raised you, was my granddaughter. Welcome to Atlantis, the First Circle of Undersea.'

She's Cate's grandmother? It's her eyes – something about the colour, yes, but more the directness of her gaze – that remind me of Cate. Then the rest of what she said sinks in.

'You've called this place Atlantis? *Seriously?*'

'Most legends begin in someone's truth,' she says. 'This is one of ours, and has been for a very long time. Come. There is time for more introductions and refreshments before your initiation begins.'

Initiation? What's that? Before I can ask, the door behind her opens. Ariel comes through.

'Ariel! You're alive?' Relief wars with other emotions inside me as she grins widely and rushes over, grabs me into a hug, and I don't know how to react. We were friends, or so I thought, but she must have lied to me about knowing about the Penrose Clinic, the IVF clinic behind what was done to us. And could it really be her in that CCTV footage, wanted in connection with the Hoover Dam bombings?

Ariel makes it easy; she is, as always, in charge. She links an arm through mine. 'Come on, time for a quick tour.'

I glance back at Malina, my jailor, but she has turned to Cassandra.

'Go if you wish to do so,' Cassandra says. 'But Ariel, you must bring her to the meeting on time.'

12

'Of course,' Ariel says. 'Hurry, we haven't long and there's something you've got to see,' she says to me.

I follow her out the door she came in and down a hall. Before I can ask her anything – how she came to be here, if any of the others survived too – she begins to run, and I keep pace. We go through another door to a narrow passage that slopes up and seems to wind around and around. It's dark but motion lights come on as we go, though we're going so fast that we're almost past them when they do, so the light is mostly behind us. There's a sense of pressure in my blood once again, as if we're getting closer to the water. And then we reach a door with a hatch. I help her unwind it and we step through into what is, at first, darkness. The air is cooler, damp; my eyes adjust, and then . . .

'*Wow*,' I say.

'Told you – you had to see it.'

I walk further into the room. It's round, the ceiling curving upwards to a dome. And above us? The sea. All I can see in its inky depths are faint, moving shimmers – phosphorescence of some sea creatures. Gradually my eyes adjust, and I can see more: dim shapes of fish, squid, jellyfish, tentacles waving in the currents.

'How far down are we?'

'Twilight zone. About three hundred metres here: closer to five hundred below.'

Silvery shapes come closer, look down at us. Dolphins?

Ariel has stayed by the side where the ceiling is lower and they go to her, her hands outstretched against the transparent surface.

'Later,' she says, waves and they swim away.

She turns to me now. 'It's really good to see you,' Ariel says. 'I'm so glad you're all right.' Her words, so heartfelt –

genuine – and despite everything, I feel a rush of happiness to see her again and know she is OK.

'You, too. But you were reported missing after the hurricane? What happened at the school?'

'It's too long a story for now; I'll tell you later. We better go or we'll be late and incur the wrath of Cassandra. Believe me, that is something you don't want to do.'

She pulls the door back open and I blink as the hall lights come on. We wind the hatch door shut, then race back down the sloping passageways – faster this time – but when we get to the end and through the door there, we change to a fast walk.

'Nearly there now,' Ariel says. 'We've all been waiting impatiently for you to join us.'

'We? Who else is here?'

She starts reeling off names from swim school, some familiar, some less so, but she stops too soon. Not enough names. And all girls?

'What happened to the boys? And the rest of the girls?'

'A long story.'

'I know, you'll tell me later.'

She tilts her head to one side. 'Not exactly, but you will know.' A trace of a shadow crosses her eyes but then there are footsteps coming towards us: it's Zara, one of the girls from our swim training group.

'Hi Tabby,' she says, and smiles. 'I'm glad they convinced you to come after all.'

Convinced? They hunted me down, kidnapped me against my will, did something to Denzi. Panic about what happened to him crowds back into my thoughts and I struggle to push it aside, to

14

concentrate on here and now. *Convinced* isn't even close to the right word, and I'm thinking what to say, what not to say, when there are other voices, footsteps – people converging from all directions to where we are.

We go through a door to a large open space. What look like stone benches descend in rows along the sides, down to an open circle at the centre. It reminds me of the Minack Theatre in Cornwall that Cate took me to years ago, but the Minack was open air and cut into cliffs, over the sea. Here the seats go all the way around the stage below, and instead of the sea being below us, it is above. I glance up to what looks a smooth stone roof. The thought of all the weight of rock and then water between us and the sky? Well. As much as I love the sea, it's a strange thing.

Ariel must read my face. 'It gets easier. I've almost stopped thinking about it.'

Women and girls – all ages, including young children – are coming in through doors all around the room, along the wall above the benches. Most go down aisles and sit as they arrive, but there are more of the girls from swim school that Ariel named earlier, standing, chatting, to one side of the stage below. I follow Ariel down the stairs to join them. Soon they are all saying hi like I'm a long-lost friend, even ones I don't really know, like Jess – the girl Denzi thought was using him to try to find me.

Malina comes through the doors, descends to where we stand. 'Seats please, girls,' she says.

I start to follow Ariel and the others, but Malina's light touch on my shoulder tells me to stay with her. Again: something isn't right with her. There's a tension under the surface, behind her usual serene smile.

'What's wrong?'

'Many things which may or may not come to pass. But do not concern yourself.'

Above us, the seats are nearly full now; there are maybe five hundred people here? And although there is the usual chatter and shuffling noises you'd expect from so many settling themselves, in some way they are all looking at me, either directly or sidelong. It's making me feel like a fly caught in a glass.

A door opens above, and movement and conversation cease at once. There is total silence.

3

Cassandra and another woman step into the room. She's familiar, though I can't place her, but— Oh. Is that Ariel's mum, Dr Rose? I saw photos of her online when I was searching for information about the Penrose Clinic: she's one of the founders.

Wait. Didn't Cassandra say her name is Cassandra *Penn*? Penn and Rose: Penrose Clinic.

They seem to be in charge here. If they also founded the clinic, it isn't just connected in some way to The Circle: they are one and the same – they must be. The clinic that made designer sea-loving-swim-addicted babies like me; The Circle that caused disasters and threatens more if the world doesn't act soon on the climate crisis. How does it all fit together?

The two women pass through rows of seats to the open space at the bottom, opposite where I stand with Malina, and walk to the centre.

'Greetings, sisters,' Cassandra says. 'The time of the Chosen is nearly at hand, and the lost one is returned to us. It should be Catelyn to speak for her, but she was banished years ago and cannot come back to us now. In her absence, who will take her place?'

'I will,' Malina says. She motions for me to stay where I am and steps forward.

Cate was banished? Does that mean she was kicked out

17

instead of left? She cannot come back: strange way to word the reality. She died, stabbed while in prison, waiting to stand trial for kidnapping me. Soon after Malina caught me, I asked her if The Circle was involved in Cate's death. She said they weren't, and I believed her when she said it. But that she's not in charge here is clear; maybe they were, and she doesn't know.

I have to find out what happened to Cate. To even think they might have had something to do with her death fills me with rage. If they did, they will pay. I'm so focused on this that I hear what is said next as if from a distance.

'I challenge,' says Dr Rose.

There is a sharp intake of breath all around us that has me back and paying attention. Malina's shoulders stiffen. Is this what she's been worried about?

'On what basis?' Cassandra says.

'Fourfold. First, lost to early observation, her training and allegiances are unknown.'

'We will get to know her and she, us,' Malina says. 'That is not a bar.'

'Perhaps. Second, she broke one of our most fundamental rules by speaking of us to outsiders, requiring interventions we'd rather not have had to make.'

Interventions: my stomach twists, sick to think what they may have done to my friends.

'If she was not schooled by us, how could she know that was wrong?' Malina counters.

'Ignorance is no excuse, but I grant extenuating circumstances. Third, she missed making her promise at the summer solstice, although she did make it after the fact recently.'

'That isn't without precedent.'

'Maybe so.' There is a pause and Dr Rose turns, looks around the room, her eyes seeming to rest on certain women. 'When she finally made her promise, she included a boy. He promised with her.'

The looks of shock all around are so marked – she might have said I promised with an alien from another planet. If today is representative, The Circle is only women and girls. But there are children – where are their fathers?

Cassandra and Malina didn't seem surprised when Dr Rose began her challenge. It was as though they were expecting her to say what she did, and Malina was ready with her answers. Until that last detail. They didn't know Denzi promised with me; how does Dr Rose?

The only other person who knew what we did was Denzi himself. If she somehow found out from him, then . . . Denzi couldn't have died at the beach.

It doesn't mean he's still all right – I doubt he would have told anyone what we did easily – but a flicker of hope burns bright inside me.

'Please adjourn while we consider these challenges,' Cassandra says.

All around us women and girls stand, file out. Silently, but there is something under the surface, reactions I don't understand.

Ariel glances back from the door – meets my eye. Her face is troubled, afraid, and it's like she is trying to say something with her eyes. But then a woman comes behind her, says a few words, and she turns and is gone.

4

Malina takes me to what looks like a small sitting room and tells me to wait until she comes back for me. The door closes behind her.

My head is reeling with everything that has happened – this place, the words that were said. Many of us from swim school somehow survived the hurricane and were brought here. The time of the Chosen – what does that mean? Are we this Chosen she refers to? And Malina was speaking for me – the lost one, according to Cassandra – and then these challenges were made? It's all going around my head and I'm pacing around the sofa and chair and back again, thinking, when there is a light knock at the door.

It opens, but it isn't Malina. It's Elodie.

'Tabby, darling. It's so lovely to see you. Home at last.'

'Home? I don't know this place.'

'You will, very soon. Come, sit. Let's talk.'

I look at her, stay standing.

She sighs. 'I'm sorry, Tabby. I understand that you're angry at me. I was doing the best for you that I could in the circumstances.'

'Could you explain something to me?'

'If I can.'

'You're here – so you're in The Circle, which I'd guessed, anyway. But how does Simone fit into all of this? The Circle did something to my DNA, made me different. Was she in on it, too? And what about Ali, my dad – did he have any say in any of this?'

'Simone wasn't in The Circle. And neither of your parents knew anything about it.'

'But you did. Didn't you? And you didn't tell Simone – your own daughter – the truth about the baby she carried. Me.'

'I couldn't. But know this: she loved you. Ali did, too. Without knowing anything about how special you are.'

I'm blinking, hard. 'I know they did. But The Circle caused the hurricane that killed Simone, and you are part of that.'

'I never wanted that to happen. She shouldn't have been there.'

And she came because of me. It's my fault: that's what she means, isn't it?

The door opens and Malina looks in, hesitates when she sees Elodie. 'Sorry to interrupt. They're ready for you now,' she says, and gestures to me.

'We'll talk again,' Elodie says and leaves.

After the door closes behind her, Malina turns to me. 'Is everything all right?'

Nothing about this place or me being here could be anything approaching *all right*, but I shrug, say nothing.

I follow Malina down the hall to another door. She knocks once, opens it. Inside are Cassandra and Dr Rose, who comes over to me now.

'I'm Dr Seraphina Rose; everyone calls me Phina. I'm chief scientific advisor to The Circle.'

Now that she's closer I can see something of Ariel in her stance, her bone structure. 'Are you Ariel's mother?'

'Yes, I am.'

And what about the girl-fish under the CSME with Ariel's face. Was Ariel twins? Was she your daughter, too? This is what I want to say but I keep it back. She's not someone to mess with – I get that, even on short observation. It was finding that creature in a cage underwater that made me run away the first time: half fish, half girl, breathing underwater, eyes like Ariel's but blank. How could she experiment on her own children? On *any* children. Me and others like me.

'You've already met Cassandra, but I'm guessing not officially? She is an elder and seer of The Circle.'

'Seer? What, like seeing the future?' I say, remembering a dream I had once – that the future voices were all silenced.

'Cassandra, it is obvious how unschooled this girl is,' Phina says.

'She lacks details on our history and organisation but her knowledge and application of the four are sound,' Malina says. 'Besides, the dreaming will deal with any knowledge deficit.'

'But at what risk? She needs to be tested. Many agree with me.'

'I'm aware of your supporters,' Cassandra says, and sighs. 'There is so little time.'

'Then it must be done at once.'

Malina's face – she's alarmed. 'We can't withdraw the blockers until her training is complete.'

'Objection noted and rejected,' Cassandra says.

'I need to reinforce her training—'

'As has been stated, there is no time,' Phina says.

'She's right,' Cassandra says. 'And there is steel in this one.'

She glances at me as she says this. They're all talking about me as if I'm not even in the room.

'Have you seen? Will she prevail?' Malina says to Cassandra.

'I haven't looked and I will not. Do not question me on this any further.'

Malina steps back as if she's been slapped.

'Take her to her room for food and rest,' Cassandra says, and when Malina doesn't move, adds, 'Now. Go.'

5

Sun . . . sea . . . earth . . . sky . . .

'Concentrate on each in turn,' Malina says, but I haven't had anything to eat and this isn't very like rest. 'Please,' she says.

I close my eyes and do it properly.

Sun . . . sea . . . earth . . . sky . . .

Blazing sun, too bright to look upon. Deep endless seas, less known to most than the stars above us. The green and blue of our earth, spinning in the sky, hidden by an abomination: chemicals deliberately injected into the atmosphere to shield us from the sun, geoengineering the sky to reduce the temperature of the planet with no regard for the harm this will cause. Ali – my father – works for Industria United; he was involved in doing this, and thinking about him and what he's done makes me lose concentration.

'Focus,' Malina says, and I try again:

Sun . . . sea . . . earth . . . sky . . .

'Always remember,' she says, 'if ever you feel overwhelmed, return to this. It will keep you safe.' Something very like words Cate often said.

I open my eyes. 'What are you scared of?'

She sighs. 'You are to be tested. Depending on how that goes, you will either be admitted to The Circle, or banished.'

'I don't want to be here, so go on, banish me.'

Malina shakes her head. 'You don't know what that means. You'd be banished to the outer circle of Undersea. You'd never be able to leave.'

'I'm already a prisoner, so what difference would that make?' My anger is spilling out. I try to remind myself of my plan, the only one I could come up with while I remain their prisoner: get to know them, make them trust me, learn their plans and escape. And now I add, find out if they were behind Cate's death. Anger won't help, I know this, but it's in me, on my face and I can't push it away.

'Cassandra said Cate was banished. And she wasn't in whatever this outer circle is.'

'Well, no, but only because we couldn't find her.'

'Until she was in prison. Then you knew where she was. Was The Circle behind Cate's death?'

There is a sound, a change in the air, as the door opens behind me. Malina is looking over my shoulder with wide eyes.

It's Cassandra, with a tray. 'I've brought some supper for you, child. And we need to talk. Leave us,' she says to Malina.

Cassandra settles the tray on a bedside table as Malina leaves. Her careful eyes – kind ones, with shadows I sense more than see behind them – study me, as she sits in the chair across from the bed where I'm perched.

'There is something of Cate in you. The way your eyes flash when you're angry. The defiant look. I miss her so much.'

The real emotion in her voice undoes me.

My head droops in my hands. 'I do, too.' A hand touches my shoulder – a small gesture, but done just as Cate would have done when I was upset. I look up to her eyes. 'I thought Cate

25

was my mum, but she lied to me my whole life. Will you tell me the truth?'

'I will speak truth or stay silent if I cannot – much as she did with you, I'm sure. But choose your questions wisely; there isn't much time.'

'You and Phina keep saying that: there isn't much time. Time for what?'

She tilts her head, looks at me as if her eyes are reading something inside my head. 'There is a crisis in time coming soon,' she says, finally. 'We need you.'

'Why me? And what does that even *mean*?'

'I can't tell you any more yet. You will learn it all if you pass the test.'

'The Penrose Clinic – is that from your names? Cassandra Penn, Seraphina Rose.'

She half rolls her eyes. 'A conceit of Phina's, not mine. Somehow she wanted my name all over what she was doing.'

'So, the science behind what was done to us – that's from Phina?'

'Yes. Very much so. We've been selectively breeding our daughters for many, many generations, but in the usual way – by choosing parents based on characteristics we wanted to enhance or lessen. This was the first time we did this so directly, using precise genetic methods.'

'You said before that Cate was banished. She wasn't, was she? She left – took me – ran away?'

'She was banished in absentia – for just that crime.'

'But why did she do it – do you even know?'

'I can't tell you her story yet. We still have to learn yours.

But I will offer you a truth, unasked. Cate truly was your mother.'

I stare back at her, shocked. I loved Cate as if she was, but she wasn't. All the proof they tried to show me didn't sway me, but then, I remembered. Being small, Simone reading me stories, even my soft toys I remembered from the nursery in Simone and Ali's home. There was no doubt to me at all: they were my parents.

I shake my head. 'I don't believe you. I *remember* Simone.'

'Well, Simone gave birth to you. Cate was your mother, your sister—'

'And my friend. Yes, she often said that. But how can all of these things be true at the same time?'

'There is something of The Circle in your DNA, and it came from Cate.'

I'm frowning, thinking, and trying to make sense of what she is saying. 'So, putting some Circle DNA in me from Cate was part of the genetic engineering that Phina did?'

'Just so. You are one of the Chosen of The Circle; your birth parents were carefully selected to meet certain genetic requirements. DNA from The Circle – Cate, in your case – was substituted in part of the human DNA. In a very real way, you are my great-granddaughter.'

A connection to Cate I can cherish, but what does it mean in a wider sense? I make myself remember all the things The Circle has done. They caused hurricanes on the English south coast and New York that killed thousands – including Simone. Simone loved me so much, even though I barely remembered her; she *was* my birth mother, despite the rest of all this that she knew nothing about. And The Circle's bombs destroyed dams in the US and

27

China and killed even more people, too many to even get my thoughts around, more than I can feel as a real thing because of the scale of it all.

And some of me inside is from *them*? I can't begin to process how I feel about that.

There is recognition, sadness, on Cassandra's face – as if she understands what I'm thinking. That I need time, and may never want to claim her as mine.

'Did you hear what I asked Malina?'

'Yes. I loved Cate, very much. I would never have harmed her. Just as I could never harm you.'

That directness of her gaze reminds me so much of Cate: it makes me want to believe her, but how can I? This organisation has ended so many lives.

'Is there anything else you want to ask?' she says.

'The other stuff that was done to my DNA: why did they do this?'

'We were fairly sure you must have worked out the other addition.'

The *other*, inside me – silenced by the blockers Malina made me take. Not that she knew it – she just meant to silence the voices, the chorus to my life. Always there if I listen to their whispers, sometimes so loud I can't block them out myself. But she didn't know about my other half, inside and always part of me. The one who can call dolphins, who saved my life when Simone drowned by doing just that. *My kin.* Apart from Denzi, I've never said this out loud to anybody, and it's hard to do so now to someone I've just met.

Someone who knows all about it, already. 'Dolphins: DNA

from a dolphin,' I say, finally. 'That's it, isn't it?'

'Yes,' she says, and even though I knew it, it's still a shock to have someone confirm it so calmly.

'But why?'

'That answer I cannot give you until you are in The Circle.'

'I don't want this. Let me go.'

'I'm sorry, child. I felt that way myself, once – so many years ago. Once you join fully with The Circle, you'll understand, as I did. It is part of you anyhow, and will come with you no matter where you go.'

There is no escape. Shivers run up and down my spine. What they are, is inside me? I'm not like them, I'm not. I'd never destroy and kill like they have, and it doesn't matter why they've done it – *why* doesn't take the taint of wrongness away.

'How can you even begin to justify the things The Circle has done?'

'Judge more when you know more. Your knowledge of us is limited, and we have a very long history.'

'Thousands of years, according to those stone tablets found in caves. Was that from The Circle?'

'You found that online?'

I nod.

'Yes. All true. I regretted ruining that archaeologist's career, but it wasn't yet time to risk exposure.' She hesitates. 'Nothing we have done was my decision alone; there are things I would have changed if I could. Yet at the same time, my hands are behind much of it. I can't deny this or stay apart or make excuses. It is what it is.'

'So, The Circle has been around for thousands of years. How

about this place – your Atlantis. You said you have had it for a very long time and it looks really old, but how can it be? That submersible technology can't have been around for long.'

'There are some things our distant ancestors could do of which we have lost knowledge. Creating this place was one of them. But when I was a child, there was another way to come here, using tunnels under the sea. They were destroyed by bombs in the Second World War – accidentally, no one knew they were there. We maintained contact with our sisters here over many years until finally we had the technology – the submersibles and so on – to be able to join them.'

'That war was a long time ago. Does that mean some of you have lived down here all of their lives?'

'Some, yes.'

'How old is Atlantis?'

'We don't know all of our history, or how far back it goes, or when this place was built.'

'The voices – past ones – can't they tell you?'

'In theory. In reality, the further you go back, the fainter and more tenuous the voices become. The strength to go back that far is beyond what we can do – what I can do, at any rate.

'Enough questions for now. Have something to eat and try to sleep; you need your energy for what is to come.'

She gets up, opens the door, looks back.

'I know this is hard for you. Focus on joining The Circle; then you'll understand. And if you disagree with what we have done or will do, argue with us! You are one of the Chosen; we have to listen. Sleep well,' she says and then she is gone.

6

I count down a few minutes after Cassandra is gone then try the door, expecting it to be locked. It opens. I look out into the long corridor we passed through to get here.

Why would they lock it when there's nowhere to go? I'm under the sea and, even assuming I could find a way out, I don't know what the high pressure so far below the surface would do to me. I don't know how to use a submersible even if I could find one.

What next?

I sit back on the bed next to the table where she'd put the tray. Sandwiches – fish, of course. The bread – it's sort of pale green? Some kind of tea that doesn't look like tea as I know it. There are many things to think about, but just now all I can do is remember how long it's been since I've eaten. From what Cassandra said, many of them have been living down here for decades, completely cut off. They must have perfected living off the sea. I take a cautious bite of sandwich and it's like nothing I've ever had before. The bread has a seaweed sort of tang, and there's some interesting spices on the fish. Though weird, it's all good and soon gone.

Everything that has happened since we arrived is spinning through my mind. I don't know quite what I expected to find at the stronghold of The Circle, but somehow, this isn't it. Always

31

trust your instincts – something Cate often said. My instincts are: no matter the things The Circle might have done, Cassandra cares about me.

But that doesn't mean I can trust her. Knowing some of the things they're capable of doing, I can't let my guard down with her, or with any of them. Even if her feelings are genuine, would I come first if there was a clash between me and what The Circle wants? I doubt it.

If Cassandra really cared about me, why kidnap me and bring me here against my will? Why did they go to so much trouble to do so? That I'm part of their plans somehow is plain – and their plans, whatever they are, took precedence over any feelings she has about me.

I thump my head with my hand, dismayed, when I realise I should have asked her about Denzi. She might be like Malina and refuse to answer, but I should have tried. His face fills my mind. How it felt to be close to him. He made me feel safe, in a way I haven't since I was with Cate. Where is he now?

We were on our way to meet with a policeman to tell him about the connection between The Circle and the Penrose Clinic. And The Circle found us, tracked us by the dolphins we love. I should have thought of that – pods of dolphins near the shore always attract attention. Anyhow, Malina told me they'd been tagged and were being tracked in case they led to me.

I make myself remember: every bit of it. How they found the two of us on that beach and we ran for the sea – and then, something happened that made Denzi fall to the ground. He lay still, motionless. And I kept running.

If Denzi is like me, doesn't that mean that he's one of their Chosen? If that is true, why didn't they bring him here with me? Though there don't seem to be any boys in this place.

I sigh, lie back. Face the ceiling. I can't get around the fact that just because it looks like one of them spoke to Denzi at some point about the promise, it doesn't necessarily follow that he's still OK now.

Especially as it came from Phina. I get the definite sense that me being here doesn't seem to be part of her plans. And Ariel is her daughter: has she been in on everything from the start? Did Ariel make friends with me because her mum told her to keep tabs on me? I know Ariel lied to me about Penrose. And that video in the news of a girl wanted in connection with the Hoover Dam bombings in the US – it was Ariel, I'm sure of it. These things make me think she must have been part of The Circle all along.

Ariel seemed to make a special point of being my friend – she really sought me out – and now I'm questioning everything she ever did or said. I lived alone with Cate most of my life, always moving, never staying anywhere long enough to get to know people. Maybe that is why I'm so unsure of Ariel now. I have so little experience of friends: how do I even begin to judge her motives?

Though there was Jago: we met on the beach, one of the last places I stayed with Cate. Apart from Cate, he was my first real friend. He went out of his way to help me when I was running from The Circle; his friends did, too. I don't have any of these doubts about Jago. I know, in my gut, I can trust him.

The other thing I should have asked Cassandra was about this test they say I have to do. Whatever it is, Malina was worried, even scared. Cassandra didn't seem too pleased about it, either, though she said I have steel in me . . . Huh. Not feeling that at the moment.

If I fail, I get banished – effectively imprisoned for ever by the sounds of things. So maybe passing their test and joining The Circle is what I must do to have any chance of finding out who killed Cate and what happened to Denzi, then learning The Circle's secrets and escaping.

I try the tea. It's nice – a bit sweet, spicy, like-but-not-quite-like cinnamon.

I stifle a yawn. I'm weary, right into my bones. I've slept little since Malina caught me and some of the kin in her net in the sea.

At least they're all right, even though I can't sense them any more. She let them go when I agreed to go to her.

Malina argued against stopping my blockers today, said I needed more training. What was it she said when I had the first injection after she caught me? That I was very sick, that the voices were dangerous if I didn't know how to . . . individuate – I think that is the word. She's scared I can't tell myself from the rest of them; she said to focus on the four if I'm feeling overwhelmed.

I lie down, pull the covers over me. It's cold enough to want them here so far under the sea. Above, it has been endlessly hot for so long – that's global warming for you – and it feels good to be warm and cosy under soft blankets.

My eyes are too heavy to stay open any longer.

No more blockers: how long will it take for the voices

to return? For the other half of me to come back, to make me whole again?

Rest . . .

A blue eye inside a spinning circle. The eye is still, staring, the circle shines bright as it spins. Not able to resist, I reach for it. It cuts my hand. Blood — so much blood. Mine, then someone else's?

At first, I'm scared, then . . . centred. In the centre with all the circles around me.

I'm so alone. Despair is gripping and strangling me inside . . .

But then something is tickling, reaching for me. I struggle to push the dream away, to focus. What is it?

Tenuous, at first — wisps, almost there, then gone, then back again. Is it my missing dolphin half coming back to me?

I'm reaching inside myself, searching and seeking and now I'm sure it is there, but rejecting my outstretched hands. And THEN:

All at once, I am whole! We are back, together, belonging to each other, and there is no sense of where one ends and one begins. We are one.

It isn't a great reunion.

RAGE rips through me that is both mine and against me at the same time, so strong it's bruising, incoherent.

Until finally six words are shouted so loud inside me that I flinch:

HOW COULD YOU BRING US HERE?

'It's not my fault.' I think through all that has happened and there is gradual understanding. But, if anything, the anger inside me is more intent, focused, in one place.

It's HER.

'Who?'

An image forms in my mind, of Phina. But she is younger.

She did this to me. To us. And all the rage – and pain – focuses on her. *She is my enemy.*

'Then she is *our* enemy.'

Part 2
London

Hayden

@HaydenNoPlanetB

The threat of fires to the Amazon gets the news coverage, but climate change is just as deadly to the world's largest rainforest. Models predict that a tipping point turning the Amazon from rainforest to savannah could occur at as little as 20% deforestation. One in ten of all known species call the Amazon home – and it is already at over 17%. We must act now.

#NatureIsScreaming

7

Another funeral.

I didn't know her well. Lily Ng was just a half-recognised face and name to me, but I had to be here. No matter how hard it is. I was there when it happened; the car that ploughed into our protest could have hit me, could have hit any of us. Bishan said we must stand together, especially now, just like we do for the climate. And I know he's right.

Numb unreality gives way to *pain*. Rage, too, at what happened to Lily and the other two whose funerals have been and gone over the last week. Each loss is – *deserves* to be – agony in its own right.

But they also take me back to Eva's.

I'd missed that protest – the one where Eva was hurt and later died. I had a dentist appointment. Like dental hygiene is more important than the climate emergency? But Mum insisted and I caved, went to have my teeth cleaned.

If not for that we'd have been together, Eva and me: best friends since we fought over who got the Superman costume at the first day of nursery. It was me who got her involved in climate protests to start with; it's my fault she was there at all. If I'd been with her, maybe that bottle would have hit my skull instead of hers, or maybe I'd have seen it coming and pulled her out of the way. Or perhaps in the way that one small change can influence another, and another, until everything is different – maybe it wouldn't have happened at all.

Bishan, next to me in the church, nudges my shoulder with his, and I meet his dark eyes. He nods, says nothing. He knows how I feel. He feels the same weight of guilt; he led both protests that ended in violence – his arm is still in a cast from getting broken at the first one. I swore to him that it wasn't his fault; he swore to me that it wasn't mine. We were right to protest against climate change, the sixth mass extinction, our stolen futures. Those who stood against us – the mob throwing bottles at the first protest, the driver of the car that ploughed into us at the second – they're the ones who did this. They're to blame, not us.

But it still doesn't *feel* that way. Maybe it never will.

I try to listen to the service, but the words seem to hang in the air without making sense. I can't stop looking at Lily's parents, her little sister. Her mother is sitting bolt upright, so rigid it's like she's not even breathing. Her father has an arm around Lily's crying sister and is whispering something to her.

Until a month ago I'd never been to a funeral; now this is my fourth. There is something inside me that cracks open more with each one. I want to stand up and scream and scream that this isn't real, it can't be; say it loud enough and it'll drown it all out and take it away.

I breathe deep. In, out; in out. Move my glasses just a little down my nose so I'm looking over them and Lily's family disappears in a blur.

But I can still hear her sister crying.

* * *

When it's over, Bishan and I leave to walk to the Tube together.

I scan the sky when we step outside: a uniform greyish-white or whiteish-grey, either way, weird. 'I can't get used to this,' I say, pointing up.

'Dad's been talking about starting some class action against Industria United and the geoengineering coalition.'

'Class action?'

'Yeah. Basically saying that the UN Convention on the Rights of the Child has been breached by taking away clear skies and introducing pollution into the atmosphere.'

'Any point?'

'There's no precedent, so hard to say. Might be worth a try, but they've got bottomless pockets to fund defence. It'd take so long to get through the courts that by the time we get there the climate might have passed enough tipping points that it doesn't matter any more.'

'Maybe they could get an injunction against further geoengineering until the case is resolved?'

'You know about this stuff?'

'My mum is a lawyer too, remember?'

'Oh, yeah.' He winks. My mum and his dad may both be lawyers but what they do is worlds apart and we both know it. His dad wants to save the world; my mum is more about helping the insanely rich stay insanely rich.

'Are you all right?' Bishan says.

'Not really. Glad that was the last one.'

'Amen to that. Are you still coming tomorrow?'

'Of course. How are numbers looking?'

'So-so. More dropouts, though some new names, too. Any word yet from Denzi?'

I shake my head. Too many have left No Planet B because they or their parents are scared there might be more violence, but I know Bishan was hoping Denzi wouldn't be one of them. Having the son of the Home Secretary involved gets us publicity – maybe better police protection, too – but it isn't just that. There's something about Denzi that makes you want him on your side.

'I get that I didn't know Denzi for long, but somehow I think when he joined us after Eva died that he really meant it,' I say. 'He wouldn't just change his mind. Even if he did, he'd tell me, not ignore me.'

'You're worried something has happened to him?'

'Yes. The last time we saw him was at the protest – he went to try to help with the injured, remember? And before that, he was the one who helped get Eva to the paramedics. He's not the sort to just slink away.'

'If he got hurt or something, it'd be in the news, for sure.'

'I guess. I've still got this uneasy feeling that something is wrong, though.'

'Have you checked social?'

'He's on the usual sites, but only now and then. He hasn't posted lately, but that isn't unusual for him.'

'Try his dad, maybe?'

'I have – left a message with an assistant something-or-other. No reply.'

'Are you just a little obsessed with this guy?' Bishan raises an eyebrow and I know what he means, but he's got it wrong.

And is this the moment when I explain why?

No. I just *can't*. Not now, maybe not ever. And anyhow, it doesn't matter what I say or don't say any more.

It's too late.

8

I'm rummaging for chocolate, biscuits, *anything* in Mum's not-very-secret, secret treat drawer when Dad comes in. He taps my shoulder and hands me an apple.

'Organic. Local. Just like you wanted, so why not give it a try?'

I roll my eyes, take a bite.

'How was it?' he says.

'Awful.'

'Funerals aren't usually much fun,' he says, and his eyes hold mine a moment. He'd said I shouldn't feel I had to go if I didn't want to, but didn't try to talk me out of it, either. It's as though we've reached a point where he knows there are some things I have to decide for myself, and part of me loves him for that and part of me is scared, like I'm on a bicycle for the first time and he's not there, running alongside to catch me when I fall. But I can't say stuff like that.

'I meant the apple,' I say. 'When you're thinking chocolate and get apple? It's just all wrong.'

Now he rolls his eyes, takes the apple off me and has a bite, then reaches into his pocket and holds out a bar of my favourite. Not the dark, organic, sustainable kind, but the extra-sweet, tooth-rotting, milky kind. When I reach for it, he waggles it up high.

'I'm proud of you. You know that?' he says.

I blink, hard. 'Yeah. Now give me the chocolate before I kick you in the shins.'

It's late and I should be asleep, but I can't stop thinking about Denzi. Where is he?

I check his social again; no updates. I search his name online, but just find the same things as last time I tried: he wins swimming trophies. He went to some exclusive, expensive boarding school, and was also at swim school for the summer for elite swim training. The school was washed away when the hurricane hit but he wasn't there when it happened. He's seventeen – two years older than me. Only child of Home Secretary Pritchard. Parents divorced when he was a baby. Mum, Leila Klein, lives with her husband in the US.

But this time, something twigs in my memory. Leila Klein: her name is familiar. Why?

I search her: oh, yes. She was high up in Big Green, the umbrella group of environmental groups in the US. It got totally discredited by leaks showing kickbacks from oil companies. Huh. That was the last thing we needed. Big Green didn't start the backlash against environmentalists, The Circle did that, but they fanned the flames for sure. And now Eva is gone, and so are Lily and two others. Still more of us were hurt, like Bishan with his broken arm; others have life changing injuries – one in a wheelchair, another with head injuries so bad they can't talk.

Focus: on the rage. It's the only thing that will stop me from crying again. If this Leila Klein was getting kickbacks, she's part of the problem. But then I see the next link and shock makes me forget my anger. Oliver Klein, journalist – her husband –

found dead in his hotel room, just days ago. Investigations are continuing, but no one else is wanted in connection with his death. That's code for suicide, isn't it? There's a photo of him; he is survived by one daughter. He was distraught over his wife's involvement with the Big Green scandal. They're all but saying he killed himself because of it.

Imagine having to live with *that* – the guilt. It'd be horrific. Even if she did take kickbacks, maybe that is something we have in common.

I search Oliver Klein. There's an outpouring about his death from all kinds of people – politicians, writers, activists. He was involved in Black Lives Matter, and there is a photo of him interviewing the parents of an unarmed black man shot and killed by police – the photo was taken the day before his own death.

Switching to social, comments about Oliver Klein's death are split between disbelief – he'd never have killed himself, it's a cover up, he must have been murdered by a far-right group, and belief – that he did do it, some blaming his wife, others his despair over the continued murder of people of colour by police, that his last interview was the one that pushed him over the edge.

Leila Klein doesn't seem to be on social herself, but there are comments about her all over the place, most not pleasant. Maybe she left because she was being trolled?

That's odd. There's a photo of her taken a day ago, in arrivals at Heathrow. She's in London? Now? Only – I check the dates – nine days after her husband's body was found.

What would be important enough to bring her here?

What *else*: her son, Denzi. It must be.

If I can find her, maybe I'll find him.

46

But how?

I take off my glasses, rub my eyes. I can't think straight any more, not tonight. My head hurts and I'm so tired, and not just because it's late. It's been another day of too much emotion and pain after weeks of the same.

Eva swings from the side of my thoughts, where she always lurks, to centre, and it hurts like being kicked in the gut. I study her, every detail, in my memory. Will this hurt less next week, next month, next year? Will I start to forget things, like that little dimple she had when she smiled, the way her hair was always in her eyes? The cute way she bit her lower lip and turned her head to one side when she was thinking about something. I don't want to forget *anything*, no matter how much it hurts to remember and know that I'll never see her again.

I, Hayden Richards, loved my best friend, Eva Kowalski, and not just as a friend. *I loved her.* There, I've admitted to myself what I've always known, despite how hard I tried to deny it.

Would telling her have been worth the risk of losing her friendship? Could she have felt the same about me?

I'll never know and that is what hurts most of all.

9

I'm on clipboard duty the next evening.

I hand the forms out to the new faces, but there aren't many. There aren't enough of us to even fill all the seats – seats that are usually full, with people sitting on the floor in front and standing behind. The ones who always come, that have stuck with us, are quiet, subdued. I guess a week of funerals will do that.

There's the *tap tap* of a spoon on a mug and what chatter there is dies away.

'Hi everyone,' Bishan says. 'Welcome to this meeting of No Planet B. Thanks for coming tonight. Look, there's no way to get around the pain of what has happened to us. We need to talk about it. We also need to think how we can learn and change to make that kind of violence less likely to happen, or to have less of an impact if it does. But no matter what we do, there will always be a degree of risk in standing up for what we believe in. Don't be too hard on your friends who aren't here. They may come back to us in time. If they don't, they have the right to decide what is best for themselves and their families.

'First up tonight, I've got an important update. Many of you know that I attended a meeting this afternoon with the Metropolitan Police, along with representatives from other London-based environmental groups. The Met say they want to work together with us to prevent more tragedies. It would mean giving them advance notice of our demonstrations and other activities for the purposes of protecting both protestors and the public. This is something we've resisted doing in the past. They assured us that they won't interfere with our reasonable right to protest – whatever that means. They will advise on ways to make us less vulnerable to attacks, including timing and location and so on.

'Any thoughts?'

One of our long-time members waves a hand. 'You can't trust them,' she says. 'We have to do what is right for the planet, not their staffing levels. Some of the best stuff we've done has been spontaneous. It'd put an end to that.'

Someone else is shaking their head. 'Maybe this is the way to get more to come back, new people to join in – make them feel safer?'

It goes back and forth; everyone has an opinion and wants it one way or the other. This isn't going to keep us together – it'll tear us apart. There are already so many groups and factions within groups, even just in London. Ours is one of the biggest lately, but it won't be if we split down the middle.

I wave a hand in the air.

'Quiet, please,' Bishan says. 'Hayden?'

I'm uncomfortable with so many eyes on me and swallow, mouth dry. *You can do it, H* – Eva's voice inside of me.

I push my glasses back up my nose. 'There are some strong opinions here but it doesn't have to be all or nothing, does it? We can choose to cooperate with the police when it suits us. We don't have to do it all the time. If there's a reason we want to do something without warning, we can still do that.'

There are murmurs, nods.

'OK, let's take it to a vote,' Bishan says. 'Show of hands for Hayden's way?' I look around. Most – not all, but most – hands are up.

I hang back at the end, wait as people leave in twos and threes. Until it is just me and Bishan.

'Good one earlier,' he says. 'You should step up more often to say what you think.'

'Thanks, but I dunno about that. I was just worried we'd end up split down the middle and get nothing done.' I hesitate. 'There are so many different groups as it is. Wouldn't we make more of an impact if we all work together?'

'Probably. We've talked a few times about that. No one could ever agree on anything and it kind of fell apart.'

'Typical,' I say, and hesitate. 'Have you got a minute?'

'Of course.'

'It's about Denzi. I was doing searches last night for any news of him and found out that his mum is Leila Klein.'

'That name is familiar, not sure why.'

'She was in Big Green.'

'Oh. Interesting.'

'There's more. Her husband died recently – sounds like it might have been suicide. But I found a snap of her in one of these who's-who photo things online. She's in London, arrived yesterday. And when she got here, it was only nine days since her husband died in the US. I bet it has something to do with Denzi. Why else would she leave home at a time like that?'

'Where was she in London?'

'I don't know. The photo was taken at Heathrow. Can you think of a way we could find her?'

'Maybe try hotels, see if you can work out where she's staying?'

'Like just phone them up and ask if she's there? Wouldn't they think that was weird, be suspicious? Though, maybe I could call and ask to be put through to her. If it's the wrong hotel, they'll say she's not staying there. If it's the right one, they put me through?'

'I'm not sure they'd put you through to a guest unless you know the room number, but they'd probably let you leave a message, so that could work. There's a lot of hotels in London, though. It could take forever. And what if she isn't even staying in London?'

I sigh.

'Need some help?'

I smile. 'Really?'

'You'd owe me a favour. Are you sure?'

'That depends. What sort of favour?'

I need some help getting this lot going again after everything that's happened. I think they'll listen to you.'

'*Me?* Like, talk in front of people? I'm no good at that.'

'How do you know unless you try? But if not, we'll find some other way to get you more involved. Deal?'

'I guess so.' I hear myself saying the words and there's an echo inside – *don't agree to things when you don't know what you're agreeing to*. My mum the lawyer turns up in my head sometimes.

But just like in real life, I mostly ignore her.

10

'I printed a list of hotels in London,' I say, and hold up a stack of pages. 'Then I went through and circled the ones that are mid- to high-price range to try first, as being maybe more likely for someone like her to book from the US.'

'Remind me to get you more involved in logistics,' Bishan says.

I divide the pages into two piles, hand one to him. He rifles through the sheets and whistles. 'OK, hit me: how many hotels are there in London?'

'*Lots.*'

'Out with it.'

'Over fifteen hundred.'

'Ouch. Lucky I get unlimited calls with my phone.'

'Me, too. Let's get started.'

We sit either end of the dining table with our lists, pens.

I hate talking to people I don't know on the phone; I'm not that keen even with ones I do know. It's hard to work out what whoever it is at the other end means when I can't see their face.

But I'm just going to have to do it, aren't I? I listen to Bishan make one call first, then enter the number at the top of my page.

It rings so many times that I'm thinking no one will answer. Just as my finger is inching towards end call, there is a click. 'Good morning, Hilton Hotel, this is Anne. How may I help?'

'Hi, I need to speak to one of your guests, Leila Klein. Can you put me through to her?'

'Just a moment.' There's a pause, then, 'I'm sorry, there's nobody here by that name.'

'Oh, sorry, I must have got the wrong hotel. Bye.'

I put an 'X' through that one and move on.

A few hours on, we've gone through maybe a quarter of the ones I circled and I'm looking for biscuits to go with some tea. 'This is impossible,' I say. 'And boring. I understand if you've had enough.'

'Well, that depends.'

'On?'

'What kind of biscuits have you got?'

I put down the digestives and go into the treat drawer. 'Double chocolate?'

'Oooh, nice.'

It's about three quarters of an hour later when Bishan waves at me from the end of the table. 'Yes, that's right. Can you put me through?'

A pause. 'OK, I see.'

'No, not now, I'll catch her later. Thanks.'

He ends the call with a big grin.

'You found her?'

'Yes! She's staying at the Radisson in Leicester Square. They wouldn't put me through but said I could leave a message. I wasn't sure what to say, so I didn't. Could always call back and do that if you want to?'

'And say, what? Hi, you've never met me, but I'm a friend of

Denzi's and wondered if you could tell me where he is and why he isn't returning messages? She'd probably think I was a nutter. Or a stalker.'

'Yeah, fair enough.'

'I think this needs to be done in person. There probably isn't much point in fronting up at the desk and asking for her – if she asked to not be disturbed, actually being there won't make any difference. But I could go there and watch for her coming or going?'

'It's getting late now. We can give it a try tomorrow?'

'You'll come with me? Thanks, Bishan.'

'We can talk through some other stuff at the same time.'

11

The next morning, I meet Bishan in Leicester Square and we sit on a stone wall opposite the hotel. There are enough people wandering around that we shouldn't be noticed. We study every photo we can find of Leila Klein online, and we watch.

'There is something we need to talk about and here you are, a captive audience,' he says.

'OK. What is it?'

'We need some new faces to galvanise support. Your face for a start.'

'For what?'

'Video messages on social media and interviews, if we can get them.'

'Whoa. Why me? I'm not good at public speaking, and not exactly photogenic either.'

'You can learn – I did. And you are so. You're the girl next door – the one everyone wants to be friends with. And besides, you have a story: Eva.'

I feel something twist in my chest when he says it.

'You want me to talk about Eva? On camera?'

'It's hard, I get that. It really is. But that's the point. A young girl has died, others too. We need to get across why they were there in harm's way, why everyone else should be standing up to the bullies and thugs for all of us now. Hearing from someone directly affected will make people listen.'

And I get it – why he's asking, what it could do. But can I talk about Eva like that? My memories of Eva – my feelings for her – are *mine*, not for sharing.

'I don't know if I can do it.'

'What do you think Eva would say if she were here?'

Go on, H. Her voice is in my head. 'She'd say do it.'

'Just give it a try. And if you're shite at it, or really can't do it, you'll be off the hook.'

'OK. I guess I can try,' I say, reluctance in my voice. It feels wrong somehow to use my feelings for Eva like this. But if it can help our cause – one she believed in – what memorial could be better for her?

'Let's do something now, before you have too much time to think about it. OK? It's just a trial run, so no pressure. I won't use it unless you want me to.'

'All right. But keep your eyes on the hotel at the same time.'

'I will. I promise. Right. So here we go.' He starts recording on his phone, facing the camera. 'Hi. I'm Bishan Khatri of No Planet B, London. I'm here with a friend, Hayden Richards. She's been with NPB from the beginning – she even brought her best friend, Eva Kowalski, to join us.' He turns the camera around to me. 'Hayden, tell me what Eva meant to you.'

Tears are welling up in my eyes. I blink. 'I loved her. We've been friends since we were little kids at nursery. We did everything together.'

'Tell us about Eva.'

'She was smart – top grades at school – and funny. She had a really silly sense of humour. She loved animals and had always particularly loved polar bears since she saw them on a trip when she was six. That's really why she wanted to get involved in climate change protests. We read about how polar bears are interbreeding with grizzly bears as their habitats are changing with global warming. Polar bears might be lost as a species – another casualty of the sixth mass extinction that threatens so many.'

'What do you think about The Circle? Their aims, what they've done?'

'They've killed people; destroyed habitats and animals, too. They say they want to end global warming but they're nothing like us. I don't understand how anyone could think we're like them: we want to protect, not destroy. And now the oil companies and governments have done this horrible thing – using chemicals, like sunscreen on the planet, making the skies dead, grey in the day, black at night. Their geoengineering isn't going to make things better. They're putting tonnes of chemicals in the atmosphere so they can burn even more fossil fuels and say it doesn't matter. But it *does*. They're still poisoning the seas, the whole planet. And it's like The Circle is being used as an excuse to ignore all environmentalists. It's so wrong.'

'Can you talk about the day when Eva was hurt?'

'I missed that protest. My parents made me go to the dentist. I wasn't there when she was hurt, or when she died.'

'What happened to her?'

'You probably saw it on the news. People were yelling terrible things, calling them terrorists. Somebody – they haven't been able to work out who – threw a bottle that hit Eva in the head. Her little brother was there – he's only twelve. He was trying to drag her away from the mob of people to get help. She died later in hospital.' The tears I've been struggling with are on my face now. I hold up a hand, shake my head. Enough.

Bishan puts his phone down, his good arm around my shoulders. I'm fighting to get control, pushing the pain back down for later.

Finally I pull away, wipe my face on my sleeve. 'You've kept watching the hotel, haven't you?'

'Yeah. No sign of Denzi's mum.' He hesitates. 'Do you want to look at this video now?'

'No. Maybe later.'

We take turns watching so one of us can wander off for a walk, stare at our phones, whatever. The hours tick slowly by.

'Maybe she's not staying there any more,' Bishan says. 'Should we try calling again?'

'I'll do it this time so it's a different voice,' I say. I dial the number; speak to reception. Hang up. 'She still doesn't want to be disturbed. Maybe she's sleeping off jet lag and getting room service.' I sigh.

'Sorry, but I'm going to have to go soon,' Bishan says. 'But let's have a look at what we recorded earlier? I edited it a bit when you went for a walk.'

I nod. 'OK. You watch the hotel, I'll watch the video.'

It takes me a moment to psyche myself up enough to press play. And it's hard to watch, hard to hear what I'm saying and what I'm not saying. I said I loved her but nothing about *how* I loved her. I kept that back for me, but is that right? I don't know.

'What do you think?' Bishan says when I hand back his phone.

'It's not totally crap, I guess. Do you think it'll help?'

'I do. It won't stop thugs from being thugs. But so many people seem to be in this frozen state of knowing we have problems, but somehow being unable to stir to do something about it. If it makes them really think about it and what we are doing, maybe even join us, help the cause – that'd be great.'

'OK. Do it.

Bishan grins.

Once he's gone I stay sitting on the wall, thinking. Trying to work out how I feel about that video and talking about Eva like that – taking my private pain and making it something anyone can see. And Bishan said some stuff about maybe doing interviews? The thought makes me feel sick inside.

He'll probably tweet it and whatever, and no one will even notice. And why would anyone want to interview me, anyhow?

Time to go. I get up, stretch, cross the road to the hotel: might as well have one last try. I go up to the reception desk.

'Good afternoon. How may I help you?'

'Hi, could you put a call through for me to one of your guests?'

'Name?'

'I'm Hayden—'

'The guest's name.'

'Oh. Leila Klein.'

He taps on his keyboard, peers at a screen I can't see.

'I'm sorry, she's asked to not be disturbed. Would you like to leave a message?'

If I'm not lucky enough to catch her I'll have to try a message, and a note is better than recording – I can think about what to put in it and how to say it. 'OK. Give me a minute, I'll write a note.'

I take a notebook out of my bag, go to sit on a chair in the lobby.

Chewing the end of the pen – bad habit – I'm frowning at the notepad, thinking what to write, when someone walks towards me. I move my stuff off the chair next to me, thinking they want to sit on it.

'Hi . . . Hayden? I heard you at the desk.'

I look up. A girl, a few years older than me and *everything* more than me: flawless ebony skin, slim and in stuff that says designer and dark sunglasses and she's . . . *perfect*.

She tilts her oval face to one side. 'Is that your name – did I get it wrong?'

I give myself a mental slap. 'Yes, sorry. I am. Hayden, that is.'

'Were you asking for Leila Klein?'

'Uh, yes. Do you know her?'

'Yeah. Tell me what you want and I'll pass it along.'

And I'm thinking, fast, what I should or shouldn't say, and now she's closer, taking off her sunglasses, and I'm noticing more. The telltale signs: red-rimmed eyes. And remembering when I read about Oliver Klein's death: he left one surviving daughter.

'I'm so very sorry about your dad.' The words are out before I have time to think if I should or shouldn't say them.

She blinks hard. 'Who are you?'

'A friend of Denzi's.'

She looks torn between staying and getting away as fast as she can.

'Please. I'm really worried about him. I was hoping Leila might know where he is? Do you?'

She hesitates. 'OK, Hayden. I'm Apple. Come on, let's get a coffee and have a chat. There's a place around the corner.'

12

We find a table in the corner, sit down with our drinks.

'How do you know Denzi?' Apple says.

'From climate protests, with NPB – that's No Planet B, London. There was this kind of riot at a protest in Hyde Park a few weeks ago. My best friend was injured and Denzi tried to help her. She . . . she died. Just hours later.' Having just relived this with Bishan and talking about it again now, the raw emotion hits me hard.

'I'm so sorry. I heard about that – saw some stuff online.' She doesn't say anything else, waits for me to get myself together. I focus on Denzi, get my breathing under control.

'Denzi came to Eva's funeral – that's where I met him. And he got involved in NPB. Came to this other big demonstration we had in honour of Eva's memory.'

'The one where some kids were killed when a car rammed the crowd?'

'Yeah. I haven't seen him since then; he's not answering messages. And I'm really worried. Do you know where he is?'

She hesitates. She looks like she's studying me – does she think what Bishan did, that I've got some sort of crush on Denzi, that I'm stalking him or something? And I can feel a flush rising in my cheeks.

'I know I haven't known him for long but I count him as

a friend,' I say, with emphasis on friend. 'And he's not the kind of person who would just ignore me – not after the way we met. But if anything happened to him, it'd be in the news, wouldn't it?'

'How did you know Leila was here and her hotel?'

'OK, this is going to sound a little crazy.' And I tell her how I saw that photo that was taken at Heathrow, then how Bishan helped me track down the hotel.

'Wow. When you decide to do something, it gets done, doesn't it?' She looks amused rather than freaked. I can see she's thinking, and I don't say anything else.

'OK. I'm going to believe you and trust you,' she says finally. '*Don't* take this to the press.'

'I won't, I promise.'

'He's in hospital, in a secure unit for kids with mental health problems. It's part of a private hospital in Chelsea.'

'What? Seriously?' And I'm thinking of the Denzi I knew, and wondering if he could have been having problems locked away that I didn't know anything about. Sure, it's possible. There was a girl at school like that last year, and no one seemed to know she was struggling until she had a total breakdown. But it doesn't ring true somehow for Denzi.

'I don't think – neither does my stepmom – that he belongs there. She's got a lawyer trying to get him out. She thinks his dad is behind it.'

'But why would Denzi's dad want him locked up like that?'

'I don't really know him. But he's a politician – I don't have great opinions of most of them – and Leila's opinion of him personally is pretty dire. Maybe he wants Denzi kept quiet about

63

something, or kept away from climate protests? I don't know.'

I process that. 'If he's been locked up for taking part in protests, I'm the one who got him involved. But surely not – who'd have their kid locked up over that? Does your stepmum think she can get him out?'

'Yes, assuming some court assigned specialist agrees with her. But it's going to take ages. Especially if people are on a go-slow because of who his dad is. She got in to see Denzi once, but only had a moment alone with him, and they spent most of that talking about what happened with my dad. Now they got an order that she's not allowed to talk to him without medical supervision, so if Denzi knows anything about why he's there he might not be able to tell her.'

'Is helping Denzi why she came over here so soon after . . .'

'After my dad died? Yeah. Well, that's part of it anyhow. The police think it was suicide but Leila and I agree: there's just no way he killed himself. So, who is behind it? There might be some connection with London.'

'What, with Denzi?'

She hesitates. 'Police in London called Leila because someone Dad had spoken to several times was murdered over here. It happened around the same time as Dad's supposed suicide.'

'Ohmygod. Seriously?'

'Yep. So, she was coming anyhow. Wanted to see Denzi when we got here, was told she couldn't, found out why. Looked at Oliver's phone and found he'd been speaking several times to Denzi and didn't tell her, which straight away seems odd. Anyhow, Leila is with the police this afternoon talking to them about all this. Maybe they can help get Denzi out if they want

64

to talk to him— Hang on.' There's a muffled vibration from inside her bag and she fishes out her phone. Glances at the screen and smiles, answers the call.

'Hi Ems.

'Yeah, thanks. I know. Wish you were here, too.

'Look, can I call you back?

'Love you too. Bye.

'Sorry about that. Anyhow, I should get back – I want to be there when Leila returns. Not sure I've reassured you about Denzi being OK, exactly. But not knowing can be so hard, don't you think?'

'Yeah. Unless what you know is worse than anything you can think of.'

'Emmie, who just called – my girlfriend – was in New York when the hurricane hit and I was so scared something had happened to her. Denzi was with us in Washington then, too. There was a girl, Tabby, that he was really worried about from swim school. Last I heard from him she was still missing and he was trying to find her. We don't see each other often, but kind of bonded over both of us worrying about someone.'

'Your *girlfriend*?' The words are out before I can think.

She raises an eyebrow. 'Yeah, got a problem with that?'

'No, of course not.' I'm blinking hard again now, trying to stop my tears. 'Eva. My friend who died. I . . . I loved her, too. And she didn't know.' Apple takes my hand, holds it briefly, lets go. And I'm wondering why I've told her – someone I only just met – something I haven't been able to say to anyone.

'Keeping things inside only makes it hurt more. Believe me, I know. I've got to get back. Are you going to be OK?'

'I think so. Thanks. Is it OK if I tell my friend who was helping me find Leila's hotel and stuff where Denzi is?'

'Sure, if he can keep it to himself. Take my number . . . if you need to talk? And text so I have yours, and I'll let you know if there is any news about Denzi.'

I enter her number with shaking hands. Text: thank you.

'Got it, and you're welcome. Take care.'

And she stands, looks back when she reaches the door, nods, and then goes through.

It takes me a while to get up. I'm going to be late for dinner – again. I'm reeling with feelings so strong – loss, pain – that seem more powerful now I've said it out loud instead of less, so has Apple got that wrong? I want to keep this stuffed down as far inside as it will go.

Slowly I get under control enough to get up, walk across the coffee shop and back out to the street.

My phone beeps. Where are you?? Mum.

Sorry, on my way – be half hour or so.

I rush along to the Tube. People all around me – anonymous faces – what do they hide? Does anyone else have pain gouging into them and still somehow manage to keep one foot going forward after another?

Apple does: she must with her dad only just gone. She's so strong. I wish I were more like her.

13

'Why are you late?'

'Hi Mum. Sorry, I met Bishan. Lost track of time.'

'Dinner has suffered a little.' Dad is bringing out plates.

'You waited for me? Sorry.'

'We need to talk,' Mum says.

I glance at Dad but he's giving nothing away.

'What about?'

'Eat first,' she says.

Overcooked pasta. Garlic bread that has dried out spectacularly. Salad that has been sitting in dressing. Chew, swallow, wonder what it is that they think is so important that it gets put in the we-need-to-talk category? I've only just managed to lock everything back down inside me again; I feel like any little push, one way or the other, would upset the balance and I could fall to pieces, or explode in a rage. I can't even tell which is more likely, or which would be worse.

Mum is telling Dad about some mess at work; Dad is telling her about a new contract, the neighbour's cat digging up flowers. Clink, cutlery. Chew. Swallow.

'You're quiet,' Dad says.

I shrug.

Finally, Mum is clearing up, Dad is making tea and we're moving to sofas but when I reach for the remote a shake of

Mum's head and my hand falls back.

'What have I done this time?'

'Good question.' Mum flips open the cover of her iPad, goes to Twitter, and . . . Oh. It's the video Bishan shot today. 'Why did you do this, Hayden?'

'Well, we thought it'd be a good idea. To show our side of what happened, the impact it has had.' I almost said Bishan but managed to substitute we. Don't want them to get any ideas about him being a bad influence. Or spark off one of Mum's rants about doing things because a boy said to do them. This might have been Bishan's idea but him being a boy has nothing to do with why I agreed. 'What's the big deal?'

'Look,' Dad says. Points at the likes, the retweets. 'It's trending.' He refreshes the screen and the numbers get even bigger.

'Whoa. Serious?'

'That's not all. People are arguing about it. Some sympathetic, defending you; trolls, too, making comments I'd rather you didn't read. You should probably delete your account.'

'No way. We wanted to make an impact—'

'Well, you *have*. Hayden, we're just worried about you,' Mum says. 'Getting all this attention – it could be dangerous.'

'Standing up for things you believe in may carry risk. That doesn't mean I should hide away.'

'We're not suggesting that,' Dad says. 'You know I'm proud of how you've been involved in this cause, and we know that it means a great deal to you. And we've agreed' – a look to Mum – they've been arguing, haven't they? – 'that we won't tell you what to do about this or try to stop you taking part. Just think before you act. Think of the potential consequences and do what you can to stay safe. Will you do that?'

'Yes. Of course. Can I go now?'

They exchange another glance.

'I'm really seriously worn out. Doing that' – I wave a hand at Mum's tablet – 'was . . . well, exhausting.'

'I know, love.' Dad's arms – a hug. And Mum's hand strokes my hair. But the cracks are forming inside me. I need to be alone. I squirm away.

'Goodnight.'

Up in my room I lean on the closed door. Breathe: in, out. In, out. Until my heart stops racing.

I call Bishan.

'So, you're trending,' he says.

'Yeah. It's just . . . amazing. Though my parents were the opposite of thrilled.'

'Uh oh. Any consequences?'

'They're staying with the "I'm old enough to make my own decisions" line for now. But that isn't why I called. I know where Denzi is.'

'Tell!'

'This is between us – agreed?'

'Of course.'

I summarise meeting Apple and what she told me.

'Could there be any truth to Denzi being locked up for being a climate protestor when his dad has been supposedly championing the environmental ticket?' Bishan says.

'You said you wouldn't tell, remember?'

'I keep my word, you know that. But I wonder if there is a

way to find out from Denzi himself.'

'She said it was a secure unit – it's not like we can go visit him. Even his mum has to be supervised to see him.'

'Did Apple say what it was called?'

'No. Just that it's part of a private hospital and it's in Chelsea.'

'Leave it with me and I'll see what I can find out. But while I've got you, I've been thinking about something you said the other day, about making a bigger impact if all the different environmental groups worked together. Do you want to help make it happen?'

There was only one answer: 'Yes.'

I find myself agreeing to go to his the next morning to come up with a plan.

A few hours later, a text pings in. Bishan.

OK. My sister's friend's cousin's stepmum works in Denzi's hospital.

You're kidding.

Nope. And I'm on my way to meet her. I'll see if she can take him a note. What should we say?

I think about it for a moment, then text him back: how about this: Hi D, found out you were there from Apple. Bishan knows someone who got this to you. What is going on?? Can we help? Hayden.

Got it. I'll see if she can do it.

14

When I get to Bishan's the next morning, he motions me in – he's messaging on his phone and looks up a moment later.

'Right. So last night I went to see the woman who works at Denzi's hospital. She's a health care assistant. She delivers meals to patients. With the high security rooms, like Denzi's, the meals go in a small service hatch into their rooms. So I wrote out your note, put it in a little envelope, and she slipped it under his breakfast. Wrote on the envelope to put any reply under his plate after he ate.'

'Seriously? And?'

'I was just messaging her. We got a reply from Denzi, of sorts. It was succinct and apparently written on the envelope in ketchup: *Hi H, no pen.* He shows me a screen shot, complete with artwork of what might be a happy face. Does that mean he is happy to hear from me? Or does that mean everything is fine?

'What kind of place is he in that he hasn't got anything to write with? At least now we know he's OK.'

'Hmmm, yeah, well, it's not the nicest place he's locked up in. I found out a bit more about it.'

'Tell me.'

'It's for young people with really serious mental health and addiction issues; most are violent and/or suicidal. Denzi is being kept isolated and his identity hidden. She only knows he's there because she caught a glimpse of him when someone went into his room and recognised him from when he was in the news for helping Eva.'

I absorb what he said, then shake my head. 'There's no way he belongs there.'

'I think you're right. But to be fair, we don't really know him that well.'

'Could she take him a pen?'

'Bit harder to hide under a plate but yeah, I already checked, and she said she could leave paper and a pen under his dinner tonight.'

'Thanks.'

'Now let's get to work.'

We go through to the dining room, table already taken over by Bishan's laptop, printer, print outs.

Bishan's mum sticks her head in from the kitchen. 'Hello dear,' she says.

'Hi, Mrs K.'

'Would you like some hot chocolate?'

'Oh yes, please!'

Two of his brothers run through and she shushes them, sends them to the garden. 'They're working,' she says, with a note of pride in her voice.

Bishan's family is amazing. His parents are activists for refugee rights and all sorts; she's a freelance journalist and he's a lawyer, but his practice is light years away from my mum's. He does all the free stuff to help people, and their big house – jammed full with Bishan, one sister, three brothers, one set of grandparents and other relatives and friends that come and go – is happy, loud and falling apart.

Bishan shows me his spreadsheets of local and international environmental groups with a presence at climate protests or stances against global warming. He's got names, positions, stars for people he thinks will be up for joining forces, odd comments like who they have good connections with in the UK and beyond, who they do/don't get along with. He shows me my name on our organisation's list with the comment, 'Will work for chocolate'.

'Ha. Thanks,' I say, as right on cue his mum brings in steaming mugs of the stuff. I wrap my hands around a mug and marvel at all the information he's brought together – and the detail. I've never met anyone as organised as Bishan.

'The hard part is working out the points of overlap between groups,' Bishan says. 'If we bring them together too soon, it won't work – everyone will argue and nothing will get done. First, we need to find the things everyone will agree, then convince them the things that are the same are more important than things that are different.'

'I don't get it. If all of these environmental groups want to stop climate change, stop pollution, stop the sixth mass extinction, what is there to argue about?'

'It's all about convincing people who disagree that they agree, without them noticing.'

'You make it sound like a game.'

'Yeah, I get that. But remember the arguments we had when we started out, even just in our group. Some are all about getting people to switch to electric cars, not use single use plastic. All stuff that we as individuals can do. They're all about shaming people into doing or not doing stuff.'

'We've talked about this before – you know what I think. It's ridiculous. It makes everyone forget about corporations who make profit producing the stuff – cars, plastics, whatever – in the first place. They should be responsible for what they produce.'

'But who lets them go for profits above all else in the first place? Our governments. So who do we blame: individuals, corporations, or governments? Or maybe all three? Once you answer that, then what do you do about whichever you think is the culprit? Everyone has their own ideas. And then some of the groups don't even think about any of that and are all about dealing with problems we have now – like cleaning up polluted waters, helping climate refugees, changing crops so they'll grow in hotter temperatures.'

'It's like they've given up thinking we can change anything.' I scowl, arms crossed. 'And you're making this sound impossible.'

'Not impossible, just bloody hard work. I've started looking at groups, trying to work out their most important goals. Draw them together with their similarities and go from there.'

'Yesterday you said that me talking about getting groups together made you think about this, but you've obviously been working on this for a while.'

'Guilty as charged. But sometimes you have to wait for the time to be right.'

'You think that time is now?'

'Yes, for four reasons. One: general lack of progress and frustration on many fronts makes everyone more likely to agree to try this again. Two: the violence against protestors that has followed terrorist actions by The Circle – in the UK, and other parts of the world also – makes everyone want to draw together.'

'Safety in numbers.'

'Exactly. And we'll have more reach together as well. Three: the failure of Big Green. It was held up as a way forward but it was all about lobbying big companies and regulators, all on their own turf. The next move has to be a grass roots movement centred on activists like us around the world, all demanding change: bottom up, not top down.'

'OK, I get that. And the fourth reason?'

'You.'

'*Me*? What do you mean?'

'You, Hayden, are trending still. Sometimes we just need the right spokesperson at the right moment. You can make this happen, I can't.'

I take a moment to absorb what he said, struggling to believe it. I shake my head. 'No way. I'll help but you're the one who knows everyone, who has been involved from the beginning, who knows how to do stuff. I don't.'

'I'm not saying I won't help you – I will! – as much as you need. But we need a fresh voice to make everyone listen. They're tired of me banging on about stuff. You can do this. What do you say?'

I shake my head, arms crossed. Even thinking about doing what he says makes me panic inside. I can't put myself forward like that, I just can't. 'I'll help you in any way I can. But you have to take the lead on this.'

There's a pause. If he's disappointed, it doesn't show. Which probably means he hasn't given up. 'Well, we'll start out that way and see where we end up. Let's begin with you, your social media presence.'

'Why?'

'Look at all your followers. You need to speak to them while they are still interested.'

All my followers? I frown, take out my phone. Check on different platforms. My followers were in the hundreds, and now . . . seriously? The numbers are going up so fast I can't focus on them or think what they even mean. 'This is mad.'

'Yes, it's totally bonkers how some things take off like this and some don't. Who can say what will catch?' He shrugs.

'*You*. You made this happen. You lined me up in front of a camera, asked me the right questions, got me to say the sound bites that work.'

'You make me sound manipulative.' He grins. 'I like to think of myself more as an encouraging friend who gives nudges now and then. What is out there is all *you*, Hayden.'

'Hmmm. Well, yeah, so you've nudged me into the social stratosphere. Since you got me here, what should I say now, wise guy?'

We go back and forth on this, but he says it has to come from me, be in my words. And that we need a tag to use with my posts, something a little different that can be picked up.

'Most things I can think of are already in use,' Bishan says.

I pause, thinking. 'You know that painting, "The Scream"? By Edvard Munch? I read about it somewhere, that it was originally called "The Scream of Nature". And you know how they got the crazy idea for geoengineering from volcanoes – that big eruptions put so much sulphur and stuff into the atmosphere that the temperature of the whole planet can drop for a year or two afterwards? Anyhow, there was this huge volcanic eruption before Munch did this painting – it lowered the temperature so much it was called the year without a summer. And some think Munch painted "The Scream" in response to the insane red sunset after the volcano.'

Bishan is doing some searching. 'The Scream and Scream of Nature are coming up too much to use.'

'How about #NatureIsScreaming?'

He checks, gives a thumbs up.

Finally, I post this, across all platforms:

Eva's death was a tragedy, one very personal to me. But there can be no retreat when all that lives and grows on our planet needs us. We need to be seen and heard now more than ever: we need to come together to do this so everyone will listen. Are you with me? #NatureIsScreaming

We start going through Bishan's spreadsheets in detail. Talking about who to approach and in what order: who will watch what others do, then follow, and who will want to feel like they were in at the start. I respond now and then to comments and messages on social, too. Bishan is compiling email lists and I'm thinking about what we're trying to do, how to make it work, and finally shake my head.

'I think we need to meet face to face where possible, make phone calls when not. We don't want to get jammed into everyone's inbox with all the other cries for attention. This has to feel personal to make people act.'

He thinks for a moment, then agrees. 'See, this is why you're in charge,' he says, and grins.

I flick his hand with a finger. 'Ouch,' he says.

'I'm not. I'm assisting you.'

'Sure.'

We spend the afternoon arranging meetings and on the phones. I'm surprised how many people want to talk to me, will listen to what I have to say. Want to join in, or at least hear more and talk about what it all means before they decide.

I've got goosebumps. 'Is something actually going to happen? Could what we are doing really change things for the better?'

'I think we've got a good shot at it. Thanks to you.'

'I couldn't do any of this on my own.'

Bishan shakes his head. 'If anything ever happens to me, you've *so* got this. And I'm emailing you all the stuff as a backup.'

'Don't be daft. Nothing is ever happening to you, and I so *haven't* got this – or anything.'

'You're the girl with the platform. Use it.' He means it, he's serious.

'I'll try.'

'And that is all you can do. All any of us can do: try. Work hard. Hope.'

15

My phone vibrates in my pocket at dinner and I risk Mum's wrath and take a peek at it under the table. It's from Bishan: call me.

I get away as soon as I can after dinner to my room and touch the screen by his name.

'Hi,' he says.

'What's up?'

'Got a reply from Denzi. I'll read it to you.'

Hi H, wow – you have amazing detective skills. I'm OK, nothing wrong with me besides being locked up. There are some things I know, I can't tell you – too dangerous – that someone wants kept quiet. Hoping L can get me out soon. Give my love to A.

D.

'He knows something *dangerous*?' I say. 'What could it be?'

'I don't know. His dad being Home Secretary, I'm wondering if it is some political thing, something the government wants kept quiet that he found out about somehow? But I think we're going about this wrong, wanting to keep where he is being held from the press. Maybe some pressure that way would get him out.'

'Or, maybe, if someone wants him kept quiet badly enough, that could put him in danger?' I say, feeling foolish to even say it. He's in a secure hospital – what could possibly happen to him there?

'What else can we do?'

'I'll go talk to Apple, tell her what he said. "Give my love to A" – he's practically told me to do so, hasn't he?'

'Yeah. Oh, there is something else – there's another boy being held in isolation, like Denzi, and they arrived at about the same time. There might not be any connection but they're being isolated in the same kind of way and have the same visiting consultant who only sees the two of them, and their names aren't on their files. Seemed odd enough to my contact that she mentioned it.'

'If there are two of them there for the same reason, that suggests Denzi being held is unlikely to have anything to do with his dad trying to keep him away from protests and stuff, doesn't it?' I don't add that I'm relieved. I'd hate to think what has happened to him had anything to do with us.

'True. Anyhow, Denzi says there are things he knows. That couldn't be anything about the climate movement – he wasn't involved enough. Maybe it's time to call the police?'

'Let's see what Apple thinks, first. It's amazing this friend of yours has been passing notes for us. Will she do it again?'

'I think so. It turns out she's really pissed off at her employers. Thinks they're doing things wrong, not helping kids they're paid to help the way they should, just locking some of them up in a room like Denzi and this other boy – worse than solitary confinement in prison. So if it goes wrong and she loses her job, she said she's OK with that. My uncle's friend has a gig lined up for her at an NHS hospital.'

'Bishan, do you know basically everyone in London?'

He laughs. 'Not quite, but it's a side effect of a big, extended family. And you know what my parents are like – always collecting strays and inviting them to stay.'

I message Apple: can we talk? I've got some news re D.

16

Apple is waiting at a table in the same coffee place we went to a few days ago. 'Hi Apple,' I say. 'This is Bishan. Bishan, Apple.'

'Sit, sit. What's up?'

'Bishan knows someone who works at the hospital where Denzi is being held and passed him a note. We got a reply from Denzi.'

'Really? Leila hasn't been able to get back in to see him; they keep delaying when she tries. What did he say?'

'I've got it here.' Bishan reaches into a pocket, passes the note to Apple to read.

'Woah. Something he knows – he thinks that's why he's being held?' Her eyes are wide. 'And it's *dangerous*. What could it be?'

'No idea. We were hoping you might know something.'

'Let me think.' There's a pause and I'm not sure if she's trying to find something to tell us, or knows something but isn't sure if she should say.

'I wonder if it might have something to do with his missing friend, Tabby. Well, he *said* friend, but I'm pretty sure she was more than that to him. Don't know her surname. He spent ages trying to find her. When I thought about it after, what you told me about him disappearing during that tragedy at the protest? I can't see him leaving all of you like that without a really good reason, but maybe meeting Tabby could be enough of a reason. Did he ever mention her to you?'

I shake my head.

'Is there anything else you can think of?' Bishan says. 'We just want to help him. We won't repeat anything if you ask us not to.'

She tilts her head to one side. 'I already told Hayden that there is some guy in London – I don't know his name – who was murdered weeks ago. The London police tried to call my dad about it, thought he might know something. But he'd already died by then.' She hesitates, glances at me.

'He knows,' I say, 'that they think suicide, but you don't believe it.'

'Leila doesn't either. That's why we came here – she thinks there is some connection, why they both died. She's trying to find out more,' Apple says. Hesitates. Then, 'Leila thinks how my dad died might have something to do with Denzi. And I'm sure there is something else going on that Leila wouldn't tell me.'

'So, two unexplained deaths, a missing girl. And a locked-up boy who is afraid to tell us why he's been locked up because he says it's dangerous,' Bishan says. 'What should we do next?'

'We were wondering if we should talk to the police,' I say.

'Leila has been to see them already,' Apple says. 'She told them they should interview Denzi, find out if he knows anything about what happened to my dad and that other guy.'

'Are they going to?' Bishan says.

'Don't know yet. Leila's friend, a lawyer, told her the doctors could refuse to let the police speak to Denzi if they say there are medical reasons why he shouldn't be interviewed, especially if his dad – as custodial parent – agrees. To get around that, they'd have to get a judge to order it. We're waiting to hear back on that, and on Leila's application to have unrestricted access to Denzi.'

'Oh. But what if— No.' I shake my head.

'What?' she says.

'If Denzi has been hidden away there because of something he knows, won't the police wanting to talk to him put him in danger?'

Apple draws in a sharp breath, shakes her head. 'I didn't think of that. Oh God. What do we do?'

'Could we get another note to Denzi?' I say. 'Ask for more information?'

'Getting a note in again shouldn't be a problem,' Bishan says. 'But if he's decided he can't tell us whatever it is that he knows, he's not likely to change his mind.'

'Writing notes is even worse than talking on the phone,' I say. 'Bet we could get more out of him in person.'

'Sure, now all we need to do is break into a secure hospital and rescue him,' Apple says.

Bishan raises an eyebrow. 'Now *that* sounds like a challenge.'

17

It only takes a day to get everything in place.

'Are you ready?' Bishan says.

'Absolutely!' I say.

'Got the times and everything straight?'

'Yes. Stop fussing – it'll be fine.'

'I don't like that I can't go instead of you.'

'We've been over this. You're better at crowd control than me; you know what you're doing. And with that cast on your arm still, you're too slow.'

'Huh. I'm only letting you off having a go up front because of how important this is. Next time, you're the one with the megaphone. Deal?

'OK, yes. I'll try it. Deal.'

The crowd is swelling and Apple arrives, waves.

'OK, this is it,' Bishan says. 'Good luck.'

'Be noisy.'

'We will!'

I make my way to Apple through the growing crowd. It's slow going as everyone seems to recognise me, wants to say hello. When I reach Apple, we break away and head down a nearby lane.

'I can't get over the number of people that came,' she says. 'And you've managed this in just hours? Wow.'

'Not me – it was all Bishan,' I say. And right on cue his voice on the megaphone begins.

The protest probably seems spontaneous from the outside, but, despite the time constraints, so much planning has gone into it. It's helpful that the private hospital is near the offices of a think tank that questions climate change: two birds, one stone.

We count the doors to the right one, look up and down the lane to make sure no one is watching. I push on it; it doesn't give. My heart flips – Bishan's contact said she'd make sure it was open – but another shove, and this time it opens. A small piece of plastic that was caught in the catch falls to the ground – enough to stop it from locking but not enough to make it look like it wasn't shut.

The protest chants are loud and getting louder.

At the end of the hall is a security door; the swipe card to get through it is where she told Bishan it would be, under a plant.

We count down the seconds to the exact time.

Swipe pass on door; it opens. We go through. The shouting outside is getting even louder – Bishan, true to his word. People will be at their windows to see what is happening, won't they?

Down the hall, go left, there's the desk, empty – she said she'd get them away for a moment. Keys hang on a board on the wall behind the chair. We grab key six, find the door. I unlock it while Apple gets her phone ready to stream whatever Denzi has to say – in case we are interrupted, something will still get out. It won't be dangerous information any more if everyone knows it.

We open the door, go through and—

The room is empty. Denzi isn't here.

18

Apple swears. 'Is it the wrong room?'

'It couldn't be – she said key six and the key opened the door.'

'Then where is Denzi?'

'I don't know. What should we do? Try other rooms?'

'Who knows who is locked inside?' Apple says. She shakes her head. 'Let's get out of here.'

She opens the door; a quick look – the desk is still unattended. We rush to it and as I put the key back, there is the sound of a door opening down the hall the other way.

We dash to the door we came in through, use the pass to get out.

There are shouts behind us as we bolt down that hall and then out the back door to the lane and I nearly collide with a woman who is walking past.

'Sorry,' I say, but she says nothing, turns away with a flash of red hair.

We run, fast, back to join the protest. Melt into the crowd.

'Why wasn't Denzi there?' Apple says.

'I don't know – maybe they knew we were coming somehow and moved him? I don't know.'

Apple has tears in her eyes. 'I've just lost my dad; years ago, I lost my mum. I'll be damned if I'm going to lose my brother.'

'I'm sorry.'

'I know. I'm getting out of here. I'll come clean with Leila, tell her everything. OK? Maybe she can find out where he is.'

'Yeah, do it. Go.'

She slips away to the edges of the crowd. I start to make my way through towards the centre.

Bishan's eyes find mine when I'm still metres away. I shake my head.

Police cars are arriving now on the street. Are they looking for whoever broke into the hospital? No, it's riot police. Probably annoyed we didn't give them any notice or get a permit. And we're in a high-rent neighbourhood; they aren't going to let us do this here for long, are they?

Scuffles are breaking out at the edges. Shouts.

A police megaphone tells us to disperse. Bishan gives the signal to go, and then—

And then—

A sound, a bang? Like a car backfiring, but *not*, and loud enough to hear over all the noise of the protest. There is a lurch of fear in my gut. Screams – someone is screaming – and I'm looking all around to see *why*, and everything is slowing down. My heart is thudding *thump*, *thump* and I turn just in time to see Bishan clutching at his chest. Red, red. Falling to the ground.

Now I'm screaming too, and pushing through the crowd, trying to get to him, but when I do someone holds me back.

Bishan's eyes meet mine – confused – like he doesn't know what is happening. And then . . . whatever indescribable thing it is that makes him who he is, is gone. His eyes are still. Dull and unseeing.

Part 3
Undersea

Tabby

@HaydenNoPlanetB

Targets to hold global warming to below, say, 2 degrees, refer to average temperature around the world, but warming is occurring in the Arctic region at twice this rate. Ice is melting and forest fires are sweeping through the subarctic, releasing carbon and destroying habitats.

#NatureIsScreaming

19

When I open my eyes, I'm not where I was when I closed them.

OK, *think*. It was a stressful day and I was scared, tired and hungry for most of it, but could I be that wrong? I close them and go back in my mind. Malina took me to a small bedroom with a bed and a bedside table; the tray that had the remains of tea and sandwiches was on it when I went to sleep. There was one chair, a door, and that's all.

I open my eyes again but that isn't what I see, and the disconnect is jarring.

Am I still asleep? Is this another dream?

I pinch my arm, hard. *Ouch*. But I don't wake up and nothing changes.

I sit up, look around. This room is about the same size as the other one with similar contents – a small table, one chair – but more worn, basic. The only faint light comes through the half open door.

The comfy bed I went to sleep on has been replaced by a long, narrow sofa. It's hard, cold seeping through thin cushions and blankets. The walls look to be rough stone and I'm drawn to lay my hands flat against the wall by the bed. Faint vibrations send a message, through hand to bone and up my arm. Not caused by machinery, it's too irregular for that, yet the vibrations follow a pattern I recognise:

The sea.

Yes.

A single word said in that unique way inside of me, and I smile.

'You're back! That wasn't just a dream.' No matter what is going on, where I am, what might happen, there is an intense sense of relief to be who I am, again – all of me together.

Huh. I had nowhere else to be just now.

'Sure. I missed you, too. Where've you been? I mean, they gave me blockers. But you couldn't just disappear.'

I was always there. You just couldn't hear me any more. Like when you used to ignore me – it was like that.

'I didn't do it on purpose. This time, I mean.'

OK. A sense of grudging belief. *But even if you couldn't hear me, you could have said hello now and then.*

'You're right. I'm sorry. If they put me on blockers again, I'll remember to do so. Though how would you know I was talking to you and not to myself? Do you have a name from before?'

A name?

'What the kin call you and only you.'

Of course. It is this. And then follows the most beautiful sound, a short series of whistles but more like music than anything I've ever heard before. I try, again and again, to repeat it in my mind but can't get it right.

'You need a name I can say.'

You choose.

It has to be fitting and mean something to me. I think about it for a while, and then once I have it, I smile. 'Aslan. A talking lion. He was a character in some of my favourite stories when I was younger. Besides, my name Tabby is a cat; for the hidden part of me to be a lion feels right.'

Thank you. I will be Aslan. Now that we've sorted that, what next?

'Do you know where we are or how we got here?'

No.

'You're usually awake when I'm asleep.'

We both slept.

'Was it the funny tea, maybe? It wasn't like anything I've had before. What was it?'

I don't know, but they might.

'They?'

The others that whisper inside you.

'The voices? Can you hear them, too?'

No. Only your reaction to them.

'Interesting. OK, I'll give it a try.'

I tune out of where I am to the chorus inside.

Sun . . . Sea . . . Earth . . . Sky . . .

The more I focus on the four, the more they chant with me – loud and louder. Can I channel them to what I want to know?

I shift my focus to the tea, the smell and taste of it. 'What was it?'

So many voices respond at once – some quiet murmurs, others loud – that it is hard to understand anything. I try to sift through the noise, adjust my focus to one of the clearest voices.

Then everything blurs . . . *changes.*

I'm a child holding a woven basket. A woman in long skirts is gathering herbs that grow in shadows deep in a forest; she puts them in the basket I carry. This blurs to another place – a rough cottage, stone and wood. The woman is grinding the herbs we found, adding other things. It smells so good and I want some; I'm reaching a hand towards it, but she pulls it away.

'This isn't for you, child. It'd make you sleep for a week.'

Then a door opens and a man comes in. I run towards him, throw my arms around his legs. He ruffles my hair and I'm this child, in this moment. A happy time and I want to stay, but something inside nags for attention. Pulls me back.

Tabby? Can you hear me? It's Aslan. *Tabby?*

'What's wrong?'

You were gone a long time.

'I was? Did you see that?'

See what?

I'm bemused, struggling to shake it off. 'It was like I was in someone's memory. Going by the clothes they wore, it was long ago. At least I think that is what it was.' And it didn't feel like much time passed when I was gone, not to me, and again – the disconnect is jarring.

You were in a memory that wasn't your own?

'I think so.'

Whoever it was they didn't want to let you go. It was hard to reach you.

'What would have happened without you to call me back?'

I don't know. Maybe you'd never leave it.

I shiver, not wanting to think about it but unable to stop. Could I have stayed there – my body lying here, unaware – while my mind was living someone else's memories? For how long? I didn't know who I was any more, so how could I – *why* would I – come back without help?

Did you find out anything?

I shake it off. 'Yes – it was the tea that made us sleep. So I guess we were drugged so they could bring us here without waking us up. But where are we?'

I don't know. Let's go see.

I get up, shiver and rub goose-pimpled arms and legs, cross the room and look through the door. There is a dimly lit corridor sloping down to the left, up to the right.

'Left or right?'

Up.

Right it is.

20

We walk. The dim light stays constant but I can't see where it comes from – there are no visible light fittings and the light seems even, diffuse, almost as if the walls are gently glowing. It's a warren of corridors with a constant gentle curve. Doors open to other rooms, all sorts: bedrooms, like the one I woke up in, with sofas, and bigger ones with beds, but cold and devoid of any bedding; what look like storage rooms, but the shelves are bare; larger spaces that might have been kitchens, with cupboards, tables, chairs, but every cupboard is empty. There are no people in sight; nothing else moves. It's cold and I'm shivering.

There was a blanket where I woke up. I'll go back for that, I decide, and wear it like a shawl around myself.

Er . . . which way?

I have no idea, and the more I wander around, the more nothing looks familiar. With the gradual curve of the walls, I'm wondering if this is all a big circle and I'm coming back on myself, but I can't tell because it all looks so much the same.

'Seriously, what the hell was the point of dumping me here?' I say out loud, then pause to see if anyone watching, listening, might answer, but beyond my breathing there is only silence.

I try Aslan inside. 'Oi. A little help?'

The equivalent of mental snoring answers back.

Great.

If I splay my fingers, hands on the walls, I can feel the same deep vibration in my bones that I felt when I woke up: the sea. I didn't notice it where I was when I went to sleep.

When I arrived with Malina yesterday – assuming it was yesterday and I haven't been sleeping for days – Cassandra said we were in the First Circle of Undersea. Maybe this is a different circle?

Malina said if I'm banished, I'd be sent to the outer circle. If it is easier to feel the sea here, being *outer* makes sense. Have I been banished already? Did I somehow fail a test in my *sleep*?

That's ridiculous.

Unless, maybe, *this* is the test: to find my way out of a maze.

What would be the point of that? My tummy rumbles; I'm light-headed. I need something to eat, but even more, something to drink. Maybe they've sent me out here to starve.

Why would they go to all that trouble to capture me and bring me to Undersea just to do that?

I'm starting to get a bit freaked being so alone.

Answers may hide within, a voice whispers, and it's not in the familiar cadence of Aslan. I spin all around but no one is there. Goosebumps prickle my skin. There is laughter now – inside me. That's where it came from.

So that's it, is it? Like with the tea – ask a question? I'm uneasy. There were so many voices inside me when I did that, and it felt like they all wanted my attention. Then when I focused on one of the voices, I lost all sense of myself until Aslan pulled me away and back to reality.

Aslan sleeps now, but will surely eventually wake up if I need help getting free again?

97

OK, let's do this.

I sit down cross-legged on the floor. My head spins and I lean back on the wall to steady myself. Vibrations from the sea run through me and there is a lurch of longing to be *in* the sea, not underneath it. If my obsession is back, the blockers must be completely gone from my system.

Focus.

I hold an image of my surroundings in my mind and ask a question: 'Where am I?'

A chorus of voices shout in my head, but nothing like music – it's discordant, out of tune, loud and getting louder. My head *aches* and still it's louder and louder, and there is upset and alarm and amusement and every reaction and emotion I could imagine rushing through my mind at once.

I clamp my hands over my ears but it doesn't help because the sound is inside of me. It's overwhelming and I'm reaching for Aslan but there is no answer. Now I'm panicking.

Malina said to do something if I'm overwhelmed – focus on the four. And I try, but I'm being pushed and pulled in all directions, torn apart inside, and I *can't*.

I need help – I need Cate.

'Help me, Cate.'

Cate wraps her arms around me. I know it isn't real, it's something in my mind, but it's a calm space – the eye in a storm.

You know what to do. Don't you? she says.

Focus.

Sun . . . Sea . . . Earth . . . Sky . . .

The voices calm.

Sun . . . Sea . . . Earth . . . Sky . . .

They synchronise more and more.

Sun . . . Sea . . . Earth . . . Sky . . .

Now in perfect unison.

What next? I shy away from asking where I am again after the reaction that I got before. Maybe I'll try something else, something I need if they want to keep hijacking my mind.

I focus on my thirst, my hunger and the question: 'Is there anything here to eat and drink?'

Multiple voices shout *YES*. I focus on one and the others fall away.

I get up, using the wall to help me stand. Someone inside my mind leads me out this door, down a corridor, taking several turns, and then a gentle slope up leads to a door.

I push on it – it's heavy, and resolutely staying closed. I try again and finally it gives a little, and now I can see why it was stuck. There's something tangled and caught under the door – like the vines of some sort of plant, but more white than green. I reach in and yank it out from under the door, push it open wide enough that I can look through.

Wow. It's like some sort of garden?

There is a profusion of growing things, but most aren't in soil; instead roots grip uneven walls and curl around bars spaced along the walls. Branches curl around each other in a profusion so wild that what might have once been paths are completely overgrown, and on the ground are things like fruit that have fallen and been left to rot leaving a sickly-sweet smell of decay in the air.

I open the door a little more and push my way in. It's like trying to get through a hedge.

Some things I almost recognise, as if they are descendants of more usual things, like vegetables, but most look as if they are more related to mushrooms than anything else. The growth is lush but strangely deadened – it lacks colour, with whites and greys and beiges. Is it chlorophyl that makes plants green and extracts energy from the sun? Sunlight doesn't reach down this far. No sun, no chlorophyl.

'What is good to eat?'

The chorus comes back, voices shouting for attention, but less discordant than before – they all want me to eat their favourite thing so they can taste it. There is a fruit-like tuber with a faint bitter taste almost like aubergine. Mushrooms with different flavours – I mean, *way* different from a mushroom. One tastes like an apple, another something citrussy, then another more like pineapple. Engineered to bring tastes of sunshine down to these depths?

There is amusement inside with the voices. **Other way around. Began here. Taken above.**

I frown. 'How can tastes we know as plants above have started under the sea?'

Sea is first mother.

Words I know from Cate: life started in the sea, moved to land. But then it must be that some came back to the sea to build and live in Undersea.

More amusement but not more answers.

There is water – it drips down to the plants from above and I catch some on my tongue, then use some flat leaves to catch more. It tastes odd, a bit gritty, but I'm so thirsty I don't care.

It's desalinated.

It must be seawater, salt taken out to make it drinkable.

I'm getting pushed and pulled in different directions to try more morsels. A lot of it is good and I'm trying this and that and another and wondering why this place has been abandoned, left to rot?

This circle preys on the weak. Most would not choose to come here.

I remind myself I need to leave, work out what to do. I'm full enough now but voices are tempting me to try another taste, and I do – round like white radishes but taste like marshmallows. Really?

I've got to get out of here. I pull my way back through to the door, and there, to the side – a plant I didn't notice on the way in, a tangle of what look like roots that twist around other plants. I'm drawn to it by the faint smell and sniff closer: like hot chocolate.

Try it, try it, voices say, and I break off a piece of root, chew it. It's more bitter than sweet, like one-hundred-per-cent chocolate, and I can't decide what I think of it, and reach for more. Some of the voices shout *No* and, too late, I feel alarm from some, mockery from others. I spit out what I haven't already swallowed.

'What have I eaten?'

Laughter echoes inside me.

My head is spinning even worse than before. I lean against the wall. My vision is going funny, like what one eye sees is tripping up against the other.

Then everything blurs . . . *changes*.

★ ★ ★

The garden is now neat, ordered. A woman is pinching off shoots on a pale plant. A girl is trimming another. They're dressed oddly, in loose clothing of pale hues. I'm bent low staying out of sight, reaching for a treat.

'We see you!' the woman says. 'Go to your lessons.'

'Just one? Please . . . ?'

'OK,' she says, 'just one.' A pinch of a tangy mushroom and I rush back through the door – something is scratching at me and I trip, but when I look back, there's nothing there.

The disconnect jars – I'm both here, now, when it's overgrown and I'm alone, and a long time ago. This child isn't me; it's a memory. I fight to tear myself away from it.

The child that I was a moment ago runs down a corridor without me.

I walk back along the corridors as I did before, but nothing is the same. There are women and girls, voices murmuring in rooms as I walk past. Some walk by me now and then, but they ignore me, walk through me as if I'm not there. But it isn't me who is a shade, it's them – they're not here, not in my time. This is all from before.

So long ago that my skin prickles with the sense of its passage.

Now I'm flying fast through the air, being taken to another memory, and there is nothing I can do to stop it.

I'm small, looking up. So many come to visit but they all have tasks too pressing to play, and their faces carry sadness. Where is Maman?

An auntie says my name, Lia; she takes my hand. She says it's time to say goodbye.

A blur of movement – another room. Maman is in bed? Lying so still, and when I touch it, her hand is cold. The aunties say I must say goodbye, but if I do, does that mean I won't see her again? And I shout at her to get up and the aunties explain that she can't, say she will never do so again, and then I'm screaming.

I'm bundled away.

I follow behind them later when they carry Maman away. They don't know I'm there. They go to a room I've not been in before, and up to a faint outline in a wall. An auntie presses a round space in the rock at the side of it and I see it's a door; it slides open.

They take Maman through and I slip in after them.

I don't like this place. It's cold and dark and smells . . . wrong. But I can't let them take Maman away from me.

Impressions blur, contract – join together in fragments.

A corridor, a room – shiny metal things, and they're doing something to Maman.

Fear – running – hiding. Darkness.

Lost. Alone. Cold, hungry.

Yet . . . not alone. Empty sockets for eyes, ancestors look down on me from the walls.

It's much later when the aunties find me. They carry me to where I last saw Maman and say I may join her now.

They free me from myself and Maman's arms are around me again.

★ ★ ★

103

I'm pulled into one room, then another, like a captured will-o-wisp. To be a woman, a child, another woman, to live their memories. And as they did, I love, I cry, I laugh, dance, live and die. Countless times. And each one wants me to live their story so they can do so again.

But somewhere there is another story I need to live:

My own.

But who am I?

21

Another memory, another life ends. A new one tries to claim me, but something nags inside me. Isn't there something I'm supposed to be doing? I'm puzzled. And something is tickling inside my mind.

I need to focus:

Sun . . . sea . . . earth . . . sky . . .

Close my eyes. Concentrate.

Sun . . . sea . . . earth . . . sky . . .

Everything and everybody – each memory, each voice – spin around me. They are part of me, yes, but also separate.

Who am I?

It comes back slowly. Tabby. Yes, I'm Tabby.

Where have you been? It's Aslan, a note of panic through his words, and that brings me back to myself in a rush. *Tell me what happened.*

'There were all these different voices and memories; they kept dragging me from one to another. I didn't know what to do! I couldn't get away.'

Calm down. You're all right now. Be calm and think.

'I need – we need – help to get out of here. The voices are all I have to turn to, but it's like some of them aren't on my side at all. Even those who feel like maybe they either are or could be still want me to live their memories.'

These things I do not understand. I cannot advise you. But is there one of these voices that you trust inside of you? Reach out to them.

There have been so few people in my life that I trust. Denzi. Jago, friends of his that helped me. And Cate.

The pain of losing her is still overwhelming. I imagined she was with me, helping me a few times when I really needed her, but how could she be?

'Cate, I wish you were here,' I whisper to myself.

I am, a voice says. One that sounds and feels like Cate – as if she is inside of me: a sanctuary in a sea of demands and noise.

'How could you be with me? I must be losing it, imagining things.'

No, you're not. Instead, you are beginning to understand what it is to be one of us. To carry many lives inside you. Her words are tinged with sadness.

Could it really be Cate?

I'm both weary and empty, as if being caught in the memories and emotions of others left no room for my own. I've always been aware of this background chorus inside me, just accepted its presence, though it's never been as strong and loud as it is now, or so demanding of my attention. Now that I've seen through their eyes, lived part of their lives through their memories, they are more real.

'These other lives – who are they?'

They are your ancestors.

I take that in. Cassandra explained to me how Cate is my mother in a true sense. So, if the voices inside me are my ancestors, and she is one of my ancestors, does that mean she really *is* inside of me? The pain of having lost her was so strong.

Is this a way to take some of it away?

'I thought you were gone for ever. I thought I imagined you helping me when I needed it, that I made it up because I missed you so much. But you're really there, inside of me?'

I've been here whenever you've needed me.

I can't stop my tears. And Cate is here, inside me, rocking me in her arms. This craziness is all worth it if it means I get to keep her in my life.

'Are our ancestors always so noisy, and demanding – dragging me around to their memories?'

Hearing your ancestors tends to be strongest in your teens when you are more susceptible. But most of us can only return to the past when we join with the seer in the dreaming – you ate the dreaming plant which amplifies it all. Some very few – like Cassandra – can access it all the time at will. She is a seer, and so she can also hear the future voices.

'Our descendants?'

Yes.

I digest that. 'But sometimes the voices have been there when I haven't been near this dreaming plant.'

Yes. You are a descendant of Cassandra; you may have the same skill to see the past as you will, whether or not it comes with the future.

There is a question I need to ask Cate. I'm afraid to at the same time. What if she has me live through it as one of her memories? But I have to know – who, why – and she is the one who must know. I can't avoid it any longer.

'Cate, why did you die? Who killed you?'

There's a pause, as if she's thinking of what to say and how to say it.

I will explain all that I can, but not yet. You're not ready.

'Tell me now – please.'

You have to trust me on this. You do trust me, don't you?

Despite all the things she didn't tell me, I do, absolutely.

You're not ready to understand what you want to know. When you are, I'll tell you. Right now, you need to concentrate on the test.

'So help me with that, then.'

Part of the test is to find your own way. If I try to help you, they'll know.

I pause. 'I think I need to leave this place, go back to the First Circle.'

I don't know the way. But I do know that you need to rest before you try again.

'I can't, there's too much going on, back and forth, inside of me.'

Close your eyes. Rest. I'll take you back to a memory – to when it was just the two of us.

I do as she says. And everything blurs . . . *changes* . . .

I'm holding her close, rocking her in my arms. Her perfect baby smell, small feet and toes. There is this rush of love through me, so strong – I've never felt anything like this before.

'Holly, I will always keep you safe. I promise,' I whisper into her hair.

The way she sleeps – one eye open, one closed. The open eye regards me carefully, tracks my movements, as if the part of her that is awake is something else entirely, and somehow more aware than the Holly I know. When she wakes completely and her chubby cheeks crinkle when she smiles, her eyes focus on me and they are different. This sleeping eye is something else, something . . . *other*.

Is this why Cassandra tasked me with her care? She knew this one child's importance eclipsed all the others.

That scares me. I want to hold her, love her, watch her grow and be who and what she wants to be. I don't want my life for her.

But for now, that is far, so far in the future. I'll not look ahead, not yet.

I tuck her into her cot. Draw a blanket around my shoulders, watching her as she watches me.

22

When I open my eyes again, I'm calm, rested; ready to face whatever it is that will come next. And I'm full of wonder, too, at having seen a memory of Cate's from when she was my nanny. When I was still Holly – the name given to me by my birth parents.

Cate has helped you? Aslan.

'She couldn't tell me how to get us out of here, but yes, she has explained some things. The voices inside me, like her, are my ancestors. And I guess it is time to ask them, again, for a little assistance.'

I gather the will to do this thing.

I begin the chant, inside: Sun . . . Sea . . . Earth . . . Sky . . .

Sun . . . Sea . . . Earth . . . Sky . . .

SUN . . . SEA . . . EARTH . . . SKY . . .

Once they all join in, I focus on what I need: 'Help me get back to the First Circle of Undersea.'

Amusement.

Distrust.

A chorus of **Why do you want to go there?**

'To join The Circle.'

But you don't want to join.

Is there any point in arguing with voices that are inside your head? No. But I carefully steer my thoughts away from the things I don't want them to know.

'What I want or don't want doesn't matter. It is what I must do.'

You'll never get there without our help.

'Huh. So, will you help me? Please?'

Why should we?

'I said the magic word.'

A mass conversation starts going on inside of me, too many voices and opinions to even begin to follow. It's loud and getting louder.

I try an aside. 'Cate? Is there anything you can do?'

I've tried, but they either can't hear me or ignore me. I'll see if I can find someone who will listen.

The discussions continue long enough that I'm thinking of interrupting, but then, there is abrupt silence. There is a whisper from so long ago that I'm not sure I even heard it, but whoever it is silences all the others.

'Who are you?' I ask.

A sense of uncertainty, careful thinking. *Rhiannon, I was called. Yes. That was my name. Why were you banished, child?*

'I haven't been. It's meant to be a test. Can you help me?'

Puzzlement. *Then how would it be a test?*

'I don't even know what it is I'm supposed to do! How is that fair? What questions do I need to answer to pass this test?'

That will never do, no; you're looking at things the wrong way. Turn it around.

I'm annoyed, puzzled. I push the voices away, close them away inside me as if in a box while I think.

When it comes to me it's so freaking obvious that I'm surprised it took me so long.

'*This* is what I must work out: what answers I need to question.'

Rhiannon radiates glee: ancient as she is, she'd clap her hands if she had hands. As she doesn't, she uses mine.

23

I return to the strange garden, and pick a small piece of the bitter chocolate root in my hand. It's less than I had before, but I'm still nervous.

I know. Aslan.

'I get it. There's no real choice. I have to convince my ancestors to tell me what I need to know, and connecting with them works better if I use the root. Once I ask them, then I have to figure out who to believe. At least, I think that is what I have to do.'

Using the dreaming root is the best way to get their full attention, Cate says.

'It's weird having this double conversation when neither of you can hear the other.'

What do you mean? Who else are you talking to?

And I don't know what to do. 'Should I tell her?' I whisper inside to Aslan.

Do you trust her?

'Completely.'

Then do so.

'Cate, you know how we went to some of your memories of me, when I was a baby, and you wondered who was looking back when I was asleep with one eye open?'

Yes?

'It's like there are two halves of me inside. And the other half

113

isn't one of the ancestor's voices; it's separate from that. Do you know all they did to make me? The dolphin side? I might look human, but inside it's like I'm half dolphin and half human. Dolphins have a split brain, so half can sleep while the other half swims along and goes up to breathe and watches out for predators. That's kind of like how it is inside of me – half human, half dolphin. We can sleep one at a time and when one of us is asleep, the other is in charge. Or we can both be awake, and when we are, we can communicate silently. As far as I know the only time we've ever both been asleep at the same time was when we drank the tea Cassandra brought.'

Wow.

'Yeah.'

So when they gave you the underwater abilities, that came along with it?

'I think so. It took us a long time to work this out and accept each other, but now we're kind of a team. I call him Aslan.'

A great team.

Cate continues. *Sometimes I've thought you were having conversations with yourself. And it is with this Aslan?*

'Exactly.'

Does anyone know about this apart from me?

'No. At least, I haven't told anyone. I don't know if the other Chosen are the same as me that way, or not.'

I won't tell anyone, and I think you should keep this to yourself, too. Though I wonder . . . maybe that is why you were so important to Cassandra and Phina? Do they somehow know?

'How would they? Anyhow, I get the feeling Phina doesn't like me much.'

114

Phina doesn't like anybody that Cassandra does.

'I'm not so sure about her either.'

Cassandra is on your side always, I promise you.

Do I believe her? Cate wouldn't lie to me. But maybe Cassandra has deceived Cate, and now she is trying to deceive me, too. But I keep these doubts to myself.

What are you going to do now?

'I think there is only one option. I need to go to my ancestors, ask them for help again. But the thing that worries me is being able to come back once I get sucked into their memories.'

How did you do it the last time?

'Aslan called me back.'

You didn't hear me for a long while, though, Aslan says.

'Are you sure you'll be able to get me back if I can't?'

No.

'Thanks for the reassurance.'

Worse from my perspective: I don't see these memories you do or hear the voices. If you stay away, I'll die of boredom while we slowly starve.

'Great image, thanks.'

I gather my thoughts. I know how to begin and how to calm the voices – with sun, sea, earth, sky – but is there any way to stop from being dragged by them from memory to memory? If there is, I don't know it.

Malina said I needed more training. I sigh, try to think of everything she ever said in case something might help. Back before we got along, Aslan used to fight to take over; there were a few times I switched off when I was in the sea and nearly drowned. Malina taught me to visualise a rope that ties me to myself so I could always find my way and get back in control.

115

But then once Aslan and I learned to share, I didn't need it any more, and—

Hang on a minute. Back then I'd assumed Malina knew what was going on inside me, but she didn't know about Aslan, did she? Did she actually teach me that to keep myself separate from the voices?

Worth a try?

'Yeah.'

I chew on the bitter root and try to imagine that it is extra dark organic chocolate, but it isn't quite there. Needs sugar, doesn't it?

I sit, leaning against a wall, and focus, inside, on a silver rope tied around my wrist so I can't let go by mistake. To hold me together.

Sun . . . Sea . . . Earth . . . Sky

Sun . . . Sea . . . Earth . . . Sky

SUN . . . SEA . . . EARTH . . . SKY

When in perfect unison like this, the voices are beautiful music made even richer and clearer with the dreaming root.

And then . . . everything around me *changes*.

'Hi everyone. Now, who wants to help me find my way out of here and back to the First Circle?'

Amusement. Laughter.

Voices shout suggestions, competing with each other; chaos begins to take over and I can feel the tug of a memory, another and then another, each desperate to be lived again through me. I hold firmly to my silver rope.

'One at a time, please!'

Surprised silence.

Swim there, one says. *Go to a hatch – through the water locks – to the sea. Swim across to the First Circle*.

The lure of the sea is so strong, I almost forget about the water pressure. 'The water pressure is so high this far below the surface – can I survive that?'

Laughter. *There's only one way to find out?* several voices suggest.

'Thanks, but no. Isn't there something a little simpler? Like, say, a passageway that links the different circles?'

There are conversations I can't follow, more laughter.

There is a way they are linked, but you'll never find it.

'Do you know what it is?'

Of course!

'Can't you just tell me already?'

You have to ask the right question for us to help you. More mocking laughter.

'Any hints? No?' I sigh, trying to think of different ways places can be linked. 'OK, is there a hidden passageway?'

There is mocking laughter from all sides.

'I'm not in on the joke: tell me!' But they just laugh harder. It's like herding cats trying to get a straight answer – who might help?

'Rhiannon?'

They all fall silent. Moments pass.

Yes? A faint answer.

'Can you help me?'

A long pause. *You need the help of your ancestors. You have to convince The Circle of the past to keep you in the present and future*.

'They're not very helpful.'

It's up to you to change this. I can't help you any more than I already have. She drifts away again.

It's up to me: great.

Think, think. Every detail – limited as they are – that I know about Undersea; everything anyone said . . .

Cassandra mentioned tunnels leading from Undersea to the shore that were destroyed in the Second World War. But maybe there are other tunnels?

'Are there tunnels underneath that link up all of Undersea?'

A moment of silence, some conferring.

Yes.

I sift through ancestors' memories, trying to find the way to the tunnels. Some say it is one way, some another and I'm trying to work out which voices to trust, which not, but I'm not getting any closer to an answer.

I've had enough. How do I get back? My head throbs and I'm rubbing my temples against a coming headache, and then I see it, feel it. The silver rope on my wrist.

It ties me to something. What was it?

I'm frowning, trying to concentrate, to remember, but there are so many thoughts crowding into me at once.

The rope is knotted on tight like I didn't want to lose it. Should I pull it and see what happens?

OK. I give the rope a tug – nothing happens.

I start to pull it in towards me. It's long. I coil it up and it's getting heavy, and then— Oh. It's attached to itself. It's a long circle of rope?

What the actual?

There's laughter inside of me again and I don't get the joke – am I the joke? And I'm scared, trapped inside my head.

And I still don't know . . . what was it I wanted to know?

How to get out of here, a voice says, one that has been silent until now.

Oh, yeah. I need to find the tunnels underneath.

'Who are you? Will you help me?'

I'm Yvonne, but you don't need my help. You already know the way.

'I don't!'

You've seen the way already.

'I have?'

With Lia.

Lia: the little girl who followed her aunties when they took her Maman away. They went to a door that led down! That must be it.

I follow the whisperer's memory, to a dark place, built long ago. A long way lined with skulls.

Go there. Once you are there, take the dreaming root. Then I'll help you.

24

You scared me. Aslan's worry is all through his words.

'Sorry. The rope thing didn't work. It was all a long loop attached to itself – so much for Malina's theory. I only got back because Yvonne, whatever ancestor she is, reminded me what I was doing.'

Tell me what you've learned.

'OK. They wouldn't give me a straight answer about anything. A few suggested I could try to swim for it, but I might die because of the high water pressure. Others said there is a way the circles are linked, but they wouldn't tell me what it is. Another said there are tunnels underneath that link all of Undersea, but it's dark and lined with skulls.' I tell him about Lia's memories, what Yvonne said.

So let's try that.

'Weren't you listening? It's dark and lined with *skulls*. Of dead people!'

So?

'You're not creeped out by anything.'

No. I'm not.

'Apart from the skulls there was just something about Yvonne that I didn't like.'

Is that because you didn't like her suggestion?

'Maybe. I don't know. She is the one who helped me remember

who I was and what I was doing, so I guess she has helped me once already.' I sigh. 'If we go there, you'll be with me the whole time, not go to sleep and disappear?'

Of course.

'Fine. Let's give it a try.'

We stop for a snack and a drink at the garden of weirdness. Taking care to avoid eating any of the dreaming root for now, I slip some in my pocket for later.

We set out. Lia's memory came soon after I left the garden the first time, and I concentrate. Retrace steps. First to where she lived, then to where she followed her aunties later.

When we get to the room that I think has the door to underneath, there is a heavy cupboard in front of where it should be. It takes all my strength to make it move at all, and I'm afraid it'll topple over on top of me. I shift it to the side, rock it a little each way until it steps out bit by bit from the wall.

When I can finally squeeze behind it, it's too dark to see properly. I feel for the edges of the door, then up and down to the left of it, my fingers searching for the mechanism to make it slide open. Finally I find it, lower than I thought; perhaps everything looked higher from Lia's perspective.

Press. Nothing happens.

Do it again. Hold my finger down on it a little longer, and this time there is a faint grumbling noise . . . and then, a click. The door slides open.

'OK, this is it.' I take the root in my hand.

Wait. I have an idea.

'What's that?'

Don't tie the rope to yourself. Tie it to me. Then I can pull you back.

121

I think for a moment. 'Makes sense. How do we do that?'

Let's imagine it, together?

I close my eyes and concentrate on imagining the silver rope, and tying it to my hand. Aslan is here, too – he projects himself to me. The sheer beauty of what he is inside – and yes, half of me inside is most definitely a he – I can hardly breathe to see him as he was then and is now.

He's smug. *Yes. I am very beautiful. Now give me the rope.*

I pass it to him. He takes it in his teeth.

I won't let go.

I open my eyes again and step through the door. Put the root in my mouth now: bite, chew, swallow.

It's dark. Cold. I wait a moment. I can't tell if my vision has gone wonky from the root – it's too freaking dark – and I reach out with my hands until one touches a rough wall. I lay both hands on it flat. The sea vibrates through the wall and keeps me steady.

Sun . . . Sea . . . Earth . . . Sky

Sun . . . Sea . . . Earth . . . Sky

SUN . . . SEA . . . EARTH . . . SKY

The voices are more and more in unison, but then it's like they realise where we are and many of them stop, fall silent. I'm feeling their panic inside me and start backing up to the door I came through, when I hear that other whisperer – Yvonne.

You came.

'Yeah, but why is everyone so freaked out?'

Scared of where they ended, that's all. You can pass if you are brave enough. I'll show you the way.

The darkness eases and I can see the perfectly ordinary

corridor sloping down, not with my own eyes, but with the eyes of someone who has been here before and knows the way: in Yvonne's memory.

A sense of dread is creeping up my spine. This place is old, even by the standards of the First Circle which had a feel of the ancient about it; this feels even older. Most of my ancestors are quiet, taking it in as much as I am because they've never been here before – at least not when they were alive.

Something about this place has my heart thudding at such a rate that it feels like it will pound its way right out of my chest.

And then it goes dark.

Yvonne's memory is gone, withdrawn, and I open my eyes wide and wider and still can't see anything. The voices are panicking, I'm panicking—

I'll show you the way. A small voice.

'Lia?'

Yes.

'You know the way through?'

I sense rather than see her nodding her head inside me, and then . . . everything shifts and changes as Lia's memory takes hold of me.

I'm breathing fast. Where are they taking Maman? There are lights on ahead. I creep down the slope, shaking with fear. I want to run back but can't leave Maman.

There's an open door – that's where the light comes from. I swallow, step closer, look inside.

What I see makes me run – fast – paying no attention to where I am going at all and when I finally stop it's dark and all

I can see are white bones – skulls – empty eye sockets. On every space, every wall.

Lia, shrieking, tears out of me – she's gone – I'm standing where she was. The skulls. The eye sockets. The darkness.

Why did you bring us here? Voices inside of me.

'You know why: to pass through. To get back to the First Circle.'

Only the dead may go this way.

Their fear is my fear and I'm turning, backing up, to go the way I came. I try to run but trip and fall. Screams are rising up inside me, mine and my ancestors, at once—

Then there's a tug. A tug on my hand?

A silver rope is tied there. It's pulling on me hard and then harder, dragging me along the floor and away from the skulls.

I sit up. Open my eyes.

There you are. Aslan.

Flipping heck. It worked.

25

What's the problem? The dead are part of us. Why be afraid of them? One day they will welcome you.

'I'd just rather it wasn't today.'

I call Rhiannon: it's a long time before she answers.

Why did you go to the place of the dead?

'To get to the First Circle.'

You listened to the wrong answer*.* Her voice is sad.

'What should I do now?'

She doesn't answer.

OK, I can do this and I'm going to do it now. Just keep walking, right? I stand up, turn my back on the way I came.

The chorus of ancestors inside me objects and it's all I can do to tune them out. It's just a spooky room, right? Walk across to the other side of it, find your way back up and, presto, return to the First Circle.

I'm shaking. I try a step forward. As my foot moves up to step there are so many screams inside of me that it turns of its own volition and I fall back and land in a heap.

Very dignified.

'Ah, Aslan. Thanks.'

Ignore their words. Walk straight through and you'll be fine.

'You don't know that.'

No. But do you know which answers to believe? Maybe it's a lie that you can't go this way and you'll just be so scared that you never leave this place until you die.

I pause, thinking. 'OK, you have a good point. And while that does sound appealing – any suggestions?'

Go to sleep. I'll take us where we need to go; I can't hear the voices, and your dead are nothing to me.

'Like I can just drop off to sleep in this place.'

Be a passenger. Give me control, and you will sleep.

I remember how things were before I accepted Aslan as part of who I am inside – struggling against each other for control, especially in the sea. We had to learn how to share. Can I go back to how it was then?

I'll help you.

I'm in a dream, or a memory: one from Aslan? So different to the memories of the ancestors. This is vibrant, joyful, real. I'm swept along with the colours, the sounds, the sensation of being what he was before we were together.

Wild.

Joy!

Free.

Swimming, fast, furious, and then to the surface to fly through the air. Flip down and dive, dive, dive. Deep and bubbles spin.

Tag.

Chase!

One last dance.

26

Wake up.

I open my eye. Everything seems strangely doubled for a moment, then comes back together. We're in a room with lighting – no skulls or shrieking voices inside of me. I'm relieved, but also puzzled. This looks like the same room we went through to get below: empty but with a big wardrobe, pulled away from the wall.

'It didn't work?'

No. Disgust through his tone. *It was a trick.*

'Tell me.'

We walked and walked and ended up back where we started.

'Seriously? All that was for nothing?'

All for nothing.

'Rhiannon said I trusted the wrong answer. I should have listened to her.'

There is one thing I don't understand.

'Only one?'

When you were asleep and I was awake, things looked . . . different. Like in this room: that cupboard wasn't there, the walls were a different colour. As soon as you woke up, they changed back to how they were when we were here before.

'That's weird.'

I'm thinking through it all, sifting all the things I've seen here, felt, the memories, the voices. I feel like there is something I'm almost beginning to grasp but I'm not there yet.

I'm tired. Going to sleep. Don't *use the root again without me and a silver rope.*

'I won't. Go to sleep.'

I walk aimlessly, thinking. The corridors and rooms are empty again now, like they were when we first checked the place out; I mark a room by putting a chair in the hall upside down, and the gentle curve eventually takes me back all the way to where I started.

So, this place is a circle. The place below that Aslan wandered through with the skulls, also a circle. No matter where we go we end up back in the same place, so how do we leave?

I feel sick, weepy, exhausted, even though I slept for however long it was that Aslan was in control. I don't know if it is day or night and with that comes a strange, weary feeling, like I don't know if I should be awake or asleep. And running through it all is the sea. It's above and all around but I can't see it, I'm kept separate from it, and I'm longing so much to be in the water, swimming as fast as I can. Swimming with the kin. I need it like I need oxygen. It's a fever taking hold, one I can't fight.

I'm not paying attention to where my feet are taking me. I'm on autopilot, longing for the sea, the kin, so much that at first I don't notice where I'm going.

Then it registers: the winding path I'm on now, one that goes up, up. It's like where Ariel took me to the sea dome.

But it can't be, can it?

It leads to a door. One with a round wheel to open it, just like where Ariel took me.

I wind it around until the door opens. Through it is a big open space with a transparent dome curving up from the edges – it looks exactly the same as the dome we saw with Ariel, or so like it there is no difference. I must have homed in on the sea, and come here to be as close to it as I can be.

I raise my hands, splay my fingers along the transparent surface. As my eyes adjust I see more and more. Aslan stirs, wakens, and— Oh! Here they are. The kin.

We stand there, the kin all around us in the water, and even though there is this barrier between us and the sea, we are together. I start to breathe easier, feel less lost and alone.

What happened? Did you find the way back to the First Circle?

'No. I was walking without purpose and somehow just ended up here. Whatever circle we are in must have a dome, too.'

No. This is the same place we went with Ariel.

'But how can that be?'

It is the same dome: the kin remember us standing here with Ariel.

'You can communicate with them?'

Of course. Surprise. *Why would they come to us otherwise?*

'Calling them and having a conversation about memories aren't quite the same thing. Can all dolphins communicate the way you do with them?'

A pause. *I don't think so. Not in the same way. They don't have words for memories – they live in the now, though the past is part of what shapes now. I hadn't realised that I've changed so much.* He's uneasy, pulls away to think his own thoughts.

Everything is drifting through my mind as if I were floating in the sea. If he is right and we are in the same place, then that means we've been in the First Circle all along. But how can that be?

Things looked different to Aslan when I slept – when my eye was shut. Not just my sight was shut down, all my senses were asleep. I wasn't experiencing anything but dreams. I'm here with the voices from the past inside me, showing me memories, things Aslan doesn't experience. Maybe because of this he can see more clearly than I can?

If he's right – and we're in exactly the same place – then I'm not experiencing it the same way that he does when my influence is gone.

Why?

I have the ancestors; I've been living their memories much of the time. So is it like I'm seeing where we are with the eyes of the past?

Then how I experience time with the ancestors is different: it's not just one second leading orderly to another, the one before never to return. It's more like time spins around and I can step back to any ancestor's experiences of it.

Have we been in the same place all along, but in different circles of time?

Oh, well done! It's Rhiannon, using my hands to clap with glee once again.

27

Past. Present. Their circles overlap and intertwine inside me, and now that I understand, I can go to them at will. Despite that so many of my ancestors were playing with me like a cat with a mouse, most seem happy now that I've figured this out. Like children who've had a taste of freedom, they are content with a return to constraints, rules.

Most, not all. There are some inside me who will cause me trouble if they can, like Yvonne. Though maybe I should thank her also, as without Aslan's comment about how things look so different when I was asleep, I might never have figured out what was going on. But I still need to be careful – to work out which answers to question, like Rhiannon said. Or maybe it is more, to listen to those I trust? And Aslan is one of them.

'I couldn't have worked all this out without you and the kin.'

I know. Smug.

'Or you, Cate.'

You did this all by yourself. Well done! Time to front up to Cassandra and Phina?

'Let's go find them.'

We leave the dome behind, go down the spiral path towards the door and it opens before we reach it.

It's Malina. She's grinning widely and despite how much trouble she's caused me, she is so genuinely pleased that when she hugs me, I hug back, caught in emotions I can't even work out.

'I knew you could do it,' she says. 'Come on.'

She takes me to the meeting place and they're all waiting for us there: Phina and Cassandra at the centre below, everyone else sitting all around. Cassandra raises a hand, beckons us down.

We walk down the steps, one foot after another. All the seats around us are filled like they were before and the reactions cover everything:

Pleased surprise.

Disbelief, with or without grudging acceptance.

Relief, happiness – Cassandra, Ariel, Zara, the other Chosen.

Phina I can't read. There is something like a smile on her face but it is guarded, like there are things that she hides.

We take the last step down and walk over to them.

Cassandra smiles. 'Congratulations, child,' she says, and adds in a low aside to only me, 'Cate would be so proud.'

I am, Cate whispers inside me.

Cassandra addresses the room. 'Sisters, welcome Tabby to The Circle! We will dream together tonight.'

28

Cassandra and Malina take me to Cassandra's rooms to prepare me for the dreaming, whatever the hell that is. I'm feeling like I've had enough of cryptic weirdness and being told what to do; I need to know that what they want from me will lead to what I want, and not just spin more strands of a web that will hold me fast. Remember the plan: gain their trust, find out their secrets, get away, betray them.

And, most of all, discover who killed Cate and find Denzi, or what has happened to him.

'So, I gather I passed your test. Can you explain what that was all about?'

'There were two main components,' Cassandra says. 'First, to be able to channel the voices, to not be lost in their memories, and to gain the trust of our ancestors. Second, to recognise the space-time paradox and return to now.'

'Sure. That's what I did.'

'What it means is you worked out you were in the same place at different times.'

'What I don't understand is if I was in the same place all along and just seeing it like it was in the past through memories of ancestors, wouldn't I physically be in the same place the whole time anyhow? Wouldn't I walk into people in the here and now and stuff like that?'

'All times can be accessed from the same physical point of space. The memories you experienced run concurrently and independently. I can explain it more if you like, but you will understand more after the dreaming.'

'So, basically, because I figured out how to control the voices and about the space-time thing, now everyone is happy and wants me to sign up for life and have a dream-along-slumber-party. Is that it?'

Malina's eyes widen and she glances nervously at Cassandra, who just smiles.

'Something like that,' Cassandra says. 'Taking part in the dreaming is the final step to joining The Circle. It brings all of us – sisters, mothers, daughters, friends – together with ancestors. We use the dreaming drug; the plant root you found during your test is the source, though we have a more refined version that we use now. Any questions you have about The Circle and our past will be answered during the dreaming tonight.'

She begins to turn away but this time I won't miss my chance. 'What happened to Denzi?'

Cassandra exchanges a glance with Malina then shakes her head. 'In due course. When you are one of us there will be no more secrets.'

'Did you shake your head because he isn't all right, or because you won't tell me?'

'This is not open for discussion.'

I stare back at her a moment, gather my thoughts. 'So, to sum up: overall, The Circle has killed people on a massive scale. Hunted me down, kidnapped me. Put me through some crazy ordeal under the guise of a test. And now you want me to join without really knowing what The Circle is on the off chance I might find out something I want to know.'

'Malina, leave us for now, please.'

Malina gets up, worry etched between her eyebrows. Leaves and shuts the door behind her.

Cassandra sighs. 'This would be so much easier if Cate were here, if she could explain.'

'She is here. Inside of me.'

'What did you say?'

'One of the voices – it's Cate's.'

Her head tilts to the side and she looks at me carefully as if trying to read something on my face without giving anything away herself. There is something about her eyes that makes me squirm inside, but I hold her gaze.

She nods. 'All right, humour me for a moment. A question – let me see . . . ask Cate her true name.'

'Cate, are you there?' I say, silently.

Always here for you.

'I'm with Cassandra.'

Oh! I've missed her so.

'She wants me to ask you a question. What is your true name?'

It's Catelyn, because that is the name I chose. A mental sigh. *The name she asked my mother to give me, though, was Faith. I hated it and changed it when I was ten. She was the only person who insisted on calling me Faith. Here, I'll show you.*

Everything blurs . . . *changes.*

I'm lying on the floor, up on my elbows. Books spread all around. I should be reading and taking notes, but instead I'm biting my lip, concentrating: on the white paper, charcoal pencil. The drawing of a creature I dreamt of again last night. The dreams are coming more often, are more terrifying. If I can capture it on this piece of paper, name it and control it . . . it won't scare me any more.

It was a girl but not a girl – like a mermaid? No, not quite. Mermaids aren't real and anyhow, this was much scarier. Sure strokes of the pencil: her face, eyes – the eyes are important – and then the rest of her. Scales and fins, and—

'Faith?'

I'm startled, my pencil jumps on the page – a slash of black across my drawing. It's ruined. I could rub that mark out, but I'd always know it was there. I sigh, find another sheet of paper.

'Faith, it's time for dinner.'

My stomach is rumbling but I don't answer to Faith, I don't. I start drawing again, concentrating, and—

Footsteps. Cassandra sits next to me on the floor. Watches as I draw.

'Another nightmare?'

I shrug.

'I can help if you tell me.'

I sit up. 'Call me Cate and we'll see.'

'Where did you get this stubborn streak? Your mother was easier.'

'She at least calls me Cate.'

'Names are important. I've explained this to you before.'

'Yeah, so there's something in my future that needs a lot of faith and I'll be the girl for the job. But maybe I don't want to do whatever that is?'

Her hand touches my cheek, the sadness behind her eyes that is always there. What must it be like to always know what is coming? She never had a choice. I refuse to live like that.

Cate's memory bleeds away. I open my eyes, look at Cassandra, and wonder: did Cate win or lose that battle? Was the path she followed of her own choosing?

It was. I promise you: there is nothing I would rather have done than look after you.

My eyes are closed but tears still escape and trickle down my face. 'I don't know if I can do this dreaming thing, if I want to, if I should,' I say, silently.

I know. When we're alone we'll talk it through. All right?

I nod.

I think Cassandra is waiting to hear my name.

Oh yeah. I wipe my face, open my eyes. Turn to Cassandra. 'Did you always call her Faith?' I say.

Cassandra's face pales and she reaches a shaking hand towards me – touches my cheek as she did Cate's in that memory.

'Cate? She's really with you?' I nod. 'But how is this possible?'

'I've got all these other voices of ancestors, too. Why would Cate be any different?'

'We weren't there when she died. You'll understand more later but usually there is a transfer at, or soon after, the moment of death to a seer like me. I don't understand how this has happened.' Her eyes are glistening with tears.

I'm thinking back to the last time I saw Cate. We spent the night in our car, hidden in a barn – the police were after us.

'That last night I was with Cate I dreamt that she was

137

whispering in my ear all night long. Then the next morning, when the police came, it was like she wasn't herself – at all.'

Yes. You've got it. I transferred most of myself to you in your sleep. You didn't know until later as you weren't accessing your ancestors in a conscious way then.

I repeat what Cate said to Cassandra.

There's a mix of horror and pride in Cassandra to know what Cate did. 'She wouldn't have been able to live like that, not for long. With most of herself gone.'

Tabby, there are things I never had a chance to say to Cassandra. Can I speak through you?

'How?' I answer, silently.

Let me in . . . and I can be you. Just for a moment.

There's a rush of fear to think of letting anyone – even Cate – take over like that. But isn't that like what Aslan does sometimes? And we share – we don't fight for control any more, now that we understand.

'Yes. I trust you,' I say, silently. 'Do it.'

There's a strange feeling, like something is pouring into me, trying me on, and then . . . I'm not here any more. I can't feel the chair I'm sitting on – I can't feel anything physically, not breathing, not anything, and I'm struggling to control the rising sense of panic.

'Cassandra? It's me, Faith,' Cate says using my lips, throat, air movement to make sounds, but I can't feel that either. Instead I'm hidden inside, listening. Is this how it is for all of my ancestors? Just along for the ride, not really taking part ever again?

'I'll call you Cate now if you want,' Cassandra says. 'Why did you do this to yourself? How?'

138

Cate sighs. 'It doesn't matter. I knew I would die; I saw it. Cassandra, you knew, didn't you? That I could see. Even though I always denied it.'

'I'd guessed. But how did you do this – cut so much of yourself away and still live?'

'Rhiannon – one of the first ancestors – told me how. I won't share it. It's not easy.'

Something happens then – there is a barrier, one put up by Cate? And I can't hear what they are saying to each other any more, and it's like I'm locked inside, alone in darkness. What are they talking about? Why can't I hear it? Just as I start to panic, it eases.

Then there are arms I can't feel hugging me, and I can hear again. 'Cate or Faith or whoever you want to be, I love you. But let her go now.'

Cate is crying, something I sense as if from a distance, but don't experience myself.

'I love you, too,' she says. 'I'm sorry I didn't say it more.'

'I know. But you can't stay. You know what you have to do. Goodbye, Cate.'

Cate nods. Slowly she bleeds away and I slump back into myself, dizzy, nauseous, my face wet with my tears and Cate's, the two mixed together. Wearing my body again takes a moment to settle, for me to feel like I'm in control.

'Tabby? Are you back now?' Cassandra says.

I nod. Manage to look up to her.

'Cate told me she'll talk through what will happen tonight with you when you are alone. Now, go back to your room. Rest, and prepare yourself for what is to come.'

I nod, get up, wanting to get away, to be alone. Or as alone as I can be with a full complement of ancestors in residence.

'Tabby? One more thing. Listen to me carefully. Never, ever let an ancestor use your body like that again. Once you've done so, you can't come back unless they allow it. It's too dangerous.'

And I start to object: Cate was always going to let me come back; I trust her.

'She loves you, but it is a hard thing to be only a memory inside someone. The longer this is so, the harder. Don't put Cate – or anyone else – through that again.'

29

Ariel is sent for to show me the way to my room. And I'm guessing that isn't the only reason.

'Are you a bit freaked about the dreaming?' she says.

'Cassandra told me, but I don't really understand what it is'

'I didn't either. But to tell you, to describe it — I don't have the words. It's amazing! It's like everyone is connected, all of us, all of our ancestors too. I'm part of something in a way I've never been before.'

'I haven't had a great time with some of my ancestors.'

'Yeah, I'm guessing that would have been wild when you didn't know what was going on and how to deal with them.'

'Let me guess: I'll understand it all after the dreaming?'

'Yes. You will. And here we are.' Ariel opens the door, comes in with me, sits on the chair while I sit on the bed.

'Go on,' she says. 'Ask me anything — but you really will know everything—'

'After the dreaming? Got it. OK. Did you know about The Circle and your mum all along?'

She tilts her head a little. 'Depends what you mean by that. I mean, my mum has always been scary, you know? And I knew weird things were going on. But I didn't know it was the actual Circle that had been on the news; that freaked me right out once I knew.'

'Doesn't it still?'

Ariel looks back at me, taking time to answer. 'In a different way, I guess? Look, The Circle has been around for ever and done a lot of amazing things. Then came Cassandra and everything changed.'

I'm surprised. 'Are you saying it is because of her that they did the hurricanes and bombs and stuff?'

'Yes. Because she saw the future and told everyone. She wasn't supposed to do that. As a group they decided they couldn't let what she saw happen and came up with a plan to try to stop it. But then Cassandra and my mum had a big falling out about what they should or shouldn't do. The solution they came up with? *Us.*'

'The Chosen.'

'Yep. Apparently, we're going to come up with all the answers to save the world,' Ariel says. 'Or not. And it's up to us – not Cassandra or my mum or anyone else – so no one who supposedly knows what is going to happen can hold sway.'

'So, the dreaming doesn't include future stuff.'

'No. Only seers do that.'

'Cassandra and who else?'

'She's the only one.'

Maybe, she isn't. Am I a seer, too? There have been moments when I've thought I sensed future voices. Am I the only one of the Chosen who can do this?

Maybe that's why they went to such an effort to find and bring me here.

'What about the boys, like Denzi? He's one of us, I'm sure of it. Why aren't they here?'

'This is all about the sisterhood. No boys allowed.'

'There are children here, so does the stork bring them?'

She smirks. 'They don't fly underwater, so no. The ones who are born here are test tube babies.'

'Like us.'

'Yes, but not like us – as in, not the Chosen. They're just regular Circle kids.'

There is a tap on the door and a tray is brought in – with some of that nifty tea that makes you sleep, and what, on her way out, Ariel assures me is really decent chocolate: they add sugar to the bitter root to make it more palatable.

Soon it will be time to drink the tea and eat the chocolate and see what happens.

I'm scared.

There were so many things I wanted to ask Ariel but didn't. I'm not sure I can trust her – that's the reason, isn't it? I couldn't bring myself to ask what I really wanted to know. Did she seek me out because her mother told her to? Did she take part in the Hoover Dam bombings?

'Aslan, are you awake?'

I am here. What is wrong?

'I have to make a decision and I don't know what to do.'

Tell me.

I explain as much as I can.

This dreaming, would it make you closer to your kin?

'I guess.'

That is a good thing. Yet one is our enemy. Phina's image and Aslan's anger, together.

'Yeah. There may be others, too – kin who have done

143

things that are wrong and may not want what is best for me. For us.'

Is there an elder you trust? One you can ask what to do?

'Yes. Cate. Another thing: Cate said I should keep you and what we are together to myself, and I'm sure she's right. If I do this dreaming, will they all know?'

Ask Cate.

I pause. Gather my thoughts.

'Cate?'

There's a long pause. Then *Hi*.

'Are you all right?'

Just about. Seeing Cassandra like that . . . well, it was hard to say goodbye to her.

'She said I shouldn't let you, or anyone else, do that again.'

I know, and she's right. Are you ready for the dreaming?

'I'm scared,' I say. 'I don't know if I want to do this.'

Ah, I see. Why?

'A mixture of reasons. I was brought here against my will. When I was taken, my friend Denzi was hurt and no one will tell me if he is all right or where he is. No one has asked what I want. There are things The Circle has done that are horrendous.'

All good reasons, Cate says. *But somehow, I can sense that you still want to. Don't you?*

'I don't know. Maybe joining is the only way I'll find out what happened to Denzi, be able to help him if it isn't too late. And maybe I'm curious, but that isn't enough of a reason.'

It is who and what you are. Even if you think you can walk away from The Circle, the ancestors will always be part of you, inside. You can embrace this or fight against it, but it will still be

144

so. If you join with the dreaming you will have a better sense of who you are and how to deal with the past lives inside of you.

'You make it sound like I don't have any choice.'

There is always a choice, but maybe the options are different than you supposed at first glance? Before you decide, consider some context. If I hadn't been taken away from you too soon, I'd have explained all of this to you and we'd have come here together. You'd probably have felt differently about it then, wouldn't you?

'I guess so, though not about all of it – they still *killed* people.'

The promise we made together every year – that I believe in passionately, and I know you do, too – is The Circle promise. To honour and protect sun, sea, earth and sky above all else. Even human life.

I pause, thinking through what Cate said, but I still can't reconcile the things they've done. Something that feels so wrong just *can't* be right. And there is still so much I don't understand.

'Can you explain something to me? Why did you take me from my parents so we had to live on the run? Wouldn't things have been easier if that hadn't happened?'

She's quiet for so long I'm wondering if she won't answer.

OK. You can't tell anyone about this. Cassandra saw – so did I – that you would be of key importance to the Chosen. There are . . . factions, within The Circle. They don't always agree on the best way to do things.

'Do you mean Phina and Cassandra?'

In part. Cassandra felt you needed to be hidden away, to become who you are meant to be without being influenced in any way by these factions and their views. We were also concerned that if we didn't, someone else might have taken you, either to do you harm

145

or to attempt to indoctrinate you with their views.

'Are you saying that Phina might have kidnapped me, maybe even had me murdered, so you and Cassandra hatched a plan to get me away?'

Yes.

Even though I'd guessed as much, I'm still shocked when Cate confirms it.

'What about Simone's mum, Elodie. Did she know you were taking me away from Simone?'

There's a pause. *This may be hard to hear, Tabby. Elodie is one of Phina's supporters. We didn't inform her*.

'Are you saying my *grandmother* might have been involved in a plot to kidnap or kill me?'

I don't know for sure if she was involved in that part of things. I do know that you need to take care around Phina and Elodie. Some of the ancestors will be on their side, also.

'Is Yvonne one of them?'

Yvonne? Is she an ancestor?

'Yes.' I explain what happened during my test – that Yvonne led me below saying she'd help, then left me there.

I didn't know she'd died. Yvonne was a scientist and was one of those involved in searching for ways to end the Anthropocene – the age of man – without harming any non-human life. She worked closely with Phina, so best to take care around Yvonne also.

'The other thing I need to know: if I decide to do this dreaming thing, can I keep my own secrets?'

Yes. It's just the past that is shared.

'My past?'

No. Not until you have died, and even then you can decide

146

what to share and what not – to an extent. The living may see your memories if they have the skill and know to look for what you are hiding.

'OK,' I say, thinking through what she said. 'But if I join the dreaming, won't you be part of it with me? And then if someone with the skill to examine your memories looks into your past, won't they know all about you and Cassandra and the rest of it?'

There's a pause and I sense Cate's sadness, her looking for the words to tell me . . . *No.* No! She won't be there? Is that why she said it was so hard to say goodbye to Cassandra – because she'll never speak to her again, not even as an ancestor in the dreaming?

'Aren't you going to be part of the dreaming? And of me? Cate?'

No. For just those reasons, it's too risky. And anyhow, I can't.

'I don't understand. What is going to happen to you?'

Rhiannon explained it all to me. How to give you part of myself before I died, but because of the way it was done – while I was still alive – I can't be one of the ancestors and can't be part of the dreaming. Once you've joined, I'll be gone.

'You mean you're going to die – again?'

Something like that. It's OK. I've known this for a long time. Most people die, don't they, and are just gone?

'I won't do it, then. The dreaming. I can't lose you.'

It won't stop me from leaving soon anyhow. This, what I am in you, was only ever a temporary thing – an echo of who I was, and echoes fade until they are gone. Be strong. The Circle – and sun, sea, earth and sky – need you.

I'm crying. Losing her once was agony; how can I go through this again?

I told you I'd explain about how I died when you were ready. It has to be now. Earlier with Cassandra, you know how I transferred to you that last night? That is when I died. My body carried on without me, without much more than basic reflexes. It would have died soon after that, no matter what. I was a dead woman walking. It was my choice.

'Why? Why would you do this?'

It was the only way that I could see to help you. Never feel guilty about that, Tabby. It was my choice. I had faith in you but knew you still needed me to become what you needed to become.

'I don't understand. Even if you were dying, someone stabbed you. Didn't they?'

Yes. But I wasn't there to see who stabbed me, or why. But you know what? It really doesn't matter – it was just a shell. Nothing that makes me who I am was there. I'll show you.

Then she is taking me back. To her memories so that I can remember them for her and keep her with me in that way.

A day on a beach with her mum and older sisters.

Arguments with Cassandra.

Saying goodbye to her mother – she died? I didn't know.

The day she first met me.

The pain she felt, taking me from Simone and Ali knowing how much they loved me. Knowing it was the only way to keep me safe.

A kaleidoscope of happy and sad and all in-between.

A last word from me, Cate says. *If you join The Circle in the dreaming as one of the Chosen, you will decide our future. If we have done wrong, tell us so. And we will have to listen.*

And then she says goodbye.

I love you, Tabby.

'I love you, too.'

You'll do the right thing. I know you will.

It's almost time. I'm ready.

I drink the tea, then chew the chocolate. Ariel is right, it tastes pretty good, but it's like dust in my mouth.

I curl up on the bed, blankets pulled up, waiting for whatever will happen to begin.

Part 4
London

Hayden

@HaydenNoPlanetB
Global warming and subarctic forest fires are melting permafrost that has been frozen for thousands of years, releasing carbon they've kept safe for as long. Once it is released this cannot be reversed.

#NatureIsScreaming

30

'Hi. I'm DCI Palmer. We need to ask Hayden some questions.'

My arms are crossed against me, holding in the pain. My eyes are heavy, swollen from crying, but I can't cry any more.

'Does it have to be now?' Dad says.

'It's OK,' I say before he answers. 'If there is anything I can do to help get whoever did this to Bishan, I want to do it.'

'Thank you, Hayden. Can you tell us about the planning of the protest? Why this location was chosen?'

'Oh. Well, it was Bishan who chose it.'

'Do you know why? Or why your group didn't honour its commitment to the Met to register the protest beforehand?' I don't answer, not sure what to say.

'I've interviewed a healthcare assistant from the hospital nearby who came forward after the shooting.'

'Yeah?' My mind is trying to process this and what it means – does he know what Apple and I did? Is he here to bang me up for trespassing or something? In the face of what happened to Bishan, that seems so unimportant. 'What has that got to do with Bishan and whoever shot him?'

'We'll get there. She said she left a back door unlocked and a door pass. So that friends of Bishan's could get in to see a patient. And she also saw a note written by the same patient days earlier, that began, "Hi H."'

'What is this about?' Dad says.

'Perhaps the protest was where it was to make some noise to cover Bishan's friends getting into this secure hospital. And the patient they wanted to meet with is now missing. Do you know anything about this, or where he might be?'

'What about Bishan?'

'We'll get to—'

'No. *Now*. Who shot Bishan? Isn't that why I'm talking to you?' I say, even as, slow on the uptake in my current state, what he said just drops. Missing? Denzi is missing?

'Could you tell me where you were throughout the protest? You were there when it began – you've been spotted on CCTV at the site of the protest – but you went off screen to the side where the hospital is located, and you didn't reappear until a number of minutes later. What were you doing?'

Does he think I had anything to do with what happened to Bishan?

Maybe, I did. And I'm blinking back tears, breathing, trying to get control.

'I think that's enough,' Dad says.

'For now.' He hesitates. 'I'm so sorry you lost a friend that way. I can only imagine how difficult it must have been, being there, watching it happen. But think about what we discussed today. We will need to take this up again another day.'

His sympathy seems so genuine despite the questions. I thought I couldn't cry any more, but I was wrong.

I get up, run from the room and upstairs to my bedroom. I hear the front door a short time later.

I struggle to pull myself together, to focus. I wasn't expecting to be asked about that. Denzi had been pushed right out of my mind by Bishan. I visualise a door slamming in my head, but it's too late to stop the memory replaying in my mind. I cringe as Bishan falls to the ground – all the blood, the confused look in his eyes, like what is happening to me? All of it rushes through my mind.

The whole thing with Denzi – what was I thinking, that I was some sort of superhero who could rush in and solve problems? Without that we wouldn't have been there. It wouldn't have happened.

Bishan – at Eva's funeral – said it wasn't my fault. Just like I told him those other kids who died at the next protest weren't his fault. Now I've got another not-my-fault-but-totally-feels-that-way and it's one too many.

31

Much later I get myself up. Splash water on my face and open my laptop.

I've been avoiding the news the last few days – I can't watch the carefully blurred footage of what happened without filling it all in, remembering every detail. Likewise, I'm not going to the BBC website or anything like that – it'll be there, won't it?

Instead I do a search – Denzi Pritchard.

And nothing new comes up. Surely if he was missing it'd be all over the news? Though nobody seemed to know he was in that hospital, either.

I think through what this DCI said as much as I can remember with the state I was in. He didn't use Denzi's name, did he? Just referred to him as a *patient*. If he was sure it was me who went into the hospital, I must have known who the patient was. So why didn't he use his name?

Maybe he was just fishing to see if I knew anything. Or, if he does know it was me, to see if I'll answer his questions truthfully. I didn't lie, just deflected, but it still sits uneasily in my gut as being not a good idea with the police.

Everyone – the news, Mum and Dad, me – have assumed Bishan was killed by some right-wing crazy with a grudge against environmentalists, but maybe that isn't so.

What if instead, whoever killed Bishan is involved in Denzi's disappearance? Denzi said he had dangerous information; Denzi's mum pushing the police to interview him might be what made him disappear. And Bishan was the one who arranged us getting into the hospital – maybe whoever did this thought he was a danger, too.

If there is any chance of that being true, I have to tell the police what we did and why. Or maybe somebody will be after me. And what about Apple?

She's texted and tried to call a few times and I haven't answered, haven't been up to interacting with anyone. But maybe it's time.

Phone out, I text Apple: hi

Hi. WTF is wrong with this world? I still can't believe what happened.

Me either.

Are you ok?

No. Not really. Can we meet up? Need to talk.

Course. Where?

Not sure I'll get out of the house again before I'm twenty. Can you come here?

Yes.

I give her the address. I won't tell them you're coming in case they say no. Text when you're nearly here.

32

I'm watching at the window upstairs when Apple gets out of a taxi at the front.

Dad is at the door by the time I get down the stairs.

'I'm not sure Hayden is up to having a visitor just now—'

I come up behind Dad. 'Yes, it's fine. Come in.'

'Uh, OK.' I can see the questions in Dad's eyes but introduce them quickly, link an arm with Apple and we go up to my room. Shut the door.

'Denzi's missing,' she says, without preamble.

'So it's true?'

'You know something? Tell me.'

I gesture and she sits on my desk chair. I sit cross-legged on my bed and repeat everything the DCI said as well as I can remember.

'Was that DCI Palmer?'

My turn to be surprised. 'Yes, I think that was his name. Why? Did he go talk to you, also?'

'Not exactly. He's the DCI that Leila has been talking to about the two murders.' She flinches at the word *murders* – one of them being her dad. 'She'd been trying to persuade him to get a court order to interview Denzi. When I got back from the protest, I told her everything we'd done and that Denzi wasn't there. She fronted up at the hospital – once she could get through the police cordon.' She hesitates.

'Where Bishan died.'

'Yes. I'm sorry I wasn't there to face that with you. I'd got as far as the Tube, heard all this noise, and when I tried to go back to see what was happening, they wouldn't let me through.'

'I know. Thanks.'

'Anyhow, they said Denzi had been checked out of the hospital by his doctor, but they didn't know where he went.'

'Then why did the DCI say he was missing?'

'Leila's asked them to file a missing persons report on him.'

'Wow. Do the police know what we did?'

'Leila told them what we did and that Denzi wasn't there to push the police to investigate what happened to him.'

'So this DCI isn't going to be happy with me, not confirming what he already knew.'

'Probably not. Sorry again. I tried to call but . . . well, you know.'

'Sorry I didn't answer. I was – am – a mess.'

'It's fine. I understand.'

'Were they bothered about what we did – going in the back door to Denzi's room?'

'We didn't actually break in or anything, but they weren't delighted. Anyhow it doesn't look like anything is going to be done about it. I'm not sure if that friend of Bishan's who helped us get in is OK though.'

'Normally I'd take that straight to Bishan's dad the lawyer to see if he could help. But just now?' I shake my head.

'Yeah. I get it. Isn't your mom a lawyer, too?'

'It's not really her thing. Helping people I mean.'

'Ah, I see. Maybe you should give her a chance?'

'Yeah. Maybe. Thing is, I haven't told them anything about what we were doing.'

'Uh oh. You really should, you know. Would moral support help?'

33

'Hi. Hayden? Pleased to meet you.'

'Hi, Mrs Klein,' I say, and it seems weird to be meeting her in person after spending so many hours trying to track her down, then watching for her at her hotel with Bishan — and the pain twists inside to remember.

'Call me Leila. First of all, I'm so very sorry about your friend. That must have been such a shock.'

'Yeah. Thanks. And sorry about your husband, too.'

She and Apple are introducing themselves to Mum and Dad, and I have a sick twisting feeling in my gut. They're going to be so upset with me. We sit down in the front room and I can see the questions in their eyes as to why Apple and her stepmum are here.

'I understand you and Apple have been up to some mischief,' Leila says.

'I guess you could say that,' I say.

'What's this about?' Mum.

'I'm sorry, I should have told you about all of this before. I don't think I was thinking clearly after . . . well. Anyhow, I still should have told you.'

'Go on,' Mum says. All eyes are on me. I swallow, mouth dry.

'It's about my son,' Leila says. 'He was incarcerated in the hospital next to the protest.'

'We were trying to get in to see him,' I say. And see Mum and Dad glancing at Leila. 'She didn't know – it was Bishan, Apple and me.'

I explain about Denzi not answering messages, how worried I was, how Bishan helped and I met Apple.

'He arranged for the protest to be there and then we snuck through a propped open door to see Denzi. But when we got there, his room was empty. He was already gone.'

'So that explains why they were asking about the hospital,' Dad says.

'Do the police know?' Mum's lips pressed into a thin line. Reaction held in check by Leila and Apple being in the same room, but later? I don't like my chances.

'Yes, I told them once I found out,' Leila says. 'The hospital are saying Denzi was checked out by his doctor, but they don't know where he went after that. I'm trying to convince the police that he's a missing person but everything seems to be on a go-slow. Something about who his dad is, I suspect.'

Mum raises an eyebrow.

'Denzi Pritchard. Home Secretary Pritchard's son.'

They get up to leave soon after that.

Apple gives me a hug at the door.

She's so strong. How is she like that? Her dad only just gone; her mum dead years ago. Her brother is missing. She's away from home and her girlfriend and still, somehow, she's trying to help me.

'Let's talk,' Mum says, and draws me down next to her on the sofa. 'Let's see if I've got this straight. You and Bishan actually staged a protest next to this hospital to sneak in and see this boy?'

'Yes.'

She glances at Dad. 'We'll have to get that DCI back so you can tell him the truth.'

'OK.'

'I just can't get over the thought that it could have been you: that you could have died.'

'But I didn't.'

There are tears in her eyes. 'I couldn't stand to lose you. Your dad convinced me to let you have your way with being part of these climate protests, but no more.'

And they're waiting for my reaction, but there is none. Not now. I feel too numb, like nothing is real. Like I'm looking in a mirror and wondering who the girl I can see actually is.

I make excuses, go to my room. Lie on my bed and stare at the ceiling.

There it is: the excuse. I can't be involved any more because of my mum. I can just walk away, let it be somebody's else's problem. I've done enough – lost enough. Haven't I?

Usually if Mum tells me I can't do something, it's like waving a red flag at a bull: cue arguments, slamming doors. Getting Dad on my side and trying again. But this time I understand why she wants to keep me away from it – she wants to keep me safe. Dad didn't say anything earlier but it wouldn't surprise me if he feels the same.

But what would my life be like? What would it mean? If I just go to school. Do homework. Watch some TV and try the impossible: to forget.

Eva would be so unimpressed. Bishan, too.

34

DCI Palmer comes by again – this time Mum and Dad are both with me.

'Hi Hayden. I understand you wanted to talk to me?'

'Yes. There are some things I didn't know how or what to say before. But I know you know about Apple and me going into the hospital.'

'Ah, I see. Tell me, in your own words, why you went there, what you did.'

I go through all the details: how I was worried about Denzi, met his sister, Apple, and found out Denzi was in the hospital. How Bishan arranged passing notes back and forth, and then set up the protest next to the hospital so we could sneak in and speak to Denzi. But he wasn't there.

I hesitate. 'The press are all going on about anti-green terrorists, and I know Bishan's parents have confirmed there have been threats made against him. But do you think what happened to Bishan might be because of Denzi somehow? And what about Denzi – where is he?'

'We're pursuing all possible angles at this point. Now, going back to when you left the hospital. Could you tell me what happened after you found Denzi's room was empty?'

'We left his room, put the key back over the desk and rushed down the hall. Someone saw us and called out, so we ran the rest of the way and out the door to the lane behind the hospital.'

'Was there anyone in the lane when you came out?'

'There was someone walking past – I half ran into them. Said sorry and kept running.'

'Can you describe them?'

'I don't know, it was just an instant and we were in a bit of a panic that somebody might be chasing us. It was a woman,' I say, and frown, trying to remember. 'I turned towards her when I said sorry, but she was looking the other way so I didn't see her face. But now I think about it, that's odd, isn't it? To not turn to see who it is when somebody runs into you?'

'Can you remember anything else about her? What she wore, how tall she was, any details?'

'Um, I think she was taller than me but I'm not really sure. Don't remember what she was wearing – nothing that stood out.'

'Did you see anyone else?'

'No. We just pelted around the corner and back to the protest.'

'If you remember anything else' – he puts his card on the table – 'give us a call.'

'Do you think that woman I saw has anything to do with Denzi being missing and what happened to Bishan?'

'We need to interview all possible witnesses. Thank you for answering these questions. But if you ever have occasion to be talking to the police again – try to be more forthcoming from the start.'

'Don't worry, she will be,' Mum says.

They talk a moment longer, he says goodbye, starts heading

for the door. I'm sure there's more, something about the woman I saw. I tuck the card he left in my phone case, still trying to put myself back there in that moment . . . Oh, yeah.

'Wait. Red hair. She had long, red hair.'

Part 5
Undersea

Tabby

@HaydenNoPlanetB
The Atlantic meridional overturning circulation is an essential regulator of the earth's climate, taking warm, salty water near the surface north and cooler, denser water south. But melting ice in Greenland is diluting the cool water so it doesn't sink, and the whole thing is slowing down – it's heading for a complete shutdown.

#NatureIsScreaming

35

When I open my eyes I am not in a place I have seen before – I'm not even in a form I'm familiar with. I feel as I always do – like a physical being – but when I hold out my hands, there is nothing there. This should be terrifying, yet strangely I'm not scared. I'm curious.

'Tabby?' Cassandra says, but in my mind, not my ears. She holds out her unseen hand. I take it, and it feels reassuringly solid and real. 'Welcome to The Circle. Welcome to what we are, what we have been, and may yet become.'

Words are too small to encompass what unfolds as I join with my sisters. I'm both my own self and everyone else at once, and I can see their thoughts and wishes as easily as my own. We are together, a collective; not individuals, but part of a whole that is more than each of us added together.

Just when I think I may be overwhelmed, our focus shifts back in time. To where life began.

The sea is first mother, where life began on earth.

We serve the four, always. Sun, sea, earth, sky – the four interlink and must do so for life to exist.

And life *burns*, so bright; it ends. That is what it is for – what it does.

But must all of the earth and life upon it reach a point of no return, where the totality dies and is gone for ever? As we live

169

and die, planets live and die. So do stars.

What is the answer?

Is there an answer?

We don't know. And we have sought this knowledge since we began. We have the means inside us to access the past through our ancestors as we do now; we've selected and strengthened this ability to learn from our shared past. As our understanding of time grew, so did the abilities of our seers, like Cassandra and Alicia before her. Circles of time intersect, overlap – and complete each other. Time can go backwards and forwards, fast and slow; seers began to develop the ability to follow the future strands to see what was to come.

But the very act of observing the future changes what is yet to be: the observer and observed interact in ways they would not otherwise. And if failure is known, expected, is that the real reason it is assured?

In just such a happening many hundreds of years ago, it was foreseen that many of us would die – be hunted as witches – and not harvested to stay with The Circle. And so this happened and much knowledge was lost. Abilities and techniques we had, such as when Atlantis was built, are gone from us now.

Did the *seeing* make it certain to happen? A decision was taken to breed this ability out from most of us.

Are we witches?

What are witches? If what is meant by a witch is a wise woman with a connection to nature, then yes. But it isn't a word we claim, even though at times it is thrust upon us.

As we were changing ourselves to breed out the ability to see the future, the ability to enter the dreaming was waning.

170

We found a way to focus our minds and bring it back: the tea and the root help. But more and more of our daughters do not dream even with this help, and cannot join The Circle. Our numbers have been gradually declining.

So in some very few of us the ability to look ahead was honed and selected, to protect the joining in dreaming, but where seers were once common, now they are rare.

Throughout history my sisters have been there. Guiding, choosing who to help and who not. And I'm seeing – living – *feeling* – all of this, and at the same time I'm separate. In my own mind and my own skin I'm a point in time – temporary, a blink. But as part of The Circle, we have created, guided and shaped our charges from the beginning. Intervened and helped when we could. The hands that rock the cradle have rocked this earth – we are its mother in a very real sense.

The planet's history is long, but in a cosmic sense, humanity is so very new: if time from the beginning of the big bang to now were made a year, humanity wouldn't appear until less than a second to midnight on New Year's Eve. The changes humanity has wrought on our earth in short millennia – especially in the last few hundred years – are shocking.

We weep together for the lost and missing. Each life – whether human, fluttering butterfly, grand dinosaur or tiny beetle; every fish, grass or slender tree. So much has been lost and is being lost; even now while we are dreaming, more species disappear for ever.

I meet my ancestors one by one, and not just as voices in my head. Now that none of us has physical form, they are as real to me as I am. All my sisters who still live are here too – many live in Undersea, others are scattered around the world: all of us come together as one with the dreaming.

There are some hugs and tears from my ancestors, apologies for not helping me more, but it was the nature of the test – they had to be sure of who and what I was. And are they sure now? Yes: they all agree and hold me close until I believe in them and they in me, and I'm a cherished part of The Circle.

I lived alone with Cate for most of my life – never had friends until I met Jago, let alone any other family – and now I've gone from nought to a hundred in a second. Now I *belong* to something. I'm part of the biggest family that has ever been and know them all – their thoughts, feelings – intimately.

Cate is not amongst us. I'd hoped so hard that she was wrong – that she'd join when I did. Suffering the pain of her loss all over again is immense, even more since I cannot share why this pain is so fresh, so recent. All but Cassandra think she was lost to us from the moment her body died. Yet the pain is eased by all those around me who have memories of Cate's life like I do. Together, we gather the pieces to make a whole; to see who and what she was, and cherish her memory.

There are other dreamers that joined for the first time not long ago, and they seek me out: some of the Chosen didn't survive when the sea swept through the school. I see it all – as it happened – through their eyes; feel their panic and fear as they died. Then their joy as they were harvested by The Circle to return to us now.

But the survivors and those harvested are all girls: what happened to the boys?

Surplus to requirements. They needed some to ensure

continuation of us as a new species. Some were saved for this purpose.

I'm shocked.

Denzi? What happened to him? The love and tenderness of my sisters fills me, seeks to displace my feelings for him.

Yes, Denzi is alive.

He is one of us – has Circle and dolphin DNA. Doesn't he?

Yes. We had to make sure of the continuation of both with such a small number of you, and that was the only way.

Where is he? Was he hurt when we ran for the sea?

No. He is well, just unconscious for a time so we could take him someplace to look after him until he is needed.

But he's one of us. Isn't he? So why isn't he cherished along with the rest of the Chosen?

His is not the hand that rocks the cradle. And they show me more memories, lives lived and lost – the pain and deaths of countless of my sisters at the hands of men.

Tears run down my face. We can change things. Make it better.

There is amusement. So young – so idealistic. I feel like a two-year-old being patted on the head.

'It is we who have the force of creation; they, destruction. Look back, through time,' Cassandra says. 'Then you will understand.'

I can see the circles of time more clearly than before. Time isn't like a line, where something happens, and then something else, all in a tight orderly row of measured minutes and hours that tick down and are gone for ever; it's more that it spins around us, goes fast/slow, forwards/backwards – you can see everything all at once if you stand in the centre of it all and see the elegant

173

connections. Like advanced maths times a trillion, it is all there and makes perfect sense.

Only a seer can harvest another seer. And I see how Cassandra inherited from Alicia when she was a frightened child, done in the most dramatic way – a knife and blood – as they couldn't return to Undersea and do it properly.

I travel back further and further at will, interspersed with glimpses of now. I can't find Rhiannon? Cassandra says she is one of the first; that she and her generation are stretched so far in time that they rarely join in. There is awe in many to know that Rhiannon spoke to me.

Although this all feels like a joining up of all of us, past and present – all equals – still, there are some I remain guarded with. Casssandra, Phina and Yvonne keep parts of themselves shielded, too. They are here and join in, but seem to hold back parts of themselves.

So do I, and not giving all of myself to my sisters feels wrong. But I keep Aslan hidden; things Cate told me, and how she was with me until now. Only Cassandra has this secret.

But Ariel shares all – at least, I think she does. She admits she befriended me when we first met to keep an eye on me for her mother. She's sorry, she says.

'I thought you didn't get on with your mum. Is that true?' I ask her.

She shrugs. 'She hasn't been around much. I get why, now. Saving the world and all that takes time, I guess.'

'When I asked you if you knew about the Penrose Clinic, you said you didn't.'

'I'm sorry. I was sworn to secrecy.'

'And did you do it? The bombings. I saw you on the news.'

She shows me: how she and others went to Hoover Dam, how they planted devices to destroy it. How they wept for life lost, but why they still did it.

If the things The Circle have done will make humanity stop destroying the world and all life on it, is it justified?

I'm taken from life to life, around the world. See the pain and destruction humans cause wherever they go – now on a bigger scale than ever. The Circle needed to do something dramatic to even get the world's attention, and when I'm inside another life, being shown how they felt and why they acted, I get it – why they did these things. But does saving many justify sacrificing a few? I don't know. It's hard to think and feel on these scales, but how many billions will die if we do nothing – people, plants, animals? How can we not try to stop it from happening?

And alongside *then* and *now* is *yet to be*. I remember something like a dream that I had: that all the future voices were silenced. But Cate said only Cassandra can see the future.

Cassandra is startled: she whispers in my mind to keep this to myself; to not look too far ahead.

But she did. She didn't know any better; she was a young child when she harvested Alicia – she was the only one with the ability to see that could be taken to Alicia in time before Alicia died. Cassandra was too young to understand right from wrong no matter how the ancestors told her.

She saw the future: humans destroying the natural world until the voices were silenced for ever.

And she did what Cassandra now tells me I must never do: she told everyone what she saw.

There was – *is*, will continue to be – a rift in The Circle between those who thought we must protect all life and sun, sea, earth and sky as we have always done, no matter how futile it may seem, and those who thought humanity had to be purged from the world, so it could heal and grow until it was ready for us to begin and seed new life again.

The Circle couldn't agree, so they compromised. Humanity would be given another chance: hence the hurricanes, fires and bombs of The Circle, their demands to stop extraction and use of dirty energy. But the condition placed on securing agreement for this last chance? Us. The Chosen.

We are designed to survive in a drowned world, to carry on if humanity is gone – whether we allow them to self-destruct slowly, or we hurry things along to rid them from the earth like fleas on a cat, to ensure it is not too damaged to sustain us.

Or – instead – we could attempt to change the course of time and history, to stop the end Cassandra saw from happening at all.

It's up to us.

And that's why we are here, and what we are. Created to make this decision; to carry out this task.

To save, or to destroy.

36

The next time I open my eyes I'm back in my room in Undersea. I look at my hands: yep, normal, perfectly visible, five-fingered sort of hands. I sit up in bed and try to take in what I felt, saw, experienced.

So you're back.

'Hi Aslan. Have I been gone for long?'

I think a few days. But it is hard to judge when you're alone, waiting.

'Sorry. You didn't experience any of that?'

Any of what? Tell me.

'I don't know where to start but I'll try. It was like I woke up in another place but not as myself. I mean, I could think normally – if any of this is anything like normal – but I wasn't actually there.'

If you could think, then you were there. Like I am, with you.

'Good point. Anyhow, everyone from The Circle was there too, and all of my ancestors. It's as if the voices I hear stepped out of my mind and were as real as me. And I could see back in time to things that happened to my ancestors, and even further back. And I could look forwards in time, too.'

Forwards? What do you mean?

'Like things that haven't happened yet – I could trace time and look ahead.'

Forwards is wrong.

177

'Why?'

If you see where you will catch the fish and go straight there, what about the chase?

'You'd get your meal.'

It is good to eat fish. It is also good to chase them.

I try to explain more to Aslan about it all, but it's hard to put it in a way he understands. But this he does: that all my life I've felt like an outsider, that I didn't belong anywhere. Denzi changed that: he was like me and when I was with him, I felt like that was enough.

But being here is something else again.

There are some like me – Ariel, Zara, all the other Chosen – in the same way that Denzi is like me. Yet here he's not considered to be part of anything, and why is that? Because he's a boy. Take that, patriarchy.

I shake my head. Focus.

The other members of The Circle – Cassandra and everyone – are like me in a different way. They're not as close as the Chosen, yet even so they are still all my sisters.

They are your kin.

'Yes. Being here is belonging in a way I have never felt before. Here I am part of something that is bigger than myself. But is the something *wrong*? The Circle do stuff that kills people, destroys things. They threaten more. The motivation may be to stop climate change, to save the planet in a very real sense. But is the *why* even important? It's still murder.'

It's wrong. Why doesn't matter.

'How do you see complex things so easily, so simply?'

We are the kin. We are for all of us. The kin followed you to be caught in a net and would never, ever leave you behind, not while you still lived. Even if we all died.

After a while Aslan sleeps and I think without him listening in.

If people were more like the kin, the things I'm struggling with would not exist. Everything is so clear to him.

At least I know Denzi is all right, even though no one would tell me just where he is. They seemed alternately worried that I care about him, and convinced I'll grow out of it soon. Huh.

That the Circle is divided is clear. Phina and her followers had to be convinced to even give humanity a second chance; Cassandra and hers convinced them to make us, the Chosen, to decide for them.

Like, *thanks*. You couldn't manage on your own and saddled us with your problems.

But I can't see clearly what is right.

Before the dreaming, I was sure what I must do: gain their trust, learn their plans, find out what happened to Denzi and where he is – then escape, find Denzi and betray them. But now? Everything is confusion. How could I betray my sisters? How can I not, if they plan more disasters or even to destroy humanity? The only points in all of this that are still clear is that I must find Denzi, and – despite Cate saying it didn't matter because she wasn't in her body any more – if there is a way to find out who stabbed her in prison? I want – *need* – to know

It is tempting, so tempting, to look ahead – to know what will happen and not have to agonise over all of this.

But Aslan is right. I need to chase the fish, or what is the point?

179

Aslan's loyalty to his kind is absolute. Before he was taken away from them, he lived for the joy of swimming, the joy of eating fish. The joy of being one of the kin. They don't kill except for food or to defend.

If humans were more like dolphins, this world wouldn't be such a mess.

Maybe that is why we – the Chosen – *can* do something to fix this planet: we are both. But I get from Cate that the sisters don't know what I am inside – half Tabby, a girl of The Circle; half Aslan, a dolphin. Phina just meant to give us the means to survive in the sea; she didn't know the implications of taking genes from a split-brained dolphin and putting them into someone like me.

And I'm desperate to know if all the Chosen are like me inside – having a conversation with their dolphin half all the time. Or maybe it is more of an unconscious, hidden thing for them, like it was for me at the start. Or maybe this central core of me and who and what I am with Aslan isn't there at all for the rest of them.

Cate said to be careful of Phina and her friends. She and Cassandra thought they might have sought to influence me or even harm me when I was a baby. Why? Is it because they sensed somehow that I'd become a seer? Cassandra said to keep that to myself. Or was it because of Aslan: Cate said to tell no one about him.

I sigh. I'll have to find a way to figure all this out, resist looking at the future, and keep Aslan a secret.

I smile to myself. Imagine if my sisters knew that half of me inside is a *him*.

37

'We're what – three hundred metres or more from the surface? Are you sure the water pressure is OK to swim in?' I say.

'Yep, totally,' Ariel answers. 'Would kill your standard human, but we're fine. Part of Mum's DNA tweaks to the Chosen.'

I'm pulling on a wetsuit alongside Ariel and Zara, the huge grin on my face matched by theirs.

'Ready?' Zara says.

'Yes!' we both answer as one.

Ariel opens the heavy door, we step through, close it. It locks and we wait as the air pressures goes up. Unwind a hatch, go through to a small chamber, a sea lock built just for us Ariel says. Wind the hatch back up and seawater starts rushing in. I am part scared, part elated.

Zara and Ariel are grinning like I am and there is this sense of being kin – that we are the same. If we weren't, why would they feel the same as I do about the sea?

Aslan stirs, wakens.

We swim?

'Yes.'

He makes a sound in his thoughts that is as close to a lion's roar as I could imagine a dolphin making. *It's been so long!*

The chamber is close to full, I draw air in deep, hold. The pressure I could feel in the submersible I can feel again, but the pain of being separated from the water is gone. The external door opens – the sea!

We swim out through the door into the dark sea and they come as if to meet us: the kin.

Some I know from before: they swam with me in Cornwall and then later they came near to Hastings to swim with Denzi and me. Afterwards – when Denzi fell and I ran into the waves – they came and took me out, out, until we were caught in a net. They were released when I gave myself up to The Circle and was hauled on board deck. They must have followed me here.

They fuss and swim around me now as if to make sure I'm OK. Then one I know well comes closer. I reach out a hand, lightly touch her. Hold on to her dorsal fin and we're off – fast and faster, carving through the water. Soaring through the sea like an eagle in the air.

A blur of water and speed, joy set free inside of me and Aslan, both. When we break the surface to breathe – Ariel and Zara and their dolphins, too – the wildness of Aslan is taking me over and my view shifts, changes. Everything more vibrant, alive. He sings in our mind to the kin around us.

They do not reply.

'They?'

Ariel and Zara: they do not reply to the kin – at least, not the way I do. They are not like us.

'The kin come to them, swim with them?'

They sense they are kin, but they do not speak.

Eventually Ariel signals that we must go back. The pull of the sea is so strong and I'm rebelling, wanting to stay and swim, free in the sea. They can't make me go back with them.

They are not your only kin, Aslan says. *The two-legged ones need you*. It is as much the regret with which he says this as anything else that brings me back.

My vision shifts back to normal as he withdraws. Our dolphins return us to where they found us – by the sea lock. It is still open and full of seawater for our return. There is a deep wrench inside, as each of the kin come close enough for me to reach a hand, a touch, to say goodbye for now, and I swim into the lock to join Ariel and Zara. They're looking at me strangely as the doors close, the water begins to drain away.

'What?' I say, once the water level is low enough to speak.

'The dolphins,' Zara says.

'You have swum with them before?'

'Yes. But not quite like today.'

We open the hatch, step through, relock it.

'How so?'

We start to peel off our wetsuits.

'I don't know, it was different,' Ariel says. 'They were so happy and excited. And there were so many of them – there must have been, I don't know, twenty ? There's never been anywhere near that number before.'

Suits off, we're wrapping up in towels.

'And it was like they all came up to you to say goodbye,' Zara says. 'What was that about?'

I shrug, not sure what to say. 'I don't know. Maybe they were checking out the new girl a little closer.' I poke at Aslan in my mind – sound asleep. Worn out and now I'm yawning, too.

He said they don't speak to the kin like he does. Is it more

183

friendly curiosity that brings the dolphins to Ariel and Zara? And with me, it's Aslan, too.

'I'm starving,' Ariel says. 'Quick shower and go for lunch? I'll come get you,' she says to me.

Before long I'm standing in the shower. The water is cool but feels overheated after the sea.

Ariel said there must have been twenty dolphins.

And I know there were twenty-two, and not because I counted them. I know each dolphin as an individual, recognise the way they swim, who they prefer to swim alongside, sense their personalities.

I may be the only one with an Aslan. Even as I cherish him and what we have together, there is a sense of sadness inside, to not have anyone to share this with.

Why would I be different?

There is something else that is different about me: that I could be a seer like Cassandra. Does that make a difference to how I relate to Aslan? I think part of being a seer is being able to stand apart from the circles of time, to be able to see and follow them and know they are separate from myself. Maybe that has an impact on how I relate to Aslan?

I remember something Aslan said too, when he told me the kin had seen us and Ariel at the dome. That the kin live in the now and that he didn't realise how much he had changed. Maybe me being a seer has changed him too.

What about Denzi? Is he like me in this way, or did I just assume he was because of how we swam together? I don't know.

I worry about him and miss him so much. Yet I know that much of how I felt being with him was this sense of wonder at being with somebody who was like me for the first time in my life. Is that all there was to it? We were together so short a time, I can't know for certain.

Maybe I have been missing something in him that wasn't there at all.

38

Ariel's arm is linked with mine as we walk into a dining hall. Zara waves and we walk through to four long tables, all the Chosen together. There are places for us across from Zara somewhere in the middle of one of them. As we walk around the table to our seats, I'm remembering being at swim school and feeling out of my element with so many people all around, and there are even more of us here than that: there are the girls that survived from our swim school, yes, but also others from similar places around the world. Were we weeded out, like some sort of survival of the fittest? I shudder inside.

Anyhow, as for how I feel to be part of such a large group now, things have changed since the dreaming. Before then I only really knew Ariel and Zara, but now everything is different. They are all my sisters; I know them more intimately than I have known anybody before – except perhaps Cate – and it's rather like I felt with the dolphins earlier. I know each of them and who they are inside, and it feels new, strange, to feel part of something. Not watching from the outside.

'Lunch is fish – what a surprise,' Ariel says.

Our plates are being brought now. Were they waiting for us?

'Ariel, you just made it before it started to go cold,' a woman chides her as she sets her plate in front of her.

'She's always last to arrive,' Zara says.

'Not any more: now it's me and Tabby who are last.'

I tilt my head to the side, thinking, as I regard my plate. 'What was with everyone being vegan before? Now that I get that the swim school was all about bringing the Chosen together and that The Circle was ultimately behind it all, why were they so for veganism then, but not now?'

'Well, apparently, they thought raising us vegan was a good idea,' Ariel says. 'In case the taste of flesh brought out our animal side.'

Zara puts her head back and does a not bad imitation of a wolf's howl and they're laughing, but I'm remembering how I was when I first tasted fish. I wanted to pick it up in my hands, rip it apart. Even now I have to remind myself to use a fork and knife.

'We're so glad you're with us,' says Lakshayaa from next to me with a shy smile. We've never met in person before, but I know who she is from the dreaming.

'Thank you.'

'Even if you had to be kidnapped,' another quips, and I realise that as well as I know them, they know me. Only things deliberately hidden weren't shared.

'Huh. Well, they could have explained themselves instead.'

'Would you have come?'

'Probably not.'

'How about now? Do you want to be here?'

Do I? I didn't want to come, didn't want to be part of The Circle, only wanted to find out what I could and then escape. I told myself I had to join for them to trust me enough that I could get away, but was that still true at the time of the dreaming,

187

or was it more because of the things Cate said?

There's no getting around it: when I had a chance to escape, I didn't take it.

'Well, I could have swum away earlier,' I say, gripped by feelings I'm so unused to that I don't recognise them for what they are. Belonging, being at ease in a group – feeling, I don't know, at peace? – just because they are around me. I don't want to lose this connection, this closeness. I'm gripped with conflicting feelings about what is right, what I need to do.

'I wondered if you were thinking about it,' Ariel says.

'But she didn't, so enough of this nonsense,' Lakshayaa says. 'And now we've got a quorum and can get on with things this afternoon.'

'Quorum?' I say.

'They said some nonsense that there had to be eighty of us Chosen to make decisions about the way forward with the climate and humanity,' Ariel says.

'Why is that nonsense?'

'It's really how many of us were needed to be able to repopulate the earth if the need should arise. Enough diverse genes and no significant recessives to cause a problem.'

I remember Denzi pointing out once how diverse a group we were at swim school: every race represented more or less equally. But the thought that we've been carefully selected to make up a gene pool? That's so weird.

I look all around. Imagine this is it: everything and everyone else in the world, gone. Are we up to that? I shake my head. Even if we are, we're only half the survival equation.

'But we're all girls,' I say.

'There's apparently a freezer full of pop-sicles. And two boys were saved as backup breeders – they're supposed to be genetically perfect, whatever that means. Denzi is one of them,' Ariel says, with a pointed look at me.

'Who is the other?' I ask.

'Con,' she says. A name I don't remember.

I'm thinking through what they've said. Can you make a whole population of a species with just two males, no matter how genetically perfect they may be? And how do they know if we can even reproduce?

'But what if we're like mules?' I say. 'They're half horse, half donkey, but can't reproduce to make more mules.'

There is silence a moment. 'That's a good question,' Zara says, finally. 'And even if we can reproduce, there's no guarantee what our children will be. My aunt was a dog breeder. Cockapoos are half poodle, half spaniel. But if you breed two cockapoos, you can get puppies that are mostly spaniel, or mostly poodle, or any mix.'

'Well, let's not ask,' Ariel says, 'in case they ask for volunteers to test it out.'

'Thinking about this is making my skin crawl,' Lakshayaa says. 'We're not horses or puppies.'

'Yeah. Breeders? *Bleugh*,' Zara says. 'Let's save the world instead.'

39

We are told to meet up that afternoon, in the same theatre where all The Circle meet to decide important things. But today it will be just us – the Chosen – making the decisions.

Cassandra and Phina are there when I come through the door and about half of us are sitting in the front rows facing them. I join them as more trickle in, in ones, twos and threes, and then finally Ariel.

Cassandra looks around the room, at each of us.

'Welcome. You are the Chosen of The Circle. Once Phina and I leave, it will be time for you to determine the path that The Circle will follow in this climate war. Do not be influenced by anyone outside your group. We have agreed to leave this completely in your hands and will not question anything you decide. You may proceed as you wish, but you must all agree before you present your decision to The Circle.'

I glance at some of the girls around me and wonder if they are thinking the same as me. Doesn't this all seem more than a little crazy? To put a group of teenagers in a room and expect them to come up with a solution to the biggest crisis in history when no one else has managed to find one?

Cassandra and Phina walk up the steps, go through the door and it closes behind them.

Now we're all looking around at each other.

'How do we even begin?' Lakshayaa says.

'Everyone had something to say before it was officially the time to say it. It's this place,' Zara says, looking around us. 'Even with no one here but us, it feels like we're being watched. Judged.'

'They said they won't question anything we decide,' Ariel says, grins. 'Let's start with deciding on a change of scene.'

'Let's go to the sea dome!' Lakshayaa says. 'Any objections?'

There are smiles all around and no one says anything against the idea, so we stand, and start up the stairs to the main door. When those who first reach it open the door, there are a few surprised faces – there are sisters watching the door? To make sure no one disturbs us, or to make sure none of us leave?

'No, we haven't solved the problems of the world yet,' Ariel says. 'We just want to go somewhere else.'

We soon reach the winding path, follow it up and open the hatch door. Once I step in and stand under the domed roof with the sea just there, so close, it's like I breathe easier. Judging by the faces around me, we all feel the same.

We mill about the edges while we wait for everyone behind us to come in, hands to the glass. Eyes adjusting to the darkness. There are dolphins, fish of all sorts, fronds that float and wave in the water; phosphorescence lights the way.

The last of us come through and the door is shut. We sit on the floor under the dome in a rough circle, and chatter dies down as each of us finds a place.

'Does anyone want to chair things?' Ariel says. 'I figure it shouldn't be me or Tabby. Since my mum and her sort of great-grandmother are on opposite sides in all of this.'

'I'll do it, if everyone agrees?' Dimitra says. Another one of us that I've not spoken to before; she wasn't at swim school but I know her, as we all know each other, from the dreaming. The sense I have of her is that she is a calm, rational, naturally in charge kind of person without being bossy. English is new to her, but after the dreaming we can all speak each other's languages. We seem to have settled on English by a majority-rules sort of default. We all nod and give thumbs up.

'As I understand things, and as Ariel said, there are these two opposing points of view,' Dimitra says. 'Phina wants to accelerate the downfall of humanity so they have less time to damage sun, sea, earth and sky. Cassandra wants to give them another chance to set things right. We're to decide between the two. To see where we are before we begin – raise hands if you are undecided?' She counts. 'Then for Phina's position?' She counts. 'And then the rest for Cassandra?' I raise my hand; she counts again.

'So that is twenty-seven undecided; twenty-two for Phina's position; and thirty-one for Cassandra's. A preference for the latter but near enough a third for each possibility, so we're nowhere near a unanimous decision.'

'Who wants to speak for Phina's position?'

Everyone looks at Ariel and she rolls her eyes. 'OK, if I have to. The way I see it is like this. Humanity have stuffed this planet and will continue to stuff the planet until there is nothing left to stuff. If we let it go that far, we might not even survive in the seas and it'll be an empty dead husk of rock floating in space. And anyhow, as we all know, Cassandra saw this would happen – all that is in question is the timing. We need to save as much of life on the planet while we can. The only way to do that is to accelerate the downfall of the human race. I mean, if it's going to happen anyhow, why not just make it happen faster?'

'You sound like a James Bond villain,' Zara quips.

'I didn't say I agree with all that – it's just one point of view.'

'Who wants to speak for Cassandra's position?' Eyes look my way.

'I don't. But I will speak for myself,' I say. 'What does giving a second chance to set things right actually *mean*? What are our options? So far, The Circle have caused disasters, and threatened more, to convince governments of the world to halt extractions and emissions. And what have they done in response? Nothing much. Unless you count poisoning the sky to block the sun while continuing merrily burning and extracting. And the hurricanes and bombs *killed* people, animals and plants – and destroyed ecosystems, too. No matter *why* it was done – how can that ever be right?'

Girls are exchanging uneasy glances, but not as many of them as I would have thought.

'But if it didn't work already, why even think about doing something like that again?' Ariel says.

'Maybe threats aren't the best way,' Zara says.

'But how else do you make them listen?' Ariel.

'My parents used to argue about this,' Lakshayaa says. 'My mum is a geologist, my dad is a biology teacher. It wasn't that she didn't agree with him that the environment is being wrecked and it's our fault – she did. She wanted there to be a solution and a way to fix things but said there just isn't one that big corporations would accept – and that they are the ones who really run the planet. Governments are just figureheads put there by whoever has the most money.'

193

Does Ali – my dad – control the government? Seems crazy to think so. Or does it? He's a VP of Industria United, the company that launched those chemicals into the atmosphere and thought it was a good thing. No one voted on it and the Prime Minister didn't do anything about it after the fact – did she know before it happened?

Around me others are saying what they think – what their parents thought – going around in circles.

Your dad is your kin – our kin – isn't he?

'Yeah,' I answer silently.

Ask him for help.

I'm looking around the room. Even though I feel I know all of them in a real sense, it's more about who they are, inside; specific details like who their parents are didn't often come up in the dreaming. But I know at least some of them were involved in the oil and gas industry in some way.

I wave a hand in the air. 'What about our parents? You know, your biological mums and dads who don't know anything about this and probably think you drowned?'

There is a mixture of reactions to that. Zara's blinking hard against tears and some are like her. Some are more just uncomfortable with it. Some even appear to be indifferent. Does the dreaming and being so close to all of us here displace their other family, the one that they lived with, that raised them? Does it make them seem more distant, less important?

'Why are you bringing them up?' Ariel says.

'Most of you probably don't know that my dad is Ali Heath, the VP of Industria United that launched this whole geoengineering thing. Who are yours?'

And it's as though my admission of who my father is has given everyone else permission; more of the others spill on the parental details they were hiding, ashamed of, even. And the more of us who tell, the more we all must be thinking the same thing.

'It's like our parents are either in oil and gas or other big important corporations, or in key positions in different governments around the world,' I say. 'This *can't* be by chance. How were they chosen?'

Ariel frowns. 'From what I understand, our parents were picked for genetic reasons. To get the biggest variation in genes and avoid harmful recessives and all that kind of stuff in case we need to repopulate the planet on our own.'

'How do they even have that kind of information on people's genes?' Zara says.

'I guess if they sign up for IVF they get screened or whatever?' Ariel says.

'But how did they get there in the first place?' I say. 'Don't you think it's weird if our parents randomly have great genes, *and* work in oil and gas or other key positions, *and* couldn't conceive, *and* signed up for IVF with the Penrose Clinic?'

'Though maybe it's more because only people with a lot of money can do private IVF, so the kind of people that went there are like our parents,' Ariel says. 'Even if they were targeted in some way – how? Why?'

'I don't know. But all this stuff about our parents has me wondering something else. What if we go to them? Ask for their help and support? If they all tried for what we want – backed the environmental cause to stop extraction and emissions – it'd have to make an impression.'

Ariel's head is tilted to one side. 'Think of your dad, and who and what he is. Do you think anything you say can change him?'

How well do I even know Ali? We'd only had weeks together, really. I know he cared for me, but how much? Would he do something like this just because I ask him to?

He's your kin. He has to help you.

People aren't the same.

'Honestly? I don't know if he'll listen,' I say. 'But I think it's worth a try. To use reason, instead of threats.'

There are nods all around.

'Should we put it to a vote?' Dimitra says.

'Wait. There's one other thing,' I say. 'They said that for us to decide anything, we all have to agree – all the Chosen. But we're not all here. I know of three still living that are missing: Isha, Denzi and Con. They need to be part of this.'

'Who is Isha?' Lakshayaa says.

'She was at swim school with us. Malina said she wasn't brought here because she couldn't handle the trip in the submersible. She's claustrophobic.'

'Well, OK. Including her seems reasonable,' Dimitra says. 'But the other two? Isn't Denzi that boy you were asking about in the dreaming?'

'Yes. And Con is the other one they've kept.'

Discussion breaks out all around me and there are a few whistles. A big group of teenage girls and only two boys? What were they thinking?

'If we're meant to be like a gene pool for the next wave of the human race, then where will all the babies come from?' I say. 'Are test tubes the plan?'

'Yeah, I think so. They've been harvesting and storing sperm until the time is right – they've got supplies ready frozen from the boys who died. Denzi and Con are kind of living backups.'

'In case the freezer full of pop-sicles fails,' Zara quips.

'Yuck. And did the . . . er . . . contributors have any say in that?' I say. 'Do Denzi and Con? Do we?'

There is silence; no one answers and as I look around at my sisters there is doubt, confusion.

'Well, we are the Chosen; we get to decide,' I say. 'They are part of us. They didn't say all the female Chosen have to do this unanimously; they said, all the Chosen.'

'Boys have never been part of The Circle,' Ariel says.

'Yes, I know,' I say. 'And I understand how some of the ancestors feel about it. But there have never been boys before whose genes carry Circle DNA – that's what Cassandra said. They only did it this time because with such a small gene pool as us they needed to make sure all children we may have will inherit Circle DNA.'

'Yeah, that's right,' Ariel says. 'Normally some children of The Circle don't inherit what we are. I think that was the case with your mum,' she says to me.

'They combined human, circle and dolphin DNA to make the Chosen. That includes Denzi and Con. I don't know about Con, but Denzi's dad is the Home Secretary. So he'd be good to have with us.'

We argue about it – around and around in circles – and there are calls to break for dinner.

'Look, we will need to compromise with each other to get anywhere,' Ariel says. 'And think how much fun it'd be to freak them all out. Let's go for it.'

'Time to vote?' Dimitra says, and there are nods all around. 'Hands up if you agree we must include Isha, Denzi and Con in our decision-making process.'

Most hands are up: Ariel's ability to sway others always surprises me. A few are hesitating, then look around the room: their hands go up, too.

'So that is agreed,' Dimitra says. 'And secondly, assuming the three of them agree, hands up if our first course of action will be to go to those of our parents who are outside The Circle, and see if we can convince them to stop their contributions to global warming, to put their efforts into being part of the solution to reverse it.'

All hands go up without hesitation.

40

'This is going to be fun,' Ariel says as we head towards the meeting. All of The Circle will be there to hear what we've decided.

'You like trouble?'

'Always. Especially if it freaks out my mum. And she is hard to freak out, believe me; I've been trying for years,' she says and pulls a face. As she does so, just for a moment – a split second – there is an odd, blank look in her eyes, and there is a strong reaction to it in my gut. It takes me a moment to make the connection: the half fish, half girl – the face so like Ariel but the eyes, they were blank.

Ariel turns back when she realises I'm not following. 'Tabby? Is something wrong?'

'I don't know. I just . . . it's OK. I'm fine. Let's go.'

We continue walking to the meeting hall. With everything else going on, the creature I saw has been pushed from my mind – maybe because even now, I don't like to think about it. But it was related to Ariel – there was no mistaking her face, almost as if some part of them were identical twins.

Does she know about her?

Should I tell her if she doesn't?

'Ariel, do you have any brothers or sisters?'

'No. I'm surprised my mother would even go through pregnancy and birth once, as she avoids anything that distracts

199

her from her work for more than a minute. Why do you ask?'

I'm not sure what to say but we've reached the meeting hall door and I'm saved answering. We go through – we're last? – and chatter falls away as we step down the steps to join the rest of the Chosen in the front rows.

Phina and Cassandra arrive, descend the steps to the centre.

Cassandra looks around the room, as if seeing everyone is where they should be, then nods. 'We understand the Chosen have reached a decision,' she says.

Dimitra stands. 'We have. It's in two parts.

'The first is that for the decision of the Chosen to be unanimous, it must include all living Chosen – so we must have Isha, Con and Denzi join us. The second is—'

Her words are drowned out by the crowd around us, all in some version of shock, denial and anger at once. Cries of, 'It's wrong', 'This must never be allowed' and other variations of 'No' sound all around us.

'This is impossible,' Phina says, her lips tight in a line, and I sense more than see Ariel's delight.

'Silence, please,' Cassandra says, waits a moment for the noise to die down. 'Explain yourselves.'

'You told us whatever we decided you would support, and that no one could influence our decisions,' Dimitra says. 'You also said that all the Chosen must agree on any decision we make. We are not all the Chosen with these three missing, so this must be rectified before we can fulfil our duty. We came to this freely and all agree this must be done.'

'She's good,' Ariel says, a low aside to me.

There's silence for a moment. I can almost see the sisters

around us silently conferring with their ancestors.

'She's right,' Cassandra says, finally. 'We have to support their decision.'

Phina's eyes meet hers. For a moment I think she'll argue, but no. She nods. 'As always, you are correct. They will have to join the dreaming, though, to become part of the Chosen.'

Looks are being exchanged around us – the sort that say they know something we don't.

'How should we implement this?' Phina says. 'Bring them here?'

There are more horrified gasps all around.

'Wait,' Cassandra says. 'Before we start making plans, what was the second part of your decision?'

Dimitra nods. 'Assuming Isha, Con and Denzi also agree, all of us will go to our birth parents – well connected in business and government around the world – and seek their support to cease extraction and emissions immediately.'

'Very well,' Phina says, and there's something about her face, the way she stands, that doesn't feel right. She's lost, hasn't she? Maybe she is resigned to the decision, supporting it because she agreed she would do so – but that feels wrong for who she is. It's almost like . . . what we've decided to do is what she wanted.

'Plans will need to be made quickly,' Cassandra says. 'Malina will assist you after dinner. Meeting adjourned.'

41

Everyone around me is getting up, starting up the steps to go for dinner, but I stay, watching Cassandra and Phina say a few words to each other. Then they head up the steps behind the others.

'Aren't you coming?' Ariel says.

'Yes. Sorry.' I get up and we fall in behind everyone else.

'Is something wrong?'

'I don't know. Phina seemed to agree too easily – I don't trust her. I get the feeling there is something going on that we don't know about in all this.'

'We got what we wanted. And careful what you say – she's my mum, remember.'

'Sorry,' I say and hesitate. 'Is it OK if I ask you something?'

'Ask and I'll let you know.'

'Do you trust her? Your mum.'

A pause. 'Yes. All she wants is for this planet to survive, to support life. To protect sun, sea, earth and sky. She might have different ideas about how to make that happen than your great-gran does, but that doesn't mean she can't be trusted.'

'OK. Sorry,' I say, apologising yet again.

She's looking at me closely. 'Out with it. Whatever else it is you're trying not to say, say it.'

'Don't you ever get *angry*? About what was done to *us*, and to our unsuspecting parents? Sorry, I guess it's a bit different for you – you seem to be the only one whose mother was in The Circle and in on all of it.'

'What, get angry at being made extra amazing? No. Look, I talked to Mum about that when I first found out about it all and was struggling to take it in, you know? And she said she wanted a perfect daughter, one who could save the world. And that she got exactly that.' Ariel looks embarrassed. 'Perfect me, huh.'

What about her other daughter? Is she perfect, too?

Ariel said she doesn't have any siblings – she doesn't know. And I don't know if I should tell her.

Plans are discussed and made over dinner. We decide a few of us who know one or more of Isha, Denzi and Con – me, Ariel, and Zara – will go to them. We'll start with Isha in Brighton, and then on to Denzi and Con. Malina tells us that they're being held by The Circle in a house in London. If they agree to do so, we'll join with The Circle in a dreaming so they can officially become one of us.

After that, if they agree with our decision to seek our parents' help, that will be implemented. The Chosen will begin dispersing to their homes around the world now so they will be in place when the decision is made – we can join the first dreaming with the new three wherever we are at an agreed time and day. After we've done what we can with our parents, we will meet again in a second dreaming with Phina and Cassandra to relay progress and decide next steps.

'We need to set out as soon as possible,' Malina says. 'There isn't much time.'

'Everyone keeps saying that,' Zara says. 'Is it really that close?'

'Yes. There are key tipping points in climate change that we're edging closer to all the time. Think of it like this. At the moment we're climbing a mountain with a knife's edge at the top and a sheer drop to the other side. If we go over the edge, getting back up again will be extremely difficult – impossible, even. We need to reverse the climb before we get to the top, and we need to do it fast.'

'How close are we?' I say. 'How much time do we have?'

'We don't know in enough detail to tell you an exact day.'

'Are we talking days? Weeks? Months?'

'Our best estimates are weeks to months.'

The room falls silent. My stomach is in a knot and I can't eat any more now.

Ariel finds her voice first. 'How long will it take to get to Brighton?'

'Our closest ship is hours away. Once it reaches us, we'll go up to meet it using submersibles, which will take a while with so many of us. Then perhaps a day of sailing after that. I've got the submersibles being prepared now.'

'What do we need to take with us?'

'Not much. Clothes. We've got mobile phones for each of you. There's a Circle contact on her way to Brighton who will meet you and have Isha's details – Paula is her name. I'll go to London and assist you there.'

They're all still talking about details of what, where, when, but I'm fading out. There is a way to know how much time we have – to take the guessing out of it.

I close my eyes and focus, inside:

Sun . . . sea . . . earth . . . sky . . .

Sun . . . sea . . . earth . . . sky . . .

Once the voices are in perfect unison, time spins in circles all around, me at the centre. Focus, first, to the past – what has led us to this precipice? Hundreds of years pass in a blink: the digging, the coal, then oil and gas; the harm burning them has wrought on the world. The poisons, abuses and injustices: pain, loss and deaths. Losses so profound I'm caught in agony.

And there – just there – is the future. All I have to do is look, and then . . . I would know.

But what if it is what we all fear, what then? There would be nothing to hope for, nothing to *live* for. I'd crawl inside myself and disappear.

I shake my head. No. I won't look. Aslan was right: it is better to chase the fish.

'Tabby? Tabby!' There is a hand on my shoulder and slowly I come back to here, now. Open my eyes and there are concerned faces around me.

'Are you all right?' Zara says.

'Yes. I think so. Thanks.' And I look from one to the other, and know each of them intimately – the things that make them happy, sad: how they feel inside in their most guarded places. They are closer to me than anyone ever has been before.

'We are in this together – we'll do everything we can. Won't we?' Dimitra says. 'There has to be enough time to do what we need to do – there just has to be.'

It would be faster to swim. Aslan.

'You're right,' I say to him, silently.

Of course. A note of surprise that he could ever be other than right.

'We can get to the places we need to go faster if we leave Undersea from the sea lock,' I say. 'Swim there with dolphins.'

Everyone looks to me now – some surprised to think that'd be possible, some less so.

'She's right,' Ariel says. 'I've seen how they are with Tabby; they'll take us if she wants them to.'

'When should we leave? Should we go now?' Lakshayaa says.

'Have a few hours of rest first: you all need it,' Malina says.

Soon we're getting up to go to our rooms to try to sleep a little.

'Wait a moment, Tabby,' Malina says. She pauses, waits until the last of the others have gone through the door.

'Where did you go? What did you see?'

Cassandra said to keep it to myself that I can see the future but Malina knows? Or guesses.

I shake my head. 'Nothing. I didn't look.'

That night I'm staring at the ceiling. In the midst of all the things there are to worry about, something else is bothering me still, and I can't quite work out what it is. We made our decision – we're giving humanity a second chance. We came up with something we can try without using violence or threats. This is right, I'm sure of it.

Yet something is niggling away inside.

Even though we were told our parents were chosen to make us genetically different, there are so many things about us that are the same.

We're not random – nothing about us has ever been random. We've been made to order by The Circle. But the driving force behind all of it is Phina; she's the one who engineered us to be what we are.

Our parents were picked for us – chosen carefully, they said. Phina made us and set everything into motion around us. Do we even have our own free will to decide anything, or was it fixed from the beginning by who and what we are?

I can't shake an uneasy feeling that we're somehow playing into Phina's hands. Is what we are going to try to do so hopeless that she knows we'll fail?

I sigh. Even if it is, I'm still convinced: we have to *try*.

Part 6
London

Hayden

@HaydenNoPlanetB
*The ice sheet that covers Greenland is beginning to disintegrate:
melting on the surface is accelerated by reduced snowfall and icebergs
are calving into the sea.*

#NatureIsScreaming

42

Can we meet up? sorry for short notice – this afternoon?

It's Apple and my mind races to Denzi: is there any news? She must know what I'm thinking. Haven't found D but might have a lead, pings in straight after.

A lead? What could it be?

I haven't been out of the house voluntarily in days, sadness and fear combining to overwhelm me so much that I haven't wanted to go anywhere or see anyone. I haven't been able to properly look at the barrage of messages and emails that have been flooding in either. I've tried a few times and, ignoring the trolls, it was a mixture of sympathy and expectation – for Bishan's death and wanting me to step in and take over what we were trying to do. And right now I can't handle either.

Dad pried me out of my room yesterday and made me go out for lunch with him – usually a treat, but I felt exposed being out in the open. It was even worse on the Tube. I couldn't stop scanning around the whole time, as if everywhere I went there might be someone hiding with the gun that killed Bishan. Maybe I'm next on their list.

Of course if that were true, they'll always know where to find me if I never leave the house.

I sigh. This can't go on for ever – school goes back in a few weeks. A thought I really can't get my head around.

I could call Apple instead of going out to meet her; maybe I should. My finger is reaching to do so, but then falls back. There's something about being around Apple that makes me feel better. Despite what she's been through, she's so strong. She makes me feel like I can be, too.

Of course. When/where?

A shower and clean jeans later, I head down the stairs, hear Dad in the kitchen and go in.

'Hey,' I say.

'Hey.' He clocks the brushed hair, change of clothes. 'I was just going to make some tea. Want some, or do you have plans?'

'I'm going out. To meet Apple.'

Eyes widened – surprised? And pleased. He grins. 'Sounds good.' He hesitates. 'Want me to take you?'

I shake my head. 'No. I'll get the Tube. It's no drama.'

'OK. If you're sure.'

'I am. Thanks.'

He kisses my forehead. 'It'll do you good. But if you call, I'll come get you, no matter where you are. All right?'

'Yeah. Thanks.'

My heart is beating faster. I walk out of the kitchen and to the front door.

OK, idiot. You can't stay home for ever, can you? You're going to open this door and walk down the street. It's too hot to rush so you will set a calm, measured pace, and you will *not* look around the whole time for hidden snipers.

Step 1: open the door. Good.

Step 2: step through, turn and lock said door. Excellent.

212

It's early afternoon, lightish traffic. A few mums pushing prams. Friends on a bench. The guy from down the road with his dog. A grocery delivery a few houses along. Apart from the dead, grey sky, everything is just perfectly normal, right?

Now walk.

One step, then another. I make myself breathe slower and gradually my heart rate starts to come down. Everything is fine, there's nothing to worry about.

I look right at the corner and it's clear to cross. I start to step forward and someone grabs my shoulders from behind, pulls me back, and a scream is almost there when I see: the cyclist going the wrong way. The one I nearly stepped in front of.

'That was close,' says neighbour with the dog.

'Thanks,' I manage.

'Are you OK?'

'Yes. Yes, I'm fine. Thanks.'

I cross the road, looking both ways this time. Then head down the steps at the Tube, still shaking. Well, there you go: I'm sure that was the most dangerous thing I'm likely to come across today – getting knocked over by some guy on a bike. Get a grip.

The rest of getting to the café in Islington that Apple suggested goes without a hitch, but I'm relieved when I find it, go through the door. Apple waves from her table – one in a back corner. She's facing the room.

'Hi,' I say and slip into the seat opposite her. But I'm uneasy sitting with my back to the room. 'Sorry, do you mind swapping seats?'

'No problem.' We both get up and she gives me a quick hug, and sit down again. 'Thanks for coming.'

'Are you staying in the UK for a while still?'

'Yep. Decided to have a gap year. We're moving out of the hotel and in with Leila's sister. She said stay as long as we like. And I couldn't face going back to university like everything is normal when it isn't.'

'Yeah. I get that. I feel the same way about school – it's back in a few weeks. How can I go sit in maths and solve equations when everything is so messed up?'

'Leila said to me, life goes on. You need to study and think about your future. I said it'll keep for a year. Guess you don't have a choice, though.'

'Not really. School isn't optional – if I don't go they can even fine my parents. So, you said you might have a lead. What's going on?'

'I've been thinking. What if, instead of being held somewhere, Denzi has run off? I told you there was this missing girl he was trying to find: Tabby was her name. Anyhow. Look what I found.' She takes out her phone, goes to a link.

'I went to his school's website. His school was completely destroyed by storm surge when the hurricane hit the coast – he would have been there for summer swimming training if he hadn't come to the US because Leila was in an accident. Anyhow, there's this link to a swim school page set up by parents of some of the kids that went missing when the school was flooded.

'And there's this post – missing: Tabby Heath. It's posted by someone named Jago who says he's a friend of hers, but it was posted weeks after the hurricane. And what he says is kind of cryptic – that Tabby wasn't at the school when the hurricane

214

came but she is missing and if anyone has any information etcetera to contact him.'

'Are you going to?'

'I already have. He's meeting me – us – here.' She glances at her phone. 'Should be soon if his train is on time. He's coming up from Cornwall.'

Just as she's putting her phone back down on the table, it rings. She answers and then turns, waves. A boy waves back, walks towards us. This must be Jago – sixteen or seventeen, fit. Tanned with dark hair.

'Hi. Apple?'

'Yes. And this is Hayden.'

He pulls a chair over, sits between us. Looks at me and then looks again. 'Have we met before?'

'I don't think so. But I've been on the news a bit.'

'Oh, yeah – the climate activist, right?'

'Uh, yeah.' Weirded out at being *recognised* by someone I've never met. And being called a climate activist. What have I done lately? Nothing.

'Thanks for coming all this way,' Apple says.

'I didn't want to talk about this on the phone or email, so here I am.'

'For Hayden, I'll recap?' Apple says, and he nods. 'I was just starting to tell her when you got here. Denzi – my stepbrother – was looking for a girl named Tabby who went missing after the hurricane, but not from the storm. She was at a hospital in Bristol and disappeared from there. And Denzi was at a climate-change protest – Hayden was with him – the one where a car killed and injured protestors driving into the crowd.

215

I couldn't work out why he'd leave his friends when that had just happened, so I jumped to a conclusion: that he was meeting Tabby as I couldn't think of anything else that would make him leave his friends just then. Denzi is missing now and, I thought, maybe if I find Tabby, I'll find him. And that's why I contacted Jago about his post.'

'And here I am,' he says. 'OK. So, Tabby is a friend I met earlier this year.' He hesitates like there is more to say but then goes on. 'She moved away but came back to Cornwall on her own just weeks ago,' he says, hesitates again. 'It's hard to know how much to tell you – so much of this was in confidence.'

'We won't tell anyone unless you agree,' Apple says, and I nod.

'So, she was hiding out and the police were looking for her, as a missing person – or so I thought to begin with. But I don't think it really was the police, and whoever it was, they were getting closer and closer to finding her. She left for London and said she was meeting a friend there but didn't give his name. And according to Apple, that was the day before that protest.'

'So, the timing fits that Denzi could have met up with Tabby, but we don't know what happened then,' Apple says. 'From what Leila said about when Denzi was in hospital in London, there may be a few missing days in between.'

'He was in hospital?' Jago says.

'This is more stuff you can't repeat unless we agree, OK?' Apple says, and Jago nods. 'He was found on a beach in Hastings, supposedly passed out on drugs. He just isn't into that kind of thing. It was some sort of set-up. He was taken to a secure hospital in London; no one knew he was there except his parents.

And his mom, Leila – my stepmom – was trying to have him released. Denzi told us via notes that he had some dangerous information, and that might be the real reason why he was being held. So, we – me and Hayden – found a way to get into the hospital to see him. But when we got in, his room was empty. He wasn't there.' Apple hesitates, looks at me.

'It was my friend Bishan who set it up so we could get into the hospital to see Denzi,' I say. 'Bishan . . . he was the climate activist who was shot and killed just days ago. It happened there – next to the hospital – after we came out. Apple was gone but I saw the whole thing.'

'Oh God, that must have been awful. I'm so sorry.'

'Yeah. It was,' I say, and try to push away the images that come whenever it is mentioned. 'Anyhow, everyone thought it must have been some crazy climate-change denialist that did it, but . . . maybe it wasn't. I don't know. They haven't arrested anyone for it yet.'

'So if Denzi wasn't at the hospital when you went there, then where was he? How did he get out of a secure hospital?'

'According to what the hospital told my stepmom, his doctor checked him out,' Apple says. 'But since then no one knows where he is. Oh, and I haven't told you this bit yet, Hayden. Leila has been trying to find his doctor, the one who checked him out. It looks like she may be missing, too.'

'His doctor is missing?' Jago says. 'Either she's involved, or something has happened to both of them.' He shakes his head, pale under his tan. 'Assuming Denzi's dangerous information is the same stuff Tabby told me, he might have been right about that being why he was set up and held. Are you sure you want

217

to know? Even if you do, I'm not sure I should tell you. Look, another friend of ours was going to blog about what I'm thinking of telling you and she ended up in a car accident and in hospital.'

'Is she all right?'

'She had a head injury and looks to be making a full recovery. But she's got a specific type of amnesia – she can't remember stuff for a few months before the accident.'

'So, whatever it was, she's forgotten it.'

'Yeah.'

'There are some other things that might help you decide what to say,' Apple says. 'My dad died recently, back in the States.'

'I'm so sorry.'

'Yeah. Thanks. Authorities say suicide but we – me and my stepmom – don't believe it. He was an investigative journalist and we thought maybe it was faked because of something he was working on, but we don't know what. Then, just days later, police in London got in touch; they've been investigating a murder and the victim had been talking on the phone a few times with my dad. And then my stepmom found out from phone records that my dad had also been talking to Denzi and not told her, which is odd. That's why we came from the States – to try to see if there is any link between all of this. So Denzi is missing; my dad and this other man in London are dead. I don't know if all of this is connected to whatever it is that Denzi knew. But whatever it is that you know, we need to know in case it is. And we really need to go to the police.'

'OK.' Jago is thinking. He looks around us – no one is close enough to hear over the café's background music but he still lowers his voice. 'Tabby was an IVF baby.'

'Denzi was too,' Apple says.

'It was done with an IVF clinic called the Penrose Clinic. Long story, but Tabby found out there is a link between the Penrose Clinic and The Circle.'

43

I'm staring wide-eyed at Jago. Some IVF clinic is linked up with The Circle?

Before we can say anything, a waiter is here wanting us to order. My mouth is dry: 'Tea, please,' I manage to say.

He moves away again.

'The actual, freaking *Circle* is connected with this clinic?' Apple says. 'And that's what Denzi knew?'

'I'm guessing Tabby told him, though I don't know for sure.'

'And that could be why he was being held – until they decided what to do with him,' she says.

'But what did they decide?' I say.

Apple is blinking back tears. 'What if us getting notes to him – and Leila trying to get him interviewed by the police – what if they . . .' She shakes her head, unable to finish the sentence.

'And what about Bishan?' I say. 'Maybe they thought he knew from Denzi. And the police know we were there – does The Circle?'

'We have to go to the police. Now,' Apple says. 'Apart from every other reason, we might have targets on our heads.'

'Yet I'm still here,' Jago says. 'They must at least suspect I know all this.'

'Maybe you're being watched, to see if you tell anyone

220

or do anything about it,' Apple says.

'Like I've told you.'

My phone case. My hands are shaking, I take out the card. 'This . . . DCI Palmer? Let's call him.'

'How do we do this?' Jago says. 'Should we go there now? What if someone has been watching me, or either of you?'

There are footsteps – Apple startles at the sound behind her.

'It's our drinks,' I say.

Waiter and his tray – two teas, more coffee for Apple. It seems to take him forever to put them on the table and walk away.

'My dad said he'd come get me,' I say. 'I could call and get him to take us?'

'Let's call Palmer first and see what he says,' Apple says. 'Want me to do it?'

I nod, give her the card.

She enters the number. 'It's going to voicemail,' she says a moment later.

'Hi, this is Apple Klein. I'm here with Hayden Richards and Jago Tremayne – he's a friend of Tabby Heath. We've put some things together between us that we need to tell you urgently. Please call soon, thanks.'

'Now what?' I say.

'Now, we wait,' Apple says.

My eyes keep darting to the door.

'I see now why you didn't want your back to the room,' she says.

'I've been pretty jumpy since Bishan,' I say. 'Now more so. I just can't believe all of this. It's like some insane thriller or something on the news.'

'Maybe I shouldn't have told you,' Jago says.

Apple shakes her head. 'You did the right thing. If telling the police means they get closer to stopping The Circle, it has to be done.'

'You're probably wondering why I haven't done anything about all this before,' Jago says.

'Yeah. A bit,' she says.

'After my friend was in that car accident, police came to talk to me. Asked if I knew any reason why someone would want to hurt her. Thing is, I don't think they were really police – I think they just wanted to know if I knew anything. So I said no, nothing I can think of. I told our other friend – the only other one who knew about this – what had happened. They went to him with the same question; he gave the same answer.

'Soon after, I visited her in the hospital. Her parents were there and I asked her dad about the car that struck her, how it happened; did the police think it was or wasn't an accident? He was surprised I even said that. Why would it have been anything but an accident? So, it's clear they never asked her parents if anyone would want to hurt her.

'So I thought I was right: they'd checked if there was anything I knew that I'd tell the police, and left me alone after that.'

He sighs. 'I should have done more. I was so upset about Ren, worried about Tabby. I was afraid anything I did might cause problems for her? But if I'm honest, I was also just plain scared. And the longer I didn't say anything, the harder it was to say it.'

'This girl Tabby has got Denzi and you both jumping through hoops,' Apple says. 'She must be something.'

'She is, but not like you mean. She's my friend.' But his eyes say she is more than what he'll admit just the same.

We all jump when Apple's phone rings. She glances at the screen, nods. It's him.

'Hi. Yes, this is Apple. Look, we're scared. We think Denzi knew something from Tabby, and that may be why he's missing – might be why my dad and that other man were killed, too, and Bishan . . . Yeah. If you can come to us that'd be great. We're at a café.' She picks up the menu for the address, starts reading it out.

I'm still watching the café, the doors, only half hearing what she is saying. Something inside me is saying *get away, run, hide*: just the same voice that has been whispering in my head for days.

Yet. There is more reason to fear now and instead of telling myself to stop worrying, I'm thinking my instincts were right all along.

There are wide glass windows at the front of the café. A black SUV pulls in out front. Someone is getting out – a woman, with red hair?

I sit up straighter. Is it the woman I saw in the lane by the hospital that day? It could be but I can't be sure.

Jago turns, looks where I am.

'It's one of them,' he says. 'Move. Now. Run!'

And we're up and he's pushing me through the 'staff only' door at the back of the café; Apple just behind – phone still in her hand – is hesitating, looking back, but must have seen the panic on Jago's face and runs through after us.

Into the small kitchen – a surprised cook, and our waiter. 'You can't come in—'

BOOM

223

Sound thunders through my head . . .

Blasts through, pushes in the door. We're on the floor, now . . .

Smoke and *screaming* and the heat of flames behind us, in the café . . .

'Get out, get out,' the cook says, and I'm coughing, struggling to my feet. A blast of hot air rushes in behind us as a door to outside opens across the kitchen.

Apple is screaming, Jago is dragging her up, pushing me out the door ahead of them.

We stagger down the lane, collapse on the ground. There is shouting and screaming everywhere – sirens, too.

Apple, she's bleeding – her back; something struck her through the door.

The phone falls out of her hand.

44

There are crowds of people, a blur of police, paramedics. All the while I'm looking around us – for red hair, or anyone who looks out of place. Does she think we're dead? Or does she know we got away, but there are just too many people around us now for her to do anything else?

It takes a while for paramedics to get to Apple with so many badly injured in the café. They say it looks superficial, it was shrapnel from the café that came through the door and she caught it, being behind us. Paramedics insist on checking me and Jago despite us saying we're OK. Though my hearing isn't right: it's like I've been standing next to amplifiers at a heavy metal concert.

I tell the police about the woman with red hair that we saw out front just before the explosion; Jago gives a more detailed description, having seen her before.

DCI Palmer is here now. When Apple is helped into an ambulance to go to a hospital, he has a police car follow behind – says they'll go in with her to keep her safe.

Then Jago and me are bundled into another police car, a driver and DCI Palmer in the front.

'We're heading to the station now. We'll have to ask you more questions. Your parents have been informed and will meet us there,' he says to me. 'Jago, we need your details?'

Jago gives his full name, address, number. 'Please don't freak out my mum.'

'Hard not to in the circumstances.'

Yeah. The circumstances: Apple called the police and then someone blew up the café before they could get there.

'You have to look for a woman with long red hair,' I say. 'I saw her out front but wasn't sure it was the same person I saw before when Bishan was shot, but Jago recognised her, too.'

'She was tailing Tabby in Cornwall,' Jago says.

'And that's why we ran out the back. Those poor people in the café,' I say, and my eyes are brimming over now, and the shock and fear are hitting me inside. Did someone want us dead and got them instead? Jago puts his hand on my shoulder as if in comfort but his hand is shaking.

'Did Apple manage to tell you what we know?' Jago says.

'She started to tell me that there is a connection between The Circle and some clinic, and then – well. It was so loud I almost dropped my phone. And then came straight to you.'

'It's called the Penrose Clinic,' Jago says. 'Can you tell somebody – tell them now?'

'You're safe with us.'

'We'd feel better if you did,' I say.

He nods. Phone in his hand. 'DCI Palmer. There is a potential connection between a clinic called the Penrose Clinic and The Circle. We'll be there soon; start looking into it.'

Jago and I exchange a glance. I feel calmer inside; it's out. The police know.

They have no reason to hurt us now, do they?

45

Mum and Dad are already there when we arrive and I'm in the biggest family hug of all time. Mum – she's crying? 'Look, it's OK. I'm fine,' I say, but then I'm crying too.

Jago is talking to Palmer – giving details of what he'd told Apple and me at the café, and Dad is shaking his head. 'Somebody seriously bombed a café to stop anyone knowing about some clinic and The Circle? I can't take this in.'

'Me neither,' Mum says.

'Everyone knows now,' I say. 'They've got no reason to care about us any more.' But I'm still shaking.

We get taken to an office – Mum, Dad, Jago and me – and told to wait, that someone will come talk to us soon. Someone brings us hot, sweet tea and I wrap my hands around it. Still trying to process what happened.

And what about Bishan? Who killed him? Why?

Suspect A: a marginal-crazy climate-change denier, either acting alone or as part of some extreme right-wing group.

Suspect B: someone trying to keep The Circle's secrets. The Circle, who are eco-terrorists, who are trying to blackmail the world into going green. Would they really kill a climate activist like Bishan just because they're afraid he might know something?

Either way, it's The Circle's fault. It's the things they've done that have caused the backlash against climate activists.

Are they so dumb that they couldn't see this would happen? It's almost like they want to fail.

A while later the door opens and DCI Palmer and a policewoman are there. 'Could we go through your statements again, one at a time?'

'Yeah, sure.'

I'm taken to another room with Mum, Dad stays with Jago.

They ask questions about it all again, over and over, and I try to remember everything I can.

Finally they've got some CCTV footage. 'Have a look. Do you recognise this woman?'

He plays it normal speed then slows it down, but it's not that clear. It's a black SUV like I saw in front of the café, through the front window – the side windows look dark like they've been tinted – a woman passenger. Long hair, could be red but hard to tell.

'It could be the car and woman I saw out front of the café, but I never had a close look at her face – it was only her hair that caught my attention. It looked like who I saw before Bishan was shot – again, just based on her hair. Could she have done that, too?'

'We're looking into it.'

Jago goes in next while we wait, and when he comes back out he tells us he saw the same CCTV and he is more certain than I was.

'It was definitely her – the woman tailing Tabby, out front the café and in that CCTV are all the same person. I'm sure of it.'

'They'll be able to find her now, won't they?' I say.

'I hope so,' Jago says. 'Despite all the horrible stuff that's happened today, there is this kind of relief inside me, you know? That what I know is out there now. It was poisoning me inside, knowing something like that and not doing anything about it.'

I'm finally alone in my own room, at home. Police are keeping an eye on our house; Jago is staying in our spare room and his parents will be here for him tomorrow.

Jago's words are going through my mind, over and again.

I get what he meant; how knowing something is dangerous, could kill people, and how doing nothing made him feel.

That's what I've been doing, isn't it? Climate change is far more dangerous than one terrorist will ever be, to people, animals, the entire world and everything in it.

What happened over the last day was insane, terrifying, heartbreaking. But it feels as if being so scared has shaken me up inside – like that cliché, that a life-or-death moment made my life flash before my eyes, and made it clear what is most important.

Sleep won't come easy tonight. Instead, I pick up my laptop.

Bishan had emailed me attachments and links with a huge amount of material about all the different groups we were trying to align. He'd sent me an updated version of his spreadsheet of all the contacts we'd made, responses we'd had, just days ago – the actual morning he died – with careful notes of everything we'd done and were going to do.

I spend hours reading through it all – all the things I'd put aside when Bishan died. I've been mostly avoiding social, but it's time to take a survey of all the endless posts I missed: sympathy, outrage from supporters and friends. Trolls, too, with their nasty comments that I report and block.

If I walk away from all of this it *will* poison me inside – as surely as extracting and burning fossil fuels are poisoning our planet.

But what can I do?

46

The policeman at the door to Apple's hospital room opens the door and I peek in.

'Hi,' I say.

'Don't "hi" me – give me a hug. But not too tight.' I lean in and her arms wrap around me briefly.

'Are you all right?'

'Yeah. Just a bunch of stitches on my back. I'm going to have some bitching scars next time I'm in a bikini. They're letting me out later today after a doctor gives the OK, then I'll just have to come back a few times for checks and to have stitches out.'

'Jago says hi, sorry he couldn't come. He's gone back to Cornwall now with his parents. And I thought mine could be OTT? His mum was practically hysterical. Anyhow, he was really worried about you.'

'Yes, he's been texting. A nice guy, for sure. Cute, too.'

I raise an eyebrow.

'Just because I bat for the other team doesn't mean I can't recognise cute-boy-with-great-ass-and-dimples when I see one.'

'After all this, I bet you want to get out of here and go home.'

'Leila thinks I should but she wants to stay – she's hoping now that the heat is up on all of this, the police will put more effort in to finding Denzi.'

'What do you want to do?'

231

'I really miss Emmie but I haven't quite decided. I feel kind of like almost dying made me want to stop, take stock. It's a second chance.'

I hesitate. 'I feel the same way. Only . . .' I shrug, words trailing away.

'What?'

'I know what I should do — what I need to — but I'm not sure I can.'

'Explain.'

'Bishan and me had all these plans. When he died, I couldn't face it, couldn't even look at any of it. Last night I did.'

'What kind of plans?'

'To bring environmental groups around the world together in a more meaningful way than has been managed before. By groups, we meant all the grass roots movements that are springing up everywhere, not so much the big organisations that lobby politicians and stuff. When I did that video about Eva's death, we got so much engagement, and everyone said they were interested in the idea and were enthusiastic, wanting to help. But once we started trying to work out the details? It was like they all wanted to consult divorce lawyers first.'

'Ugh. That doesn't sound good.'

'They said yes to everything, but after that, came all the "but"s: but only if this happens, or only if that doesn't.'

'Growing up with first my mom and dad and BLM, and then my stepmum and Big Green, I might be able to help. What are the things they want to argue about?'

'There's all these different approaches. Like some groups are focused on making everyone vegan, and recycling, and making everyone responsible for what they are doing to the planet.'

'Sounds good.'

'As far as it goes. There are others – our group included – that say that's all rubbish, it's just a smokescreen for what is really going on; making everyone focus on individual efforts instead of corporations and governments that are complicit in climate change. And looking at individual responsibility takes attention away from making corporations responsible for the damage they've caused and continue to cause.

'Others seem to be, I don't know, resigned to disaster, as if they think it's too late to really do anything to stop catastrophic climate change, and they just want to look at mitigation, helping climate refugees and stuff like that.

'And then others say that's bull, it isn't too late, it's more distraction – making people feel hopeless so they don't do anything, and don't focus on who is really to blame and do something about it.'

'And who is really to blame?'

'Either us greedy consumers, or big corporations, or governments. Or all three. And that's another thing to argue about.'

'What do you think?'

'I can stop eating steak – and I have – but the world is in a state because of so much more. Did you see on social after the Eva video there was all this stuff put up by trolls about me and my family? Things like that my parents' cars aren't fully electric so therefore, as I sometimes get driven around in one, obviously no one should listen to anything I say?' I roll my eyes. 'It's not like I haven't been nagging them for years to change them. But as Dad says, they hardly drive them and it'd mean making more cars to replace cars that don't need replacing – does that make any sense?'

'It's like putting people under a microscope to make sure they're worthy and not looking at the big picture.'

'Exactly. And *who* is behind all of this? Maybe when Big Green was discredited, that was manipulated by wealthy interests that want fossil fuels to continue no matter the cost so they can pocket more money. It's like they deflect and distract everyone from what they are doing. The more I look at all these disagreements between different environmental groups, the more I wonder: are they real, or were they manufactured to weaken and divide us?

'And then there is this big argument about what should be done. Some activists say the entire way much of the world works – capitalism – has to change. Others think we can use market strategies – do things to decrease demand for fossil fuels, and other things to decrease the supply. But can a free market where everyone wants to make money really be trusted to do the right thing?'

'What do you think?'

'I'm torn. Wouldn't it be great if we could rebuild the world to be better and fairer for everyone? But that's a hard sell to countries like yours.'

'Yeah, for sure. Say something like that in the US and you'd get shouted down fast.'

'Even here, the trolls haven't let up.' I shudder. 'I block and report as fast as I can, but they keep coming even though I haven't been posting in days. I tell myself to ignore them but it hurts when it gets personal.'

'That's tough.'

'Anyhow, it doesn't matter what idiots say, I won't give up. But I'm not sure I'm cut out for this. Bishan was so good at talking people around, like listening to what they had to say and saying it back a different way to make it look like everyone agreed, even if they didn't.'

'A politician in training?'

'Maybe.' I sigh. 'I've lost a good friend – but beyond the personal stuff, Bishan was the real deal. Like he could have been prime minister one day and been good at it – done the right things. I haven't got that knack with people that he had.'

She tilts her head to one side. 'I kind of get what you mean – but you've got something else, something he didn't have.'

'Oh, yeah? What's that?'

'You've got this, I don't know, *honesty* about you that makes people want to listen, to help.'

'Bishan said I was the girl next door.'

'Yeah. Like that. So don't try to tell people that black is white and white is black. Trust me: we don't fall for that rubbish no matter who says it. Just be yourself.'

47

I'm so tired I go up to bed early, but my eyes won't stay closed. My mind feels like it's pried open, like I've had way too much sugar and caffeine, and nothing will settle it down. Between Apple, Denzi, the police and all the Eva-and-Bishan-shaped stuff, the more I try not to think about it, the more I can't stop.

I've been putting off facing this straight on, but I can't step aside, I can't turn my back on everything we'd been working for. I could never feel good about myself if I did.

What was it Bishan said? *If anything ever happens to me, you've so got this.* It's almost like he knew what was coming.

I can't let him down.

I can't let *me* down.

What about Mum and Dad?

I sigh. This isn't about getting my ears pierced or staying up late. This isn't the kind of thing they can say yes or no to: it's who I *am*.

I prop up my phone and press record.

'Hi. I'm Hayden Richards. I did a video about how I felt when my best friend, Eva, died after receiving injuries at a climate protest. It feels like ages ago that I did that, but in reality it was only days later that I had to mourn the death of another friend.

'What can I say about Bishan? There's been so much out

there already about him, with all the usual stuff – his role in protesting climate change, the way he inspired so many of us – still there, doing all he could, even after his arm was broken in a protest; his grades in school, his family left behind and all the rest that has hit the news. So today I think I'll tell you some of the things you might not know about Bishan.

'His ringtone on his phone was Abba's "Ring, Ring". He was afraid of escalators and always took the stairs – even like in Covent Garden where it takes forever. During the last pandemic lockdown, he let his little sister cut his hair and wore a hat non-stop for months.

'He was warm and kind. Just days before he died, he spent hours and hours helping me help another friend. He didn't have to do that, but that was Bishan: if anyone asked him for help, he was there. Even if they didn't ask, if he thought he could help, he would.

'Bishan started something before he died – many of you will know about it already. Together we'd begun contacting grassroots environmental groups all over the UK and in other parts of the world about coming together. Forming something bigger than the sum of its parts, to give us a loud enough voice that we can't be ignored. We have our differences, sure, but we can do this! I have all our plans and notes together and will be carrying on.

'I can't let him down.

'We're fighting for our lives. For every person and animal and plant on this planet. I get that you may be scared. I am. But what happened hasn't changed how I feel or what I have to do.

'Will you help me?'

* * *

I watch it back a few times and wish I'd pushed my glasses a bit up my nose and maybe even tied back my hair. I shrug. I said what I wanted to say.

A deep breath; another.

Then I tag it #NatureIsScreaming and post it here, there, everywhere.

It's late but I'm giving up on sleep tonight. Instead, I watch: the likes, the shares, the comments.

Yes – we'll help you

I'll help you

You can count on me

Different versions of the same words, over and over again – in English and other languages. London, Cornwall, Edinburgh. Midlands and Kent. France and Denmark, Germany, too. Indonesia, China, Japan. Turkey. India and Pakistan. Israel and the UAE. Australia and Canada and even the USA, and they keep coming in more and more.

From all over the world.

There are goosebumps up and down my spine. Can what Bishan and me planned really happen? Can some good come from all the bad?

And even if everyone tries to come together, if they look to me – am I up to this?

Then two more comments drop in: two more – *yes, I'll help you.*

One is from Dad. And the other, Mum.

It's almost morning. I pull on a dressing gown, go down the stairs. The back door to the garden is open and they're on our swing seat in the almost light of dawn.

Mum holds out her hand, pulls me down to sit between them.

'Thank you,' I say.

'He made me do it,' Mum says.

'No, he didn't.'

'OK, no he didn't. If you're in this fight, then so are we.'

We watch the sun come up – or so we suppose. There's no real sunrise since Industria United geoengineered the sky, just a gradual lightening as the day begins.

And as if with the sun, something inside me is lightening too. I close my eyes. Fall asleep with my head on Mum's shoulder and retreat to a dark, dreamless, healing place.

Part 7

@HaydenNoPlanetB

Antarctica's ice sheets are melting, edging closer to tipping points that will see ice caps disappear. Rising seas will cause drastic changes to coastlines around the world — many densely inhabited coastal communities will be under water. We must act now.

#NatureIsScreaming

48

Tabby

We meet very early in the morning – me, Zara, and on-time-for-once Ariel – next to one of the sea locks of Undersea.

We pull on wetsuits. Last night, Malina gave each of us a waterproof backpack with a few basic supplies already inside – snacks, money, and mobile phones in a special case to cope with the water pressure. We have a number programmed to message when we arrive, and someone named Paula in The Circle will meet us and take us to Isha.

'Are you sure this will work?' Ariel says. 'That the dolphins will take us where we want to go?'

'Yes,' I say out loud. 'Are you sure?' I say silently.

Yes. Stop fussing.

We're about to go through to the first pressure chamber when there are the soft sounds of light footsteps coming towards us.

It's Cassandra.

'I've come to see you off. Have you got everything?'

'Think so,' I say.

'There is one thing you will always have wherever you go: the love and respect of your sisters. Best wishes for a safe journey.'

'Thanks.'

'Will we succeed?' Zara says, asking what we all want to know of the person most likely to have the answer. My breath catches in my throat. Does she mean will we get to Brighton safely, then London, and have the three join us? Or the much more that is the whole struggle for the climate?

There's a pause. 'Time will tell,' Cassandra says. 'Now go.'

Ariel opens the door and my eyes are drawn to Cassandra's.

Time will tell: has time told her? Does she know but won't tell us? If she knows we will succeed, then why not say so?

It is better to chase the fish.

Right. And here we go.

We step through, seal the door. The pressure rises. Then we unwind the hatch to the next chamber, step through and wind it shut. As water starts rushing in, all thoughts of time and Cassandra are gone. I'm vibrating to the touch of cold, salt water as it covers my feet, legs, climbs higher; full of excitement for *now* – to be reunited with the sea. Just before it is over my head, I breathe air in deep and hold.

The doors open.

Already the sea is dancing with dolphins all around, and the sense of *rightness* and *joy* inside me is so intense I feel like I may scream or laugh or cry, all at once.

My friend: I see her, swim over as she comes to me. Her nose bumps against my shoulder – a playful touch. A hand to her dorsal fin and we're off.

First we play, carving through the water, splashing up into the air, chasing back down to the depths. The others alongside us.

'Brighton?' I show Aslan the pier, the coastline, in my mind.

Brighton.

We set off, the others following closely behind. This will be the longest swim – the longest time – I've ever spent in the ocean. I'm completely blissed out, and at the same time so tired. Too much worrying and not enough sleep last night.

Sleep. We are safe with the kin. I'll wake you if there is need.

One eye closed, one eye open; swimming at a speed I couldn't get close to on my own. Aslan is in charge and I can rest, and there is something that feels so amazing, so right, to fall gently asleep as we rush through the sea.

49

Denzi

Darkest blue depths swirl with bubbles; seaweed brushes my skin. Skimming the ocean floor, fast and then faster until the blue embrace of the sea is a blur and I'm dizzy with it and lack of oxygen. Then up, up, to surface – my dolphin friend seems to laugh as I fall from him to the sea in a splash.

Breathe in deep.

The stars above in a clear sky reflect and shimmer on the surface, and now Tabby is here, too. She turns to me, reaches out her hand but before I can take it, she's gone, diving down deep with her dolphin.

We follow, give chase.

Sometimes we catch her, sometimes she seems to appear from nowhere behind me as if she is the one doing the chasing.

Confusion: this was in the past, wasn't it? Those two nights with Tabby in the magical sea?

Am I dreaming?

Sometimes it changes. I'm taken from the sea and questions whispered in my ear; I must answer before I can return to the deep.

I try to free myself, to climb to wakefulness, but then fall back again to the sea. It cradles me with both joy and surprise at what I am. Counts my fingers, toes, and holds me close like a precious thing.

Until the next dream takes me again . . .

50

Tabby

Wake up. We're there.

I open my eyes – well, the one that was shut.

It is just the three dolphins with me, Ariel and Zara – the others are hanging back in deeper water.

'Thank you,' I say to mine, stroke her side and she butts into my arm.

She says it is joy to help kin.

Ariel and Zara are close by with their dolphins, one eye open, one shut, but the open eye is somehow *wrong*? A bit blank, unfocused – like they're not seeing me or what is around them. I swim over to Ariel, push on her shoulder: no response. Take her hand and kick to the surface with her. Zara's dolphin brings her up also.

It's early dawn, going by the half glow in the sky.

'Hey. We're here. What's up with you two?'

They don't answer.

They've been speaking to the kin.

'What? I thought they couldn't.'

Not like us. They're different. I don't understand.

'Let's get them in closer to shore.' Zara's dolphin takes off; I pull the two girls along with me until our feet can just touch with our heads above water.

'Ariel! Zara! Oi.'

Zara turns to me, focuses slowly, with both eyes open. A puzzled look on her face. Then Ariel does the same.

Ariel looks around. 'Where are we?'

'Brighton, if I'm not mistaken. Are you OK?'

'I don't know. I feel a bit weird.'

'Me, too,' says Zara.

'Come on. Let's get ashore.'

We half swim, half walk, to the stony beach. It's too early for joggers or dog walkers; just as well, as three girls in wetsuits arriving on dolphins and emerging from the sea might attract attention. We walk part way up the beach and it's so hot already.

'Let's get these off,' I say.

Backpacks off, then wetsuits – shorts and tops on underneath. And we sit on the beach, staring at the sea without speaking for a moment.

'That feels better,' I say, finally. 'What was going on? I was calling out to both of you and you didn't answer. It was like you couldn't hear or see me, either.'

Ariel shakes her head. 'I don't know. We were swimming and having a great time before we set out. And then . . . we were here. I don't remember anything else.'

'Same,' Zara says. 'I feel, I don't know, disoriented? As if something in me *changed* and then changed back.'

They were kin and now they're not. They don't have a connection between their two halves like we do.

'That wasn't the same for you?' Ariel says.

'Not exactly.' I'm not sure what to say but they're both looking freaked out – maybe I can help? 'I think it's something like this. You know that dolphins have a split brain? So if they

248

sleep, half of their brain stays awake – so they know to go up to breathe regularly and can still watch for predators, that kind of thing.

'Yeah, I get that. And?' Ariel says.

'I think, maybe, we're a bit like that. So part of you was awake and part asleep.'

'That makes sense, I guess,' Zara says. 'But wasn't it the same for you?'

'It *kind* of was. I took a nap most of the way. But it wasn't the same when I woke up. I didn't feel that weirdness you say. Has that happened to either of you before?'

Ariel looks uneasy. 'I think it might have. There've been times when I've been swimming and it's kind of like I lose some time.'

'I'm not sure. Maybe,' Zara says.

I don't tell them about Aslan. I don't know why, but I feel this need to keep him to myself.

'Next move?' I unzip my backpack and then the extra inner waterproof shell. Take the mobile out of its case and turn it on. 'There's a message.'

Hi, this is Paula. I'll arrive Brighton about 10 a.m. Let me know when you get there.

I answer: Hi we're here.

A moment later a reply pings in. Why don't you find somewhere for breakfast once things open up? Tell me where and I'll meet you.

51

Denzi

One morning I wake up.

I'm not sure of it at first. It could be the start of a different dream? Bit by bit I become more aware of myself, of my thoughts, and that they are mine and I can direct them, not just be swept along in dreams, and that I am physically present in my body.

As if that is something I've forgotten, it feels strange. The weight of me pressing down, the feeling of gravity. Warm air against my skin. A pillow twisted under my head, and I move a little, straighten my neck. Stretch and feel stiff muscles pulling under my skin.

I open my eyes.

Dark curtains are drawn but dull light shines through underneath. A window?

My thoughts are sluggish but I know the window is significant.

The hospital: I was in that hospital, in a locked room. There definitely weren't any windows.

Where am I? Why don't I remember getting here?

I sit up. I'm in a T-shirt, shorts, that I don't recognise either. I get up and pull the curtains, look out. There's a row of houses across a narrow road, cars parked all along. Could be anywhere in London, or elsewhere; nothing is familiar. The sky is *odd* – a dull grey without cloud cover, and no way to note where the sun may be – and now I'm remembering that last morning with

250

Tabby, the way the sky looked. How uneasy we both felt without knowing why it was like this. And now – however many days or weeks later – it's still the same?

I pad across the room, barefoot, to the door; listen, but all I hear is distant traffic. Then a sort of whistling?

Turn the handle; it's not locked. It leads to a short hallway, other rooms leading off from it. It looks like a house not a hospital.

There are stairs going down and sounds of movement below. The whistling increases and cuts off – a kettle boiling?

A door opens past the bottom of the stairs and a woman looks up. I almost recoil when I see her red hair. It's Stacey, the one who was meant to be my personal protection officer but was something *else*. She chased us – me and Tabby. Tabby said she had been tailing her, trying to catch her: that she must be in The Circle.

'There you are, Denzi,' she says. 'Would you like some tea?'

'Ah, sure?' I say and start down the stairs. She goes back the way she came, presumably to a kitchen, and I run for the front door of the house and turn the knob – but it's locked. No key in sight.

She comes out again, shakes her head. 'Come on. Have some tea.'

I hesitate, then follow her when she goes through again to a kitchen.

'Where am I? Why am I here?'

She pours the tea.

'Good questions. If it were up to me, you wouldn't be *anywhere*. Yet I've been told to babysit you until Malina arrives. She might answer your questions; I won't.' She points at the fridge. 'Help

251

yourself if you're hungry. I've got stuff to do.'

She leaves and I listen to her footsteps. They seem to go towards the front of the house then pause, and there is the sound of a door clicking shut. There was a room leading off from the lounge room – another reception room, perhaps – I'm guessing that's where she went. I wait a moment in case she comes back, then, as quietly as I can, try the windows, the back door to a garden – all are locked, no keys in sight or in drawers.

I hear footsteps and grab my tea, sit at the table, just as the door opens, but it's not Stacey.

It's a boy – seventeen or so, my age. He's pale and holding on to the door frame like it's keeping him upright. It takes me a moment to work out where I know him from. Swim school?

'Denzi?' he says.

'Yeah. Con, right?'

'What the hell is going on?'

52

Tabby

A waitress brings us steaming plates of full English breakfast. She puts them down and I'm ravenous. Swimming through a day and a night does that I guess, even when you're asleep for most of it.

All three of us are food focused so much that at first we don't notice the sudden drop in conversation around us. Everyone is staring. I nudge the other two.

Napkins. Wipe hands. Pick up cutlery and eat at a normal pace until it is gone.

We've got time to kill until Paula gets here and we've all got our phones out.

'It's so hard not to dive into my social accounts and say that I'm here,' Ariel says.

'Same,' Zara says. 'I guess everyone thinks we're dead. Don't they?'

'There was a page set up by parents of kids missing from summer swim school.' I tell them where to find it.

Zara has tears in her eyes now when she reads the post put up by her parents. 'I have to tell them I'm OK. I have to.'

'Wait just a little longer. Once we get Isha, Denzi and Con on board, we're all going to our parents. Right?'

She nods. 'Right. OK.'

'There's been another bombing in London,' Ariel says. 'It says The Circle are suspected.'

'What?' I go to the news on my phone. It happened yesterday when we were on our way here. A café – almost levelled. Eight people dead, more injured.

'Why would The Circle have anything to do with that?' I say. 'It's just a café, not a major polluter or a flood defence or anything. And aren't they supposed to hold off until we've had our chance to change things?'

'Maybe it has nothing to do with them and they just get blamed for everything now,' Zara says.

'Maybe. But I don't think the police would say they are suspected without having a reason for saying it.' I'm still uneasy.

'This could be her,' Zara says. A woman, thirty or so and on her own, is at the door looking around. When she sees us, she comes to sit down in the empty chair.

'Hi, I'm Paula.' Ariel is introducing us and I'm still thinking about that bombing in London, unease in the pit of my stomach.

'I have Isha's address, her mobile number, too, if we need it,' Paula says. 'We've been watching her movements, her family. If we go after two, her mother goes to work from two until six and Isha should be on her own. In the meantime I've booked a hotel room where you can shower, change, have a sleep if you want.'

An hour or so later we've all showered and Zara and Ariel are asleep – normal sleep, both eyes shut. It's not just a hotel room, more like a suite with a separate bedroom and a sitting area.

I wander out to where Paula is sitting on a sofa reading. She looks up. 'Can't sleep?'

I shake my head and sit in a chair across from her. 'Can I ask you something?'

'Of course.'

'There was this bombing in London yesterday and the BBC say that The Circle are suspected. Did they? Do it? They're supposed to be waiting until we've tried to change things.'

She closes her book. 'Not so far as I know. Though if you think about it, every time The Circle did something they took credit for it. Have they in this case?'

'I don't think so.' Phone out, I'm checking news sites all over. 'There's no mention of it.'

'There you go. It was probably some unrelated thing. Try not to worry and get some rest. The next few days are going to be busy.'

I nod, go back to the bedroom. Ariel and Zara are still asleep on the double bed. There's a single also, and I curl up there. Close my eyes but sleep still won't come.

'Aslan?' I say, silently.

No answer: he's sound asleep after being awake a day and a night swimming.

I sigh, roll over on my back, stare at the ceiling. There are too many things niggling away inside; there's no point trying to sleep. Anyhow, I slept most of the way here so I'm not tired.

We all agreed what we were going to do – it was my suggestion to start with – so why do I feel like things aren't right?

It is *so* tempting to have a look at the future and Aslan isn't awake to talk me out of it. I shake my head: don't do it, I say to myself. Chase the fish.

In a few hours we're going to knock on Isha's door and what are we going to say? Hi, we're the Chosen, part of The Circle. Please join us in our hopeless quest to save the world. And then on to Denzi and Con with the same.

Why would they even think about coming to help us?

If Ariel had come to me with the same line a while back, I would have told her to forget it – I know it. It was only once I joined in the dreaming that I began to understand this group and what they have been, the good they have done for thousands of years. It's only recently – since Cassandra's dipping into the future – that they've gone rogue.

Their reasons for what they've done I can't deny; their motivation is, and has always been, overwhelmingly right. But their methods?

All we can do now is *try* to change things. Make them better.

I wish I could just be Tabby, a girl. Not wishing Aslan away – I'd as soon want to cut off my legs – but not struggling with all of this.

I need a friend, someone outside of everything, someone I trust to talk things through. The only one who fits that bill is Jago.

I try to go back in my mind to when we met – to what feels like another lifetime ago. In many ways it was. Jago and me, on our beach. The scratch of sand. Salt on my lips from the waves. Apart from Cate, he really was my first friend – my only friend. He had me memorise his number but I forgot it, didn't I? It was written in my notebook that is probably long gone in the sea, when my parent's house was flooded in the hurricane.

Even if I did remember it, I shouldn't call. Should I?

53

Denzi

Con watches from the door. 'No sign of her,' he says.

'OK, here I go.' The kitchen stool is in my hands – I bang it into the window. Nothing. Not even a crack. 'I'll give it a bit more.'

This time I swing it as hard as I can – smash it into the window. But it only bounces back and jars my shoulders so much it hurts.

Con is still watching at the door. 'Whoa,' he says and steps back.

Stacey stands there, the scowl on her face a bit lost as she's got an actual gun in her hands, pointed at us, and it's hard to look at anything else.

'Listen to me. I've had a bad few days so don't give me a reason to use this. The walls are soundproofed, everything is locked, all the glass is toughened, and you won't be able to break it. So just be good boys, makes yourselves some brunch, watch some TV and *be quiet.*'

'Sure. OK,' Con says and holds out his hands, palms up. 'Sounds good.'

She's looking at me and I'm saying nothing. She sighs and shakes her head. 'Anything you do,' she points at me, 'will be blamed on both of you. Got it?'

She backs out so her eyes stay on us, then goes back to a room at the front of the house and slams the door.

257

'Well, she's nice,' Con says.

'Oh, yeah, for sure,' I say, and I'm frowning, thinking about toughened glass. 'There may still be a way to break a window and get out. My other dad had a greenhouse in the garden and we managed to break a pane of toughened glass while we were building it, when a corner was clunked against the patio. This kind of glass is weakest at the edges and corners. If we can find a pane of glass loose enough that we can aim something small at an edge or a corner, it might break.'

'Then there is the gun.'

'Yeah. But look at it this way: I think it's a fair assumption that staying is going to go badly. Trying to leave could go badly, but it might not.'

'How about this. Let's eat something – because I don't know about you but sleeping for forever has left me feeling a bit wobbly and I'm starving. Let her start to think we're doing what she wants us to do. Then we'll start checking all the edges of the windows.'

'Deal.'

54

Tabby

'How do you want to do things with Isha?' Paula says. 'Do you want me to come with you?'

'About that,' I say. 'If everyone agrees, I think maybe it'd be better if I go on my own to start with? I think I knew Isha the best and she's a bit quiet. Three of us might overwhelm her; I think I should go in first to talk to her.'

Ariel and Zara exchange a glance, then both nod.

'OK, how about this,' Paula says. 'There's a big supermarket not that far from Isha's house. How about we go park up there and you can walk over and call if you need us?'

I've checked the map on my phone – it's only a five-minute or so walk. As I walk I gather my thoughts.

If I'm honest, Isha was an afterthought. I was thinking about Denzi – and by extension, the other boy, Con – and Isha's situation is different to theirs. The boys were being held as part of Phina's plans with no choice of their own. Isha, on the other hand, is at home. If she's happy being there, what right do we have to ask her to leave it behind?

And that's why I didn't want the others to come along. I want to be honest with her about everything so she can make a clear choice.

I'm thinking about what I should say so much that I almost

don't notice the police car parked in front of a house on Isha's road. I slow, check the house numbers. It's in front of her house. And her mum's car – Paula had described it in case she's home unexpectedly – is also in the drive. What's going on?

There's a park a bit further along. I go there, slip back into some trees so I can just see the police car. What now?

I bite my lip. I should message Paula.

I decide to wait, see what happens.

Minutes go slowly by – five, ten, twenty. Just when I'm thinking I'll have to go back to Paula and the others, there's movement in front of the house. Soon after the police car drives away.

What now? Her mum's car is still there.

I've got Isha's number from Paula. Think for a moment, then text:

Hi Isha, it's Tabby. I really want to talk to you, but don't want anyone to know. Can you meet me? I'm in Brighton.

Minutes pass.

It's amazing to hear from you!! Are you ok? I'll try to get out, but tricky as Mum is freaked out just now. Hang on . . .

OK.

Five minutes later: I told her I'm going to the shops, where are you?

I think I'm just down the road from your house – in the park.

There's no reply straight back. She must be wondering how I know where she lives? Just when I'm thinking I'll have to reassure her somehow, a message pings in.

OK. I'll be there soon.

I send a quick message to Paula: delayed as Isha's mother is home. Isha is getting out to meet me shortly.

OK. Keep us posted.

55

Denzi

'This is good. Thanks,' I say and take another bite of omelette. Surprised I'm so hungry, considering – you'd think being locked in a house by a crazy person with a gun would be enough to take your appetite.

'No worries,' Con says. 'I always had to cook for my brother when Mum worked late – omelettes were my speciality.'

'Toast is about the only thing I can make and usually it's burnt.'

'I'll risk it.'

I put more bread in the toaster.

'I can't get my head around what is going on,' he says. 'First, I'm locked up in some hospital I've never heard of, my family told lies – that I'd been using drugs, was suicidal. The next thing I wake up here.'

'I feel like we've been here for a while. It felt like I was dreaming for ever.'

'Me, too. Weird stuff as well. Why are we locked up here with random nutcase and her gun?'

'I might know a bit more than you do about what is going on.'

'OK, out with it.'

'Stacey – that's her name – was a personal protection officer. She was taking me places and stuff because the terror alert was so high that they were watching family of politicians.'

261

'And now she's our jailor?'

'That's not all. I think she's part of The Circle.'

Con's eyes open so wide they look ready to eject from his head. 'Shit,' he says.

'Yeah. Did you know Tabby? She was in the same swimming group as Ariel?'

'Tall, long dark hair, totally fit? Kind of shy.'

'Sounds like her. What I know comes mostly from Tabby. Parts of this are going to seem pretty crazy. Anyhow, this is the story.'

I tell him everything, not leaving things out, just pausing part way to scrape burnt toast. If we're in this – whatever it is – together, the more we both know the better.

When I'm done he's just staring back at me.

'So. We're, like, part dolphin?'

'Yeah. I think so.'

'Wicked.'

56

Tabby

'Isha! It's so good to see you.' She smiles, gives me a hug.

'You too. I thought you were missing or something? Denzi was looking for you.'

'I knew he'd contacted you – we met up in London a while back.'

'I stood him up, though it wasn't my fault. My aunt needed help with something and then I couldn't find my phone so couldn't let him know.'

'I'm glad you're all right. We were worried. Can we talk?'

'Of course. Café down the road? Or there's a few benches that way,' she says and points down a path in the park.

'Bench sounds good.'

We cut across the grass, through some trees.

'How did you know where I live?'

'Part of a long story. Can I ask – what were the police doing at your house?'

'You saw them?'

'Yeah. Waited for them to leave to call you.'

We reach the bench now, sit down.

'They came to talk to my mum about the Penrose Clinic.'

'Really? What did they want to know?'

'I wasn't in the room but from what Mum said after, they wanted to know everything about the clinic, why she went there – duh, to have me – and anything about it that she could remember. They said the clinic might be involved in something illegal but they were vague as to what. Mum was freaking out. Does this have anything to do with how there were so many Penrose babies at swim school?'

'It might. Isha, I have a lot of things to tell you and there isn't much time.'

'I'm listening.'

I tell her everything that has happened since I last saw her at swim school – as concisely as I can. Including that the Penrose Clinic is a front for The Circle and what was done to us before we were born. How they tracked me – caught me. Took me to Undersea. That she would have been taken there too if she wasn't claustrophobic. The dreaming and why I am here now: to see if she wants to join us.

'Wow,' Isha says. 'Do the police know something about all this? Is that why they were asking all these questions?'

'Know, or guess? I don't know.'

'What if they start looking at me? Will they?'

'Maybe, if they work out what was done to us.' And I hadn't thought of it that way before. If the authorities find out how our DNA was mucked around with – that we're not completely human – how would they react? What might they do to us?

'And you want me to come with you now.'

'I want you to do what is best for you. That's all.'

She stares back at me, an interplay of emotions I can't follow on her face. 'This is mad,' she finally says. 'I've always kind of known I wasn't *right*, that I was different. The first time I ever felt I was even close to fitting in anywhere was at swim school.'

264

'I get that. Me too.'

'Do you think our parents knew anything about all of this?'

'I don't think so – mine didn't, I'm sure of that. Ariel's mum did but she's in The Circle – she's the scientist behind what was done to us. And my mum's mum did as she's also involved in it. But I don't know if any more of our parents or relatives are like that at all.'

'What you say about belonging to everyone in the dreaming sounds amazing. And the Chosen: it's kind of like you're trying to save the world.'

'That sounds nuts, but yeah: we are going to try to stop humanity from destroying the planet. The question is just whether they can be convinced, or if the end is coming no matter what we do.'

'I'm not brave like you are. Even thinking about all of this just makes me want to hide.'

I shake my head. 'Believe me, I'm not brave at all and I felt the same way. If The Circle hadn't caught me and taken me to Undersea, I would have run and kept on running.'

'How do you feel about them now?'

'The other Chosen are like my best friends, or closest sisters – I didn't think I could ever be so close to anyone. The rest of it? Mixed. I don't trust all of them completely, don't believe many things they've done recently are right.'

'Thank you for being so honest.'

'That's why I wanted to come talk to you on my own. So, what do you want to do?'

'I don't know. I need to think.'

'We've got to leave for London soon. You could come with

265

us if you want to. Or call and meet us later or tomorrow in London. It's up to you.'

I walk back to Paula's car alone. I said we'd wait an hour and we do. I message Isha when it is up. There is no reply. We leave for London.

57

Denzi

We check every window – no loose panes, no corners or edges to tap. Con is foraging for a late lunch and I'm checking upstairs again when Con calls from below.

He's in front of the TV – the news is on.

'Branches of an IVF and research clinic known as the Penrose Clinic have been raided in almost unprecedented coordinated international action in London, Rome, Los Angeles and other locations around the world. Police have indicated that it is part of an ongoing investigation without further explanation as to why.

'Our reporter at the scene in London has more.'

The scene shifts to a woman with a microphone. 'I'm standing outside the London premises of the Penrose Clinic, raided today by the Metropolitan Police. Reports from onlookers say entry was forced after there was no response within and that no one was found inside the clinic. Records had been destroyed, leading to speculation that they were tipped off somehow about the raids. An unconfirmed source claims that there is a connection between the eco-terrorist group The Circle and the Penrose Clinic.'

'Wow. The news is out?' Con says.

'If they were keeping me because I know, there's no point to that any more. Is there? Stacey?' I call out.

She comes out a moment later. 'Yes?'

'Have you caught the news? About Penrose and The Circle?'

'Old news, mate.'

'Just in. A former police protection officer, Stacey Linden, is wanted in connection with the bombing in London two days ago of a café in Islington.' Stacey's face is all over the screen.

Her jaw drops.

'That isn't old news, I take it?'

She fixes an intense stare on me that makes me take a step back, but then there is the sound of a key in the front door and I'm thinking, run for the door and push through, but before the thought reaches my feet Stacey's gun is in her hand and pointed at me.

Malina steps in and looks at the gun.

'Is that really necessary?'

'Up to you now. I'm getting out of here.'

58

Tabby

Paula pulls in, parks in front of a semi-detached on a quiet road in London.

'Well, here we are,' she says. They're all getting out and I'm still in my seat.

Ariel looks back. 'Aren't you coming?'

I undo my seat belt, slowly get out of the car. Now that I'm finally about to see Denzi, I feel sick with nerves. I'm desperate to see him, but how does he feel about me after I ran and left him lying on that beach? He's been a prisoner of The Circle ever since. Why would he want to listen to anything we have to say about joining?

Maybe he'll think I'm one of them, that I'm not the Tabby he knew. And he'd be right: I'm not. Everything that has happened since then has changed me in ways he won't understand unless he joins himself.

Ariel links her arm in mine. 'Come on.'

We walk up the footpath; Paula knocks on the door and it opens moments later. It's Malina.

She smiles. 'Come in, come in.'

Ariel pushes me in after Paula.

'Tabby?' And Denzi is here now next to me, hugging me tight and I'm hugging him back, shaking, tears in my eyes.

'They've got you, too?' he says.

'Sort of.'

'Do you know Con?' he says, gesturing to another boy. I shake my head and say hi.

'Now we're nearly all together,' Malina says.

'Nearly?' I say.

'Isha will be here soon.'

'She decided to come?'

Malina hesitates. 'Her aunt is bringing her.'

'Her aunt. Is she in The Circle then?'

'Yes.'

Denzi frowns. 'Tabby, what's going on?'

59

Denzi

There's another knock on the door before Tabby can say anything else. Isha is pushed into the hall and there is the clink of the lock as a key is turned from the outside. Her face – she's been crying.

'Are you OK?' Tabby says.

'I don't know. My aunt – she's in The Circle. She came over after you were gone. Told me I had to come and my mum – she didn't know anything about what was going on and I couldn't tell her. She's just going to think I vanished or something.'

'Oh, Isha.' Tabby gives her a hug.

'Most of our parents don't know,' Zara says. 'Mine think I died in the hurricane.'

'My dad does, too,' Ariel says.

And I'm putting things together – better slowly than not at all. Seeing Ariel in that CCTV from the Hoover Dam bombing. The three of them – Tabby, Zara, Ariel – arriving together and what they've said to Isha. And even as everything inside me protests, screams *no, no*, it can't be – somehow, I know that it is.

'Tabby, are you part of The Circle?'

She turns back to me. Those eyes I could drown in, troubled.

'You are, aren't you.' I say the words like a statement not a question because I can see what she doesn't want to say.

'She didn't come to us willingly,' Malina says. 'At first.'

'But you have chosen to stay with them now?'

271

Tabby gives a half nod, looks down, not meeting my eyes.

'So all of you – do you bomb dams and cafés and kill innocent people regularly, or is that just a sideline?'

Tabby's eyes are back on mine now. 'I never have and I never will,' she says and I trust this girl, I know I do, but I don't understand how she could be a part of a group that does these things even if she doesn't.

Then she frowns. 'Cafés?'

'That bombing in London. Stacey did it – she's wanted, it's been on the news.'

'What?' She turns and looks to Paula then Malina, and gets a phone out of her pocket. Finds the story. She shows it to Malina. 'She's the one you were with when you were trying to catch me, isn't she?'

'Yes. It's her. Assuming she did it, I don't know anything about why or what she was doing. She left when I got here and I don't know where she has gone.'

'Are you saying she has like, gone rogue, and The Circle isn't behind it?'

'I'm saying I don't know.'

Paula clears her throat. 'Don't know about you but it's been a long day. Time for some tea?'

She and Malina go into the kitchen, leaving us alone.

'So could anyone explain why are we here? Why are you here? And, basically, what is going on?' It's Con this time.

'Yeah. It's a long story,' Tabby says. 'Let's all sit down.' And we find spots on chairs and sofas and Tabby's face is pained when I sit across and not next to her. But I need to see her face, to not be too close to her now.

She pauses, looks like she is having an internal debate about something.

'All right. I don't know how much everyone knows or has figured out, so let's start at the beginning.

'Many thousands of years ago, a group of wise women banded together to protect themselves and sun, sea, earth and sky. Over time they became The Circle. In the beginning they were always seeking to heal and protect. As part of this, they began selective breeding to enhance their daughters' senses to be beyond those of men. They gradually developed the ability to see the circles of time and to cherish their ancestors' memories inside of them. At times they were persecuted as witches but they carried on, and their seers became more and more adept at weaving the circles to follow the paths of time.'

Tabby continues telling the history of The Circle. Paula and Malina slip in with drinks on a tray for us and leave again. When she tells of a young girl, Cassandra, becoming seer with a blood ritual, it is so vivid it is as if it happened to her.

Cassandra saw the end coming: the silencing of all future voices. And I'm remembering now that Tabby said she had a dream like this – does that mean she is a seer? And then The Circle couldn't agree on how to handle this, what to do. And so we were made – we were chosen – to break the deadlock.

'When we met to decide what to do, we realised we couldn't make decisions without all of the Chosen being involved: that's where you three come in,' Tabby says. 'Even though only women have joined before, we convinced them we had to come to all three of you and ask if you want to join us.

'There isn't much time. We are so close to a tipping point,

273

beyond which the climate can never recover,' Tabby says. 'The planet will die; all life as we know it will die. We – the Chosen – were made to stop this from happening. You are part of us. We need your help.'

60

Tabby

Denzi's eyes: when he first realised I was in The Circle, that it was by choice? I felt his rejection as a physical thing, as clearly as if he'd pushed me away or shouted it out loud.

But this is beyond me, my feelings. This is *everything*.

I talked for so long that my voice is hoarse. Now that I'm done, I don't know what he or Con, or even Isha, will say. They might think we're all crazy, that this is some kind of mass hypnosis or something. It's all pretty unbelievable. Despite a degree of awareness of the voices inside me, I'd have felt the same way if I hadn't experienced the dreaming myself.

But before they can say anything in response, Malina and Paula come in, as if some sixth sense – or listening at the door? – told them it was time to interrupt.

'We've made a late dinner. Come, eat together. Put this aside until after.'

We get up and I stretch, stiff after sitting for so long. Make our way to the kitchen table and Isha sits on one side of me, Malina on the other. Denzi is across from me but I can't bring myself to even look at him – to see what I'm afraid he may feel about me now in his eyes.

Paula passes around bowls of pasta, salad, then joins us. I'm hungry but everything tastes like dust.

Malina nudges me. 'Eat, Tabby. You'll need energy for

what is to come.'

And she's right, so I try.

Most of us are quiet. Ariel being Ariel is trying to draw everyone into conversation and having more luck with Con than the others.

'If everyone is almost done?' Malina says. 'There are a few things I need to say. And I know the three of you have had a lot thrust on you and I don't want to make the pressure any worse than you may already feel, but there isn't much time. There's only an hour until midnight now: the time The Circle will meet in the dreaming, with or without you. I'm sure Tabby has told you everything she could to help you decide, but she – like Ariel and Zara – is new to us. Also, I'm guessing there are things she wouldn't have said that I think you should know.

'Denzi and Con. You know we have been a sisterhood for thousands of years? For many generations we've used selective breeding to enhance abilities to interpret time and join with our ancestors. These abilities are not present in men at all, but you had it engineered into you – as a safeguard to preserve the abilities in the population – in case the Chosen are the only ones who survive catastrophic climate change. Your role in all of this was only to serve as breeding stock if needed. In case it wasn't clear to you, it was only Tabby's intervention and persuasive skills that convinced first the Chosen and then the entire sisterhood that this was wrong, that we needed to change. To give you a chance to be part of us.'

'Ouch,' Con says. 'Though I am, obviously, a bit of a stud, I'm not daddy material.'

'It wasn't going to be optional,' Malina says. 'There are ways if you were unwilling.'

276

'Another ouch.'

'Just to be clear,' Denzi says, 'if we refuse to join, what happens to us? Are we back to being prisoners?'

'I'm afraid so.'

'What about me? What if I refuse?' Isha says, but then holds up a hand. 'Don't answer that. I can't just go home, knowing what I know. I couldn't live with myself if I didn't try to help. I was too scared to do what was right when you were still in Brighton. But I'm in.'

'Thank you, Isha,' Malina says.

'I'm not sure you're giving us much of a choice, but I'd already decided,' Denzi says. I lift my head, make my eyes meet his, scared what he will say. 'I've been locked up in a hospital, accused of drug use and assault. Drugged again for I don't know how long, put on ice in this house with homicidal Stacey in charge, and now this?' He shrugs. 'The bloody-minded part of me wants to tell the lot of you to get stuffed. But.

'The only time in my life I ever felt like I belonged to something was with you, Tabby. In the sea. You're part of me and I can't walk away from you. If you think this is the right thing to do, then I'm in.'

'What the hell – make it three,' says Con.

And now everyone is smiling and talking at once, but I'm silent, my eyes held by Denzi's. When we get up from the table, he comes to me and wraps his arms around me, holds me close.

'There is something else Denzi and Con need to know,' Malina says. 'We honestly don't know if you will be able to join the dreaming. No male has ever been allowed to try. You might not be able to take part at all, but if you can, there may be some risk to you.'

'Risk? What sort of risk?' Denzi says.

'Very rarely, one of our sisters doesn't survive their first dreaming. It's the intensity, the joy and pain of the lives of their ancestors.'

'No one told us that beforehand,' Ariel says.

'We generally feel that the risk is best not appreciated so you can join openly and without fear, but it's not the same for Denzi and Con. It's a complete unknown how the ancestors will receive them – they may not be very welcoming.'

61

Denzi

'I'm scared,' Tabby says. 'I'd thought there was something suspicious in the way they agreed so readily for you and Con to join. Is it because they thought it didn't matter what was decided, that you'd never be able to anyhow?'

'Well, what does it matter? We try; if it doesn't work, we're back to where we started.'

'In the dreaming you're completely taken over by memories and experiences from ancestors. They could make it hurt – a lot. Just remember, it isn't really happening to you – it's memories, that's all. Right?'

'What happens now?' Con says.

'We drink the special tea that Malina is making,' Tabby says. 'It makes us sleep. Eat the chocolate: it helps you hear the ancestors and become as one with them in your mind.'

Malina comes out with a tray of mugs and a bowl of chocolates and passes them all around. 'I suggest you find a place where you are comfortable to sleep?' she says. 'There are sofas down here and bedrooms upstairs.'

I take Tabby's hand, pull her towards the stairs. I see Con and Ariel have the same idea and follow.

We go up the stairs and down the hall. Con and Ariel disappear through one of the first doors; I take Tabby to the one at the end.

'This is where I was dreaming – the usual sort, I think – for days.' I sit on the side of the bed; she sits next to me.

'What did you dream about?'

'Mostly you and being in the sea together, swimming with dolphins.' I frown. 'Sometimes I dreamt that someone was asking me questions; I'm not sure if that was real or not.'

'I think it probably was. They knew some things – like that we promised together – that I hadn't told them.' She hesitates, looks down then back to meet my eyes. 'That day at the beach – I'm so sorry I left you.'

'It wouldn't have changed anything. They would have caught you quicker, that's all.'

'I guess. It still feels like it was wrong. Are you sure you want to do this?'

'I think so. It's not a decision all put together with reasoning and logic. My guts say do this. And here I am.' We clink our mugs of tea together. I take a sip. 'Nice. Like spices? A little sweet.'

Once it's gone, time for chocolate. Tabby hands some to me and we bite into a piece of it at the same time.

'It tastes like regular chocolate but with a bit of something else about it,' I say.

'Yeah. It's not bad like this. I first tried it as a root. Not so nice.'

'So, we'll just fall asleep now?'

'Soon.'

I lean back, pull my legs up and lie down on the bed and she does the same. Lying down, facing each other. I trace a finger along her cheek, down her neck and she shivers.

'Let's stay awake as long as we can,' she says.

'OK.'

'I was afraid you'd hate me.'

'I could never hate you.'

'But I'm part of something that used and imprisoned you.'

'You haven't had much say in any of this either.'

'No. I suppose not.' Her eyelids are drooping and so are mine. She settles closer into my arms.

She sleeps first and I try to keep my eyes open, to watch her as she breathes. I'd stopped believing that I'd see her again. Where has she gone in her sleep? Will I find her there?

I try to stay here, aware of the feel and the smell of her, her hair. Focusing on her and not what is to come.

62

Tabby

When I next open my eyes I am in the dreaming place. It is as it was the last time: what makes me who I am is with me, my physical form is not.

'Tabby!' Lakshayaa greets me then Dimitra does too. Many of the Chosen are here, others still arriving, and each I recognise before they say a word – we all have our own unique signature of energy that says who we are. Most are en route to their homes from Undersea, ready to confront their parents if we all agree. They show me what has happened since we were all at Undersea together. At the same time I think of all that has happened since I last saw them and they relive it with me.

Even the last bit, lying on that bed with Denzi. If I had cheeks, I'd be blushing.

Ariel and Zara arrive, and Isha too. She's uncertain and I hug her close, reassure her without words.

And now Con comes, followed last of all by Denzi.

Denzi burns differently to the others – the flicker of energy that is his life – Con also. And there is a sense of a pause, a silence, as everyone takes in what they are – those of us who still live, and all the ancestors. I try to go to Denzi to reassure him, but I'm caught in stillness with everyone else. I focus on him, hoping he can feel me with him.

Cassandra speaks. 'Sisters, we have Isha, Con and Denzi to welcome and cherish.'

Everything moves and I lose focus on Denzi. I'm being pulled away to a memory from long ago, and I struggle and protest against it, fight to get back to Denzi.

'Tabby, child,' Cassandra says. 'This is not for the living to decide. The ancestors have them now and will do as they will to them and to you.'

To me?

I'm dragged from one memory to another, of pain, suffering, of my sisters from both long ago and more recent. All at the hands of men.

I'm being sold.

Forced to marry.

Dying in childbirth.

Dragged from my home by a soldier.

My children killed before me.

Bought. Sold. Abused. Murdered.

Drowned, rocks tied to my feet in a lake.

Burnt alive.

Life after life, death after death, my sisters' pain is laid bare over centuries. *Me Too* on a scale unimaginable.

At best ignored, belittled, denied. At worst, raped, tortured, murdered.

My sisters are strong. They've come back from despair, pain and death to become something that seeks to heal, to protect all life.

Now they face the anguish of impossible choices with the climate crisis. And they see it as *man* versus nature – men destroy, women create and protect.

No. It doesn't have to be this way. Not all women are good any more than all men are bad.

We can grow, change. And these two boys are innocent of all these crimes against you.

I pull my ancestors to me, to my memories. Show them the Denzi I know – his kindness, the way he goes out of his way to help those that need it. The promise he made with me on a beach without fully knowing what it was, but he did it for me. He isn't the past, the ones who did these things. He would never hurt me or any other girl like they have been hurt.

If we don't accept them, we are as bad as all those men who brutalised you before. Worse, because we understand so many things they never did.

I'm released and allowed to go to Denzi now. His energy that burned bright before now barely flickers. He is in agony, collapsing in on himself as he relives what my sisters have suffered. I gather him in close, rock him like a child.

The Circle comes together: mother – sister – daughter – friend, all things to each other. Can there be brothers, too?

'Denzi: stay with me. Focus on the four.'

Sun . . . sea . . . earth . . . sky

Sun . . . sea . . . earth . . . sky

'Over and again: focus, and remember your promise.'

Sun . . . sea . . . earth . . . sky

Sun . . . sea . . . earth . . . sky

And the flicker that is Denzi grows brighter with each repetition.

'Sisters, what say you?' Cassandra says.

There is a quietness I've not felt in the dreaming before, as if

284

each sister and ancestor has retreated to themselves.

Now the Chosen join in with Denzi and me, and Con does too:

Sun . . . sea . . . earth . . . sky

Sun . . . sea . . . earth . . . sky

Then . . . the ancestors let him go. Denzi slumps against me, released from their memories.

'And so we evolve,' Cassandra says. 'Welcome. Isha. Denzi. Con.'

All join in now, voices become music that swells:

SUN . . . SEA . . . EARTH . . . SKY

And the Chosen are complete, together at last.

Dimitra draws the Chosen apart from the others. Relives the memory of the decisions we made at Undersea for Isha, Denzi and Con. They agree.

We will begin seeking our parents' help tomorrow.

63

Denzi

Awake – aware of my body. I draw air in a gasp into my lungs like one almost drowned – like one of The Circle with weights tied to my feet in a lake, thrashing and struggling until water comes into my lungs and death follows.

And that isn't even the worst that can be done, has been done, and the weight of suffering and pain makes me want to scream and die, now.

My legs are pulled up into my chest, arms around, shuddering, shaking, beyond anything like tears – bruised, battered, tortured, murdered – and guilt twists in my guts so tight it could strangle what is left of me. Like it should.

Then there are warm arms. A soothing voice. At first I can't make out the words. After a while they start to penetrate.

'Denzi, you are not this. You have not done this and will not. I believe in you.' It's Tabby.

'But I don't – I can't – believe in myself.'

'Focus on me: you are good, kind. I believe in you.

'I believe in you.

'I believe in you.'

I focus on these four words, said over and over again. Until finally the tears come.

Much later I make a new promise of my own, over and above

the one I made with Tabby before on the beach. I swear to protect The Circle and all the sisters within. I can't repair or take back anything they have suffered, but I will do everything I can to make sure it never happens again.

64

Tabby

'Tabby?' The door is thrown open – Ariel's white face.

'What's wrong?'

'It's Con. I . . .' She shakes her head. 'I thought he was OK last night. I fell asleep. But when I woke up – he's not answering, and I think . . .' She swallows, unable to finish, and dread is trickling into my stomach as we follow Ariel down the hall to the room where Con dreamed with Ariel.

He's on the bed. Eyes open, staring as if they are looking deep into me. I'm to blame.

Denzi goes forward, puts a hand against his neck. Shakes his head.

'I know this has been a terrible shock,' Malina says.

'It's my fault. Con died and Denzi might have, too, and it's my fault.'

'They made their own decisions.'

'Like Denzi said – they didn't have much of a choice. Even less than I did.'

'I understand how you feel.'

'Do you?'

'Yes. I do. One of my first students – a lovely girl – died on her first dreaming. And she didn't even know of the risk because I never told her. I accept that is the right way to do things for many reasons, but I'll never stop feeling the guilt.'

'What is going to happen to Con – to his body – now?'

'We have to leave this house this morning – that was always the plan. It's too risky to stay here any longer in case anyone saw Stacey come or go and tells the police. Once we're gone, I'll see that the police get notified Con's body is here in a way that doesn't tie anything to us.'

'We're just going to leave him here like that?'

'What else can we do?' Malina says and the sadness in her eyes is genuine, the regret, and then it twigs inside – this is his body. What about the rest of him?

'What about his memories? Will he be part of The Circle?'

'We can't harvest him away from Undersea without Cassandra, and she won't be able to come. Even if she could, she wouldn't be in time. It must be done soon after death.'

'Why Cassandra?'

'She's a seer. Oh.' She's looking at me, a question in her eyes and this time I answer it.

'Malina, so am I.'

'I'd guessed as much. But you haven't had the training from Cassandra, you don't know how—'

'I can learn. From the past.'

I take the bitter chocolate from Malina's hand and eat it quickly. 'Leave us now,' I say.

The door is closed softly behind her.

I hesitate, then take the chair next to the bed. Con's eyes are shut now – Malina must have shut them. Other than Simone, I've never been this close to someone who has died before.

Yes, you have. You're close to all of us. It's Rhiannon.

'Can you help me?'

Yes. Are you sure you are ready for this?

'No. But I'm going to do it, anyways.' I feel her approval but hesitate. 'I saw how Cassandra inherited from Alicia – with blood. But Con is already dead?'

The blood ritual is a shortcut, used in that case because of the emergency – and because Cassandra wasn't willing. Disapproval: she doesn't think it should have been done like that. *There is another way if you go to the dreaming*.

I take Con's cold hand in mine. Close my eyes.

The circles of time spin around us, twisting strands that burn bright.

Find his strand.

'How?'

I cannot say. That skill is inside of you. You should be able to find it amongst the others.

I dip into strand after strand: flashes of memory with each one that belong to other sisters. There are many thousands of them. How am I supposed to know which belongs to Con?

At the dreaming his and Denzi's energy was different somehow to everyone else's. I stand back again in the centre.

This one: there. No, wait, it's Denzi's – and I'm about to pull back. But everything he has ever thought, done, felt, it's here. I could know everything, now.

No. It is better to chase the fish.

I withdraw.

It is forbidden to know someone who is living like that without their permission. Rhiannon's voice is stern.

'I left once I knew where I was.'

Almost. Don't do it again. Now find the other.

I think of the taste of his energy, and now one strand is calling me before all the others, even though its brightness is fading. It's Con.

Just in time.

I trace his circle around and around, and all at once there is an explosion inside of me: every thought and memory and experience he has ever had, how he loved and was loved by his family, and it hurts, so much, to know they will never see him again. Everything he was and is no longer is flowing through me, ending with the trauma and pain of his first – and last – dreaming.

When I finally stand back in the centre of the circles, his is burning bright again.

Tabby? What's going on? It's Con: he is one of the ancestors now.

'I'm so sorry.'

What's happened? Why am I here like this?

I show him – how Ariel found him. That I am holding his hand now. Cherishing his memory with all of our ancestors.

Please. Will you tell my mum and brother that I never did the things they said at that hospital, and that I never wanted to leave them? And tell my brother: he's in charge.

I promise. I will.

When Malina comes in later I'm still with Con. Knees drawn up against me. Tears on my face.

'Was it difficult?'

I nod. She kneels next to me, puts her arms around me. Sings a healing song like Cate used to sing for me, but this pain won't be cured like a headache; I won't let it.

Every action has a reaction. Everything we do has consequences. The circles of time show this again and again in stark detail. Even if I wanted to, nothing can ever be forgotten.

Part 8

@HaydenNoPlanetB

Monsoons are failing in India. Industria United did this: they knew that geoengineering our climate could make this happen, and they did it anyways. The average global temperature might go down, but sacrifice zones will have increasing heatwaves, drought, and crop failure. Starvation will follow.

#NatureIsScreaming

65

Hayden

I press play, and my face fills the screen.

'Have you seen the news?

'*Nature is screaming.* The Indian monsoons are failing. Arctic summer ice is almost gone. Land ice in Greenland and Antarctica are melting at accelerated rates, disappearing faster than any of the models predicted. Ground that has been frozen as permafrost for thousands of years, keeping carbon out of the atmosphere, is melting too – and once it releases carbon, this can't be reversed. The climate changes we are seeing are so close to tipping out of control.

'There are feedback loops we know about, like that ice reflects the sun better than water. Ice melts, the water created absorbs heat, more ice melts. The more it melts the faster it melts. There may be other factors feeding back that we don't yet understand that are making the ice caps melt even faster than the worst predictions.

'What about the plants and animals who share our planet? Take polar bears as just one example of many. The more ice melts, the more they are running out of their natural habitat, heading south, breeding with other species of bear who are also losing habitat. Animals that wouldn't normally ever come into contact with each other are doing so and moving closer to domesticated animals, and to us.

'Do you want to live in a world without polar bears? I don't. But even if you're not that bothered about animal and plant species being lost for ever, all this mingling and changing of habitats risks diseases that we've never seen before, and have no immunity against, jumping across animal species and then to us. Can you imagine the world coping with two or three Covid-like pandemics at once? Or even more?

'And this is all happening under our deadened skies – the so-called planetary sunscreen of geoengineering.

'There is no time. None.

'We must act *now*.'

I pause the video. 'Do you think it's too depressing? Bishan said if we make things sound too bad then everyone thinks, why bother trying to do anything – it's too late.'

Apple shakes her head. 'No. It's terrifying, but it has to be. It's really good.'

'Thanks for helping out.'

'It's OK. With Dad gone, Denzi missing and the climate on self-destruct, a travelling-the-world sort of gap year seemed like a bad idea.'

'Yeah. I get that. OK, this is the rest of it,' I say, and hit play.

'There are so many people who understand and care deeply about doing all we can to slow and ultimately stop climate change: individuals and groups around the world. Before my friend and fellow activist, Bishan Khatri, died, we'd started a project to bring groups together: to find common ground and stand side by side.

'The thing is, too often we seem to end up squabbling with each other about our differences. How about instead we focus on the things that unite us?

'Let's be united against climate change. Have your say now: #UnitedXCC #NatureIsScreaming.'

'Maybe add a still of the tags at the end?' Apple says. 'No, hang on – how about have it on the screen the whole time, on the bottom of the video?'

'That's a good idea – do you know how?'

'Yep. Zap it over.'

Apple fiddles around with the video, adds the tags underneath. We run through it one more time.

'Good to go?' she says.

'Good to go.'

I post it – here, there and everywhere.

66

Denzi

We're driving up the road in Paula's 4WD. The sky is still this dead grey colour and I'm struggling to get my head around the fact that Industria United did it on purpose – one of many things I learned from joining with my sisters in dreaming. I can't stop staring at the streets and buildings that go past, either. My eyes are hungry for the world after being held indoors, mostly without windows, for what felt like a very long time. When we stop at a red light, the urge to rip the door open and run courses through my body – something I would have done without hesitating a few days ago.

But now Tabby's hand is in mine and I'm part of this – I gave my word. I'm not going anywhere.

Paula is driving; Malina is on the phone. Ariel, Zara and Isha have all left in different directions to go to their parents. Malina gave Isha and me a new mobile with everyone's numbers programmed in so we can all keep in touch.

Malina is off the phone now. 'Tabby? Elodie is going to meet us and take you to your dad.'

'Elodie?' Tabby says with a note of surprise in her voice. 'I thought she was at Undersea.'

'She returned with me for just this reason.'

'Who is she?' I say.

'My grandmother.'

'She's in The Circle?'

'Yeah. I haven't spoken to her for a while.' She looks like she'd rather keep it that way.

'Is she the one who was drugging you in the hospital in Bristol?'

'One and the same.'

Paula is pulling into a car park next to some shops.

'There she is,' Malina says, pointing at a red electric sportscar.

Tabby undoes her seat belt. 'Bye.'

'Good luck,' I say, wanting to kiss her, but without these two watching.

A half smile like she knows. 'Same,' she says.

She gets out and we watch her walk to this other car. A tall woman with long dark hair swept back gets out and gives Tabby a kind of a hug – the sort that doesn't quite work because the other person isn't hugging back.

'Is this Elodie all right?' I say.

'She's fine,' Malina says. 'They probably just need to have a chat.'

'OK, I'm lucky last. Time to see my dad.'

'I'm guessing maybe you two need to have a chat, too.'

'You could say that. But aren't we driving in the wrong direction?'

'He's going to meet us. We've set it up with a mutual friend? Christina Lang. I think you know her.'

'The swim-school director?'

'Yes. We're going to her home.'

67

Tabby

We're belted in and Elodie is pulling out of the car park. Cate said she is on Phina's side of things, to be careful around her – should I have refused to go with her? Maybe, but I want to talk to her too. To ask for some answers – to demand them.

Safe ground first. 'Where is Ali – where are we going?'

'His London flat. He's had it for a long while; used to stay there during the week quite often.'

'Is our house still wrecked from the hurricane? Is he having it rebuilt?'

'I'm not sure. I think since . . . well, without Simone and you, he doesn't want to go back there.'

'Does he know we're coming?'

'He knows I'm coming, you're a surprise.'

We stop at a light and she turns to me. 'It's so good to see you.'

'I didn't see you in the dreaming. Were you avoiding me?'

She tilts her head a little. 'I didn't want to, but your first dreaming can be difficult. I didn't want to upset you or make you focus too narrowly. Anyhow, Cassandra told me to give you space.'

Green light and we go forwards again, her eyes back on the road.

'Or maybe you wanted to keep some things from me and couldn't risk it coming out in the dreaming?'

She's amused. 'I like to think what I want to hide stays hidden.'

'Can I ask you a few questions?'

'You can ask.'

'Was it you who arranged for Simone and Ali to go to the Penrose Clinic to have me?'

'Yes, of course.'

'Why wasn't Simone in The Circle?'

'Our daughters don't always inherit what makes us able to dream together and access our ancestors' memories – which is why for the first time with the Chosen, we have boys with the same important genes to make sure they don't dwindle out. It was a great disappointment to me that my only daughter had none of us in her. But now I have you.'

'Was that why you got them to go there? To keep your, I don't know, legacy going?'

There's a slight pause. 'That's not how parents of the Chosen were selected. Their genomes were screened carefully for any mutation or heritable diseases and for maximum genetic variation. Simone and Ali qualified.'

'But they never knew.'

'No. It had to be the way it was. And she had a daughter she loved very much, as did Ali. Which brings us to today: you want to ask your dad for help?'

'Yeah.'

'I've known him much longer than you have.'

'Do you think it's hopeless?'

'Not exactly. Ali sometimes has the ability to surprise me. But his whole professional life is on the line with his support of geoengineering; it'd be a hard thing for him to change his stance on that.'

301

'Do you think his pride is more important to him than I am?'

'I don't know. I don't think he'd think of it in those terms anyhow. But I get that you need to try, for you as much as for him. I understand that.'

'OK.' I'm all nerves inside to know I'm going to have to try to make him see things differently. And how I'll feel if he won't even listen.

'Another question,' I say, to distract myself as much as anything else. 'Were you drugging me in the hospital in Bristol?'

'Only until we could arrange to have you transferred to a place we could explain things properly and better look after you. But you had other ideas.'

'No one was ever honest with me about anything. How was I supposed to take being drugged to keep me quiet?'

'Yet . . . do you understand now?'

Gaining ancestors' memories has let me see how sometimes we have to do things we'd rather not.

'Maybe,' I admit.

We're pulling into an underground car park. It's closed but there is a camera – reading reg plates? The doors open and we go through, then around to a level below and park.

'Here we are. But first I've got something for you.' She reaches into her handbag, takes out a small box and opens it.

And there in the box: silver waves set with blue and green stones that somehow hold the sea in their depths. Simone's bracelet. I blink back the tears. It meant so much to her, and then to me. I had no choice but to sell it – I needed the money to get away. I never thought I'd see it again.

'How did you find it?'

'You didn't make it easy but we tracked you to the place you sold it using CCTV. He was a lovely man. It took some convincing to get him to sell it back to me but I promised I'd give it to you.'

She slips it on my wrist.

'Thank you.'

'Come on, then, let's go surprise Ali.'

'Stand back from the camera,' she says, presses numbers in a keypad and faces the camera. Doors swing open.

We get in a lift and Elodie presses the button for the top floor. Penthouse it says. My stomach is churning and I'm remembering how I so wanted to contact Ali before, when I was with Jago and his friends in Cornwall, to let him know I was all right. But I was scared that if I did, The Circle would trace the call and find me. They got me in the end anyhow.

Now more time has passed. Ali is my dad but I only knew this for a short time; I only lived with him and Simone for a matter of weeks. I'd started to feel there was something there between us, that it could be good. But I don't really know him. I mean it's hard to even think we could be related, with him being a VP of Industria United, the biggest oil and gas company in the world. And it is him – his face – that has been behind what has been done to the sky.

There are all these things that we need to somehow talk about but right now I don't care about any of it.

He's still my daddy.

68

Hayden

'Can we take off your glasses?' an assistant says to me.

'Why?'

'The lights reflect in the lenses.'

'But then I can't see. I mean, at all.'

'OK.' They're fiddling with the angles of the lights set up around the studio. 'Can you turn a little to the left and down and— Yes, like that.'

'We'll go to the opticians tomorrow. Contact lenses?' Mum says.

'No! I don't want to put things in my eyes.'

'Or new glasses with a better anti-reflective coating?' Mum says. Straightens my collar.

'But these ones are fine.'

She is shooed back out of shot.

The presenter takes the seat next to me. 'Are you ready, Hayden?'

I nod even though I'm not. Being interviewed on TV by the BBC? I feel too small to fill this space.

'We are with Hayden Richards, the schoolgirl whose pleas for the climate touched so many around the world after the death of first her best friend, Eva Kowalski, and then Bishan Khatri, another friend and climate activist. Her regular posts on climate change, tagged #NatureIsScreaming, have set records. Now she's done it again.

'Welcome, Hayden. I understand you've started something a few days ago that has taken off on social media. Could you tell us a little more about what you've begun, what you are hoping to achieve, and why?'

'Many voices around the world are calling for action against climate change. We will be louder together. We are United Against Climate Change, tagged on social as #UnitedXCC, and asked everyone to post the things that unite us. It's been trending around the world.'

'Yes, and not just trending: the numbers of likes, shares and comments are breaking social media records on all platforms. Have you found an answer to your question?'

'What unites us? So many more things than divide. Compassion for each other and animals, love for nature, despair at inaction or slow action by our governments, and total rejection of geoengineering as any kind of solution. Injecting chemicals into the atmosphere has got to stop. Our governments need to promote and support renewable energy and remove subsidies given to dirty energy production and industry, and they need to hold corporations accountable for the damage they cause to the environment.'

'What is next for United Against Climate Change?'

'Watch this space.'

Apple calls that evening.

'You were so good!'

'I was quaking inside. And kept thinking who wants to listen to me? What solutions have I got?'

'Watch this space, you said. So, what are you going to do next?'

'Still thinking.'

'You need a *thing*, something big – now that people are listening to you. Something they can do, to focus attention.'

'There have been so many protests. Do they even have an impact any more? And they're bringing in more legislation to limit protests in the UK too. To keep us safe they say. Huh.' Too late for Eva and Bishan: a whisper inside me, along with a wish that they were still here even if it meant us getting nowhere.

'You need to make it united enough and big enough that governments can't stop it, and can't ignore it, either.'

'No pressure then. Has there been any news on Denzi?'

'No. They haven't found his doctor either. She was seen a few places on her own on CCTV the day after she signed Denzi out of the hospital. Nothing since then – it's like both of them have vanished. There is one thing though. Don't think it's hit the news yet.'

'What's that?'

'There was another boy also checked out of the hospital by the same doctor on the same day as Denzi. He was found yesterday—'

'Does he know anything?'

'He was dead when they found him. In bed in a house with no obvious cause of death. Police had an anonymous tip to check the house and there he was.'

'Oh my God.'

'Yeah. Don't know if there was any connection between this boy and Denzi. The police are checking with neighbours, cameras

306

in the area and so on. I'll let you know if we learn anything else.'

'Whatever happened to this other boy doesn't mean anything like that has happened to Denzi.'

'I know. We're trying to hold on to that, but where is he then?'

We say our goodbyes soon after.

Denzi has stayed on my mind but with everything else – Bishan, then UnitedXCC and all the rest – he's taken a back seat.

They must be so worried. At least the police must be taking him being missing seriously now.

The other thing Apple said, about what next moves for UnitedXCC need to be, is also running through my mind: that whatever we do, it has to be *united* enough and *big* enough. But I'm not finding a thing, a stunt, that fits.

But we don't want a stunt, do we?

And . . . it isn't just all these groups we need to bring together. We don't want just activists.

We need *everyone*.

69

Denzi

I'm the last to be dropped off by Paula and Malina, and the closer the time gets to seeing Dad the more conflicted I feel. How much is he involved in all of this? I don't know and I'm not entirely sure why it still matters so much. I mean here I am, part of The Circle now – sworn to protect them all despite things they may have done or may yet do. So what does it matter if Dad is involved in the whole mess somehow?

But when I was at the hospital Dad came to visit. He all but admitted I was being held to keep me quiet. The anger I felt then is still part of me now and I'm trying to shake it off, focus on what I'm here to do.

'Here we are,' Paula says. Pulls into a driveway.

'Good luck,' Malina says.

'Thanks.'

I get out, up the steps to the door. No more thinking time.

The door opens as I'm reaching to ring the bell: it's Dad. His face lights up and he reaches for me. I'm in a hug and despite the reasons not to trust him I hug him back, hold on tight, and something is choking up inside of me.

We step inside, close the door. He holds me at arm's length and studies my face. 'It's so good to see you. I've been so worried, and then got this call that you'd be here.'

'You didn't know where I was after the hospital?'

'No.'

'Well, let me fill you in. I was taken to a house, locked in and kept drugged, along with another boy. I've only been awake and aware for a few days.'

He flinches. 'I'm so sorry. I never knew any of that would happen.'

I step in, look around the room – sofas, fireplace. We're alone. 'Where is Christina?'

'Making dinner. She's giving us some space.'

There's a muffled beep in my pocket – is Tabby OK? 'Sorry,' I say, pull away and take out my phone, glance at the screen. No text – it's an alert, it's updating. I put it away and follow Dad to a sofa.

'No Jax or Leila?'

He shakes his head. 'They don't know about this. That was the condition placed on being able to meet with you now. What's going on?'

'I guess you must know some things about the Penrose Clinic and The Circle but I don't know how much.'

'The clinic – and Christina – have had me in a difficult place. But I promise you I didn't know anything about the connection with The Circle until I found out from the police before the news broke.'

'I saw that they've been raiding Penrose Clinic premises and that there were rumours of a connection to The Circle. Has that been confirmed now?'

'Yes. And there's more that'll be on the news eventually. It's just . . .' He's shaking his head. 'Well. I just can't believe it.'

'What can't you believe?'

'One of their biggest research sites has been searched – it seemed to have voids underground picked up by sonar. They dug down and found bodies.'

'Bodies? Of who?'

'Not just who – *what*. Things that weren't really human, but also don't look much like any known animals either. It looks like they've been doing all kinds of genetic experiments that are truly horrifying. And when I think I trusted them with you, with my son – well. What if they'd done something to you?' He shudders.

Would he be horrified if he knew what they have done to me? I know he would and there's a twist in my gut to think how he'd react. And I'm shocked at what he said has been found . . . yet, not at the same time. It shouldn't be a surprise that before they made us they'd tried different ways, different genetic combinations, and that there were failures – it could be the results of past experiments that they've found. And there was that girl-fish that Tabby saw also – something that even though I completely trust her I found hard to believe. Mostly because I didn't want to.

'Is your connection to this clinic known?' I say.

'Not yet, though I'd be surprised if it doesn't get out. If it does I'm probably finished. But that doesn't matter as much as how I've failed you. I'm sorry, Denzi. So sorry.'

He looks genuinely contrite and the anger I've been holding inside lessens just a little. But what does he mean, really?

'What are you sorry for?'

'Not fighting harder to get you out of that hospital. Not being there when you needed me. For the distress this has caused Jax, and even Leila.'

Does he really mean what he says? And even if he does, is it too little too late?

'I mean it,' he says, as if he could hear my thoughts. 'Anything I can do – anything. Just ask and I'll do it.'

70

Tabby

When Ali opens his door, Elodie goes through and I hang back a little, like she asked me to.

'Alistair, I have a surprise for you,' she says, and I step forwards into his flat.

'Ah, hello, and who is this?' And he looks and looks again. 'Tabby? Oh my God. It's really you?' And he's cupping my face in his hands and there are tears in my eyes and he hugs me tight, so tight, like he's afraid if he lets go I'll disappear.

Finally he pulls away. 'Where have you been? Do you have any idea what you've put us through? Are you OK? Your hair,' he says and I'm remembering how I'd cut it, that Jago's friend dyed the ends. 'I didn't recognise you at first. How did you find her?' he says to Elodie now.

'So many questions!' she says. 'And I understand. But give us a moment to catch our breath. I'll make some tea.' She leaves the room and he holds my hand, pulls me to sit next to him on the sofa. As he does so my phone beeps in my pocket and we both jump.

'Sorry,' I say, take it out, glance at the screen. Updating, whatever that means.

'Where have you been? Are you OK?'

'Yes, I promise. Sorry, it's hard to know where to begin.'

'Let's go back. Why did you leave swim school?'

'There was something I found out and it scared me. So I ran away.' I swallow. 'And Simone came to get me, and . . .' I shake my head. The words aren't there but what I really want to say is I'm sorry. Sorry Simone died. Sorry I worried him. Just sorry.

'What scared you?'

'It's complicated. Can we talk about something else first?'

Elodie slips back in; she puts cups of tea on the table next to us and starts to sit down.

'If it's OK, can we talk alone?' I say to her.

She doesn't like it but what can she say? 'Of course,' she says and reverses to go back to the kitchen with her drink.

I close the door behind her.

'Ali – Dad. I need your help. There isn't much time. Will you help me?'

'Of course I will. What's wrong?'

'So much. The planet – our earth. It's dying. Nature is screaming and we need to act before it's too late.'

'Is this about climate change? I told you and Simone that we were on it, fixing things.'

'Geoengineering is not the answer. Listen to me. The Circle are planning things . . . to end the Anthropocene, the age of man.'

'The Circle? Is that what you found out about that scared you and made you run?'

'Sort of. There was a hidden presence of the Penrose Clinic at swim school and I worked out they were connected to The Circle. But that doesn't matter now. We need to find a way to turn global warming around fast. Or it'll be too late.'

We talk and talk. He's trying, I can tell – to listen and not just

313

shake his head and dismiss what I'm saying out of hand, but am I even getting through?

Finally he holds up a hand and I stop. 'Just what is it you want of me, Tabby?'

'Stop geoengineering the climate. Expose your company and all the harm they are doing to the environment. Support moves to make radical changes to energy production and use.'

And then it is Ali doing all the talking, and behind all the words there's nothing he can do or wants to do to help in a meaningful way. He says some of the right things, that he'll push for greener changes in his company. He's convinced geoengineering can't be abruptly stopped once it is begun – that doing so would have huge negative rebound effects and make the global mean temperature go up even more than it would have if it had never been tried in the first place. Knowing that, they did it anyhow?

He says again that he'd do anything for me but despite that, most of what he is saying boils down to one word, two letters:

No.

Later I'm in Ali's guest room; it's my room now, he says. I haven't managed to tell him yet that I'll be disappearing from his life again soon.

We've been given until 8 p.m. tomorrow to do what we can to convince our parents to make radical changes. Then we'll meet in a dreaming with Cassandra and Phina, and share how we've all done.

A message pings on my phone: it's Denzi. Hi. How'd it go?

Not great. You?

I'm not entirely sure. He seemed to say he'd do something but not what, and I'm not sure – whatever it is – if he'll go through with it or not.

Hope so.

Your dad might still come around.

Maybe.

Get some sleep and we'll see what tomorrow brings xx

Gnite xx

I put the phone down on the bedside table. At least Denzi has a maybe; I can only hope the others are doing better than me. Nothing I say to Ali is going to change his mind, is it?

I don't understand, Aslan says. *He's your kin – our kin – isn't he?*

'Yeah.'

And he won't help?

'No. Even though he is my dad, he's almost a stranger. It can be like that with people, that those who should be closest to you, aren't. Sometimes with people, the kin you choose are closer to you than the ones in your family.'

The kin you choose – do you mean friends?

'Yes. Just that.' And as I say that I'm thinking of one friend I have who I know will always listen: Jago. And I'm gripped by a longing to see him; I miss him so much.

Then go see him, Aslan says reading my thoughts.

My eyes open wider. I could go, couldn't I? Nothing I do here is going to help. I've got a day – why not go to Cornwall?

What if I can't find him or he's not there? I wish I could remember his phone number.

Wait. What about the circles of time? I could see every single one of Con's memories when I harvested him for The

315

Circle. Why not go to my own circle, back to the day Jago told me his number?

The thought is barely formed when I'm reaching for the chocolate made from the dreaming root. I have more than enough spare from what I'll need tomorrow.

Chew. Swallow.

Sun . . . sea . . . earth . . . sky

Sun . . . sea . . . earth . . . sky

The voices of my ancestors join in.

I'm in the centre and the circles – so many of them – spin all around me. How do I find which is my own?

It is part of me. I focus closer and closer and then I can see it. I stand on it at this point in time, now. I can go backwards or forwards.

Forwards to see what will be?

The temptation is so strong. But if what I fear is going to happen, and I knew? It'd end me.

No. Go to the past. I scan fast and then faster, see everything that has happened to me – a fast rewind spinning in my mind. The last moment with Cate almost makes me stop: the last touch of her hand before she was taken from me by the police. I force myself to go further back until I'm at our beach – mine and Jago's.

On the sand, sitting so close to each other. I marvel at this girl that I was, the way I felt, the things I didn't know. So much has happened since then.

Jago knew my name. He made me repeat his number over and over again. I focus on the numbers now until they're fixed in my mind.

It's tempting to stay in this memory . . . well, at least before those other kids came and spoiled it. So much flowed on from this one point in time.

But it's time to go back to now. To live in the usual way, from one moment to another; no jumping ahead to look.

I open my eyes, take out my phone. It's sticky – have I got something on it? Wipe it off and enter Jago's number.

Press call before I can think any more about whether it is a good or bad idea.

It rings – once, twice, three, four times – just when I'm giving up hope he answers.

'Hello?' a sleepy voice, unmistakably Jago.

'Sorry, did I wake you?'

'Tabby? Is that you?'

'Yeah.'

'Are you OK?'

'Um, not really. Can I come see you?'

'Of course you can. But I'm not sure if The Circle are still watching me; will it be safe?'

'They don't matter any more.'

A pause. 'There's a story there.'

'I'll save it for when I see you. I'm in London. I'll get the first train in the morning and message you when I'm on the way.'

'OK. Can't wait to see you.'

'You, too. Now go back to sleep.'

'I'll try. Bye.'

'Bye.'

I press end call.

So Jago is your kin. And your father is not?

'Something like that.'

People are confusing.

'Tell me about it.'

I check train times on my phone, then count down the minutes and hours of the night until dawn is not far away.

Slip out of my room, down the hall. I pause at Ali's door, place my hand against it. Lean my cheek against the cool wood. Whisper, *Goodbye Daddy.*

And carefully, silently, open and shut the front door behind me.

Once down the lift and out into pre-dawn stillness, I walk as the early morning takes the sky from dull, starless black to thin grey. Does Ali really believe they've made things better by committing this crime against sun, sea, sky and earth? I sigh. Either he does, or he can't bear to admit he was wrong. And I'm not sure which is worse.

I buy a ticket when I get to Paddington Station, glad Malina had given each of us money for emergencies. Does this count? I shrug.

The train isn't crowded; I have two seats to myself. I text Jago that I'll get to Bodmin at half ten, then stare, unseeing, out the window. The sleepless night is starting to catch up with me.

Sleep. I'll wake you when we get there.

I sigh. Not sure I can.

Aslan shows me memories: of playing in the sea long before we were ever together, when he was young and free.

And I slip into dreams of joy, swimming with the kin.

71

Hayden

I'm thinking through Bishan's plans, things Apple has said. How I feel.

I can't bullshit people, try to make them see night instead of day – I haven't got it in me. I started out trying to do things the way that Bishan would have done them. He had this vision about having a series of meetings, a few groups at a time, finding things in common to strengthen ties. Doing it all in pieces and then bringing everyone together. It made sense to me the way he put it but I'm not Bishan. I can't make it work like that.

Anyhow, more and more I'm not sure that finding a way to bring activists together is the key to all of this, and so far all we've done – with Bishan and then on my own – is focus on activists. We're not enough. We need ordinary people around the world, all ages, involved in enough numbers to put pressure on governments where it hurts: the threat of lost votes, lost power.

There are climate denialists out there still, sure, but they've got their own agendas – money and keeping it no matter the cost. I really don't think anyone seriously believes them any more, so it's not like I have to convince people there is a problem. They know there is.

But what can I do to get their attention? Shake them out of inertia and make them act? All I can do is say the things that I see and understand, the way they are. And hope that is enough.

I spend half the night thinking, rehearsing in my head. Then prop up my phone and press record.

'The sixth mass extinction is happening *now*. Scientists say that every year a thousand or more species of plants and animals are being lost for ever. One day it may be us.

'A minute of silence to mourn their loss isn't enough! Let's make it an hour.

'Everyone: no matter where you are, who you are, how old you are or what you should be doing – take an hour. Just one. To say you believe that we must all unite against climate change. That you demand our governments take it seriously, that they do it now or face the consequences of being voted out in every election to come.

'And you don't have to travel or march or make speeches. All you have to do is just *stop* wherever you are. An hour of stillness and silence for all the species that have died and will die – maybe even our own – if we don't do something about it *now*.

'This Friday at noon UK time; check the time where you live at timeanddate.com.

'Join us: let people around the world come together and be united against climate change.'

#SilenceForTheClimate #UnitedXCC #NatureIsScreaming

72

Denzi

I'm staring at the ceiling the next morning in Christina's guest room when a message pings on my phone.

Put on the BBC. Love you. Dad.

Has he really done what he said he would?

I go to the BBC on my phone.

The political correspondent is on the screen, microphone in hand. 'We're live with Home Secretary Monty Pritchard, to hear a special announcement.'

Cameras focus now on Dad at a lectern in a room full of press.

'Thank you for coming out at short notice,' he says. 'I have an announcement to make and some things to say, by far the most important and critical words that I have ever uttered. Today these aren't just words that can be said and forgotten; today I will take action.

'It's been a great privilege to serve in the cabinet and be part of this government. There have been many times I've been immensely proud of things we have done for our country. But lately my feelings have changed on some urgent matters.

'Despite talk of the climate emergency and acknowledging the critical nature of action by both our country and the rest of the world, this government's environmental record is appalling. My conscience won't allow me to continue to support a government that not only doesn't throw everything it can against climate change, but also allows manipulation of key decisions in the interests of Industria United and other mega-corporations. I spoke to the Prime Minister a short time ago and resigned my cabinet post. I will continue as an MP representing my constituency, but even more, representing every man, woman, child, animal, bird, fish, insect and plant in the UK, Europe and the rest of the world as a new member of the Green Party. I welcome any MPs who feel the same to join me.'

The shock is palpable in the silent lull before the clamour of questions begins. Speculation follows that this could bring down the government.

He actually did it. And I want to go to him, now. Let him know how much this means to me.

But I can't.

My life isn't here any more. I swore to protect The Circle and this is what I must do.

I send him a message: you totally rock xx

73

Tabby

I step off the train and into Jago's arms, and I don't want to let go.

But Sascha – Jago's friend who helped me so much after I ran away from the hospital – is here too. He taps on Jago's shoulder. 'My turn!' he says and it's another hug.

'Tabby. My God, it's so good to see you,' Jago says. 'You're sure you're OK with being here? You haven't been followed?'

'I'm sure. If I have been, it doesn't matter.'

'We've got so much to catch up on,' Jago says. 'Where have you been all this time?'

'That is a long story. And I'm hungry.'

'Fish 'n' chips? Or is it too early?' Sascha says.

'It's never too early for that.'

We get into Sascha's car and are soon heading to Boscastle.

'Have you been keeping up with the news?' Jago says.

'Mostly, though I slept all the way here. Has something happened?'

'You must know that it's out the Penrose Clinic is connected to The Circle. Is that why you're not worried about them any more – because it's not a secret now?'

'That's part of the reason.'

'Anyhow, all kinds of other crazy stuff happened this morning. The Home Secretary resigned and is joining the Greens.'

'Really? Wow.' Denzi has had better luck than me.

'And there's a friend, Hayden Richards – have you heard of her?'

'The name is familiar, but I'm not sure why?'

'She's a climate activist. She's come up with this worldwide Silence for the Climate – for an hour, tomorrow at noon. The internet is just about ready to explode from all the traffic about it. It's going to be huge.

'Then there's been other stuff from other parts of the world also – a number of key resignations for climate reasons in government, corporations, all over the place. It's like it's spreading – it's amazing.'

'Are you an activist too, Jago?'

'I think I am. Kind of because of Hayden. I was messaging you – you were asleep, I now know – asking if it was OK if I told her you were coming. I completely trust her, Tabby. And you didn't answer, so . . .'

'Did you? Tell her?'

'Yes. I hope that's OK. She and Apple – that is Denzi's stepsister – are coming too; they'll be here in a few hours. They've been trying to track him down and hope you might know where he is. Do you?'

'I have seen him recently and I think he's somewhere in London but don't know exactly where.'

'That'll be some good news for them.'

'Hang on, I'll call and see if he can come too.'

I go to his number and press call; he answers straight away.

'Denzi? Hi. Your stepsister, Apple, and her friend Hayden are coming to Cornwall. Yeah, I'm here, just arrived. Come down?

OK, check and I'll hang on . . . Yeah got it. Bye.'

'Denzi is going to get a train that arrives at 3:30 this afternoon. But he says not to tell them he's coming.'

Jago gets on his phone. 'Hi Apple. Can you get to Bodmin station by 3:30 to pick up a friend and bring him to Boscastle on your way? Thanks. I'll give you his number.' I show it to him on my phone and he reads out the numbers.

I get Jago on his own for a walk after fish and chips. It's still a few hours to go before the others get here. I'd been so sad when I arranged to come see him but fragments of hope are fighting their way in.

We make our way to a bench that overlooks the sea; the one where we met when I came running back to Cornwall needing his help. So much has happened since then that it feels a long time ago, but it's really only weeks. How can that be?

We sit next to each other.

'All right, I'm all ears,' he says. 'Tell me what you can.'

'How do you always know the right thing to say?'

'Psychic, that's me.' He grins and his dimples are there.

'I've missed you so much.'

'You, too. And you're looking better than you sounded on the phone last night?'

'I didn't have a good day yesterday. I went to see my dad – have I told you that he's a VP of Industria United? I was hoping I could get him to see that geoengineering is wrong. He wouldn't listen.'

'Family can be tough. My mum is still hysterical about me barely escaping from a bombed café in London – she'll probably call in a minute because I haven't checked in for almost an hour.'

'*What*? What happened?'

He tells me about how he met Apple and Hayden, that just when Apple was calling the police to tell them about the Penrose Clinic and The Circle, a bomb was thrown into the café. 'And it was that woman with red hair who was tailing you in Cornwall.'

'I saw about this bombing on the news. Didn't know you were there. Are you sure it was the same woman? I'd asked whether The Circle had anything to do with it and got a not-as-far-as-I-know sort of answer from one of them.'

'You were talking to someone in The Circle?'

'Well, yeah. It turns out that most of my family are part of it.' I try to explain how I ended up joining too – how they caught me, the tests I was put through. Taking part in the dreaming. And I'm thinking he'll think I'm insane – making things up, a terrorist myself. But he just listens and holds my hand.

After a while I stop talking. We just sit there, look at the sea. The familiar pull to go to it is there, but I'm happy where I am too.

'Thank you,' I say.

'What for?'

'Listening. Not judging.'

'That's what friends are for. Besides, it's not like you had any real choice.'

'No. But the thing is, so many of them are genuinely decent, caring people. The other Chosen are like sisters to me now.'

'Why are you called the Chosen? What's that about?'

'Long story.' I hesitate. I've told him everything but what we are and I'm unsure whether I should, or even what to say if I decided to do so. 'We're all linked together in a way.'

He's thinking. 'Is it anything to do with the Penrose Clinic? And how you were born?' I nod. 'Is that the part you can't tell me?'

'Yeah. I mean, I can't work out if I should or how to say it.'

'It's OK. I'll be here when you're ready.'

'Thank you. Anyhow, we were set the task of finding a way to give humanity a second chance to stop climate change. We decided the way to begin was to convince our parents it has to be done, and through them make enough of an impact on the world that The Circle can back down and let everyone get on with fixing the planet. Ali – my dad – just couldn't see; when I called you I thought there was no hope. But when you told me all that stuff about the Home Secretary and others, and that Silence for the Climate. It made me think maybe, just maybe, we can do this? And I felt a little bit of hope for the first time in a long time.'

His eyes are holding mine. Time seems to be slowing down in an odd way and I can't look away.

'Tabby? There's something I—'

His phone rings and he glances down. 'It's Hayden,' he says and answers, gesturing for me to come close and listen too.

'You didn't tell us!' she says. 'You should have seen Apple. She was in shock and crying and hugging Denzi, and then hitting him with her handbag for worrying her and Leila. Anyhow, we're on our way to you now. Hang on, Denzi wants Tabby.'

Jago passes the phone to me.

'Hi. Yeah, I know – I heard afterwards then saw on the news.

It's amazing. Yeah. No. Not much luck. OK. I've missed you too. Uh huh. Bye.'

A smile is taking over my face. 'Let's go meet them? Oh, wait. Was there something you wanted to say?'

'No. I'm good. Let's go.'

74

Hayden

I can't stop grinning. There's been so much good news today! And an amazing reaction and build-up to Silence for the Climate tomorrow. And here is Denzi – looking well and happy, apart from when Apple was hitting him with her handbag. And when they talked about her dad. They're in the front together now – she's driving.

'Why didn't you call once you got away?' she says.

'It's a long story.'

'Leila has been worried sick.'

'I know.'

'Even your dad looked like he was, too.'

'You've seen him?'

'Yeah, Leila was convinced he'd been involved somehow and we went to see him last week. You should call him too.'

'I saw him yesterday.'

'*What*? And he didn't call Leila?' She swears with gusto.

'Hey, careful,' he says as the car swerves a little as she glares at him. 'I'll call her. I promise.'

A few minutes later we pull into a driveway and Jago and a girl who must be Tabby are sitting on the front step of a house. She's – wow. Fit, tanned, crazy blue-streaked dark hair, and she has this – I don't know – *presence*.

We get out of the car and Tabby gives Denzi a hug. 'You've

done amazingly. And I haven't,' she says.

He gives her a quick kiss and I glance at Jago. Do I imagine or does he flinch as he looks away?

Jago is introducing us and a woman peeks out of the front door – Jago's mother?

'Would your friends like some drinks?'

75

Denzi

It's almost time for the dreaming and I'm half excited about it and half nervous. The last time left me raw, in so much pain. Without Tabby I might have ended up like Con and the shock of finding him like that isn't something I'll ever forget.

But I'm part of The Circle now; today won't be the same. Besides, after what Dad did – and similar news from around the world – they'll have to be happy with us.

Yet Tabby has been quiet, withdrawn, since I got here. We're alone now – in a summerhouse at the bottom of the garden. Her friend Jago said he'd make sure no one bothered us but he looked a little bothered that we needed time alone.

'Hey.' I nudge her. 'What's wrong?'

'I'm not sure.' She sighs. 'It's just something doesn't feel right.'

'Stop worrying.'

'I'll try. It's time.'

We share a big mug of The Circle tea she'd made. Then she brings out the chocolate, breaks it in two and hands me a piece.

We bump our pieces of chocolate together. 'Cheers,' I say. And chew, swallow.

We lie down on the floor facing each other.

I kiss her, she barely kisses me back – glances at the door. 'It feels weird with them just out there,' she says. 'And it's time to close our eyes.'

Yet she holds mine a moment longer. I can feel sleep coming for me as hers gently close.

The dreaming soon begins.

We're two of the first to arrive. Others of the Chosen pop in one after another and we're all hugging and talking at once. Then Cassandra and Phina arrive, and the chatter dies down.

'Welcome,' Dimitra says.

'Please report,' Cassandra says.

One by one we relate our success or lack of it. Cassandra and Phina seem especially impressed by what my dad did.

Cassandra looks to Phina. 'It's not a total disaster having a male in The Circle, then?'

Phina doesn't reply but then turns her attention to Tabby. 'And? What have you to tell us?'

She shakes her head. 'My dad couldn't believe he had anything so wrong. I didn't get through to him. I'm sorry.'

The others reassure me, say I tried.

'We, the Chosen made this decision to reach out to our families,' Dimitra says. 'It was, overall, an overwhelming success.'

Cassandra and Phina exchange glances.

'You have achieved more than I thought possible,' Phina admits. 'But even if all of your well-connected parents support our aims, if any impact we see isn't enough to stop the climate accelerating towards tipping points – then definitive action will still need to be taken.'

'As we have agreed,' Cassandra says.

'Wait,' Tabby says. 'Isn't this supposed to be our decision?'

'Your role was to decide whether or not to give humanity a second chance,' Phina says. 'You reached your decision and gave them a second chance.'

'What does definitive action mean, exactly?' Dimitra says.

'This is not the time or place to—'

'Then when? Where?' Tabby says.

'When you return.'

Phina and Cassandra depart, as if they know we need a moment on our own.

'Ariel, do you know anything about what she meant by definitive action?' I say.

She shakes her head.

'This isn't over yet,' Dimitra says. 'Let's all get back to Undersea as fast as we can and remind them they agreed to go along with any decision we make and assess things for ourselves. Right?'

Everyone is agreeing, but then I notice Isha's silence.

'Isha?' Tabby says.

'I'm not going to Undersea. I just *can't*. It's being so far underwater in an enclosed space.' Her panic even thinking of it – being trapped, confined – is clear to all of us.

We all cherish her, say it's all right. That we can still be together when we dream.

'But how will I know when?' Isha says.

'There must be a way,' Tabby says. 'They used it to keep in touch when Undersea was cut off after the tunnels were destroyed. Wait, I'll find out.' Tabby zones out, comes back a moment later. 'This is how it works. We have some ancestors in common: if you need us, tell your ancestors and they'll relay the message; likewise, we'll tell your ancestors we plan to dream so you can join in.'

We all wish Isha well.

Then one by one all the Chosen leave the dreaming.

Tabby and I are last, dreaming together. I can feel her fear as she trembles in my arms.

76

Tabby

I return before Denzi, stay still on the floor and watch him sleep.

I want to believe we'll find a way to convince The Circle to stop their definitive action – whatever that means – but there is this feeling of dread, deep inside me.

Cassandra saw – I have too – that all the future voices were silenced.

Doesn't that mean whatever we do, we will fail?

Denzi's eyes open a moment later, slowly focus on mine.

'You're back,' I say.

'Yeah. Not as rough a ride as last time. But not reassuring.'

'No.'

'We'll do this, it'll be all right.'

'I hope so.'

'How do we get to Undersea?'

'By dolphin of course,' I say and see the joy in his eyes.

We get up, open the door and walk up the garden path to Jago, Hayden and Apple.

'We have to leave. Now,' I say. 'I'm sorry.'

'Why?' Apple says. 'Where are you going?'

'There's something we need to do that can't wait. There's no time to explain. Jago knows more and can fill you in.'

'Apple, can you drive us?' Denzi says.

'To the train station?'

He shakes his head. 'No. To the beach – the sea.'

'Your private yacht waiting there?'

'Something like that.'

She pauses, uncertain. 'One condition: on the way? Call Leila.'

We all pile into Apple's car – Jago and Hayden too – for the short drive.

Denzi takes Apple's phone.

'It's going to message,' he says. 'Hi. It's Denzi. I'm all right but I have to go away for a while. I'm not sure if – when – I'll be able to come back. Apple and my dad know more – talk to them. I'm sorry. And . . . and I love you. Could you tell Dad and Jax that I love them too? Bye.'

And I can see the pain he's trying to hold in, leaving these people behind. He's so different to me: he has family he's known his whole life, even if his mum wasn't there most of the time. And I found it hard enough leaving Ali.

I hold his hand. 'I'm so sorry,' I whisper and his hand tightens in mine.

We get out of the car and take the path to the sea. I lead the way with Denzi, only half aware of the other three behind us, of their uncertainty about where we are going and why.

I can taste, smell, the sea. Feel it in the wind on my face. Then the glint of blue is in sight.

'Aslan? Are the kin around to take us?' I say silently.

Always.

Tears are spilling out of my eyes as we walk across the beach.

'Tabby?' Denzi says. 'It'll be OK.'

How can he know that? No matter what, I can't get past that the future voices were silenced. We must fail.

Anyhow, how could I even hope to succeed when not even my own father would listen to me? I long for Cate – she's gone for ever. Simone is too. Even with my friends around me, I feel so alone.

You are not alone. All the kin in the sea are yours.

We near the water. The sun is low in the sky – not that we can see it under the shroud of chemicals but the light is becoming less.

The kin are coming.

I motion to Denzi to stop and we turn back to Jago, Hayden, Apple. Give them each a hug in turn. When he gets to Apple, Denzi holds her tight. Murmers how sorry he is about her dad. And Apple's eyes are full of tears when she finally lets him go.

We hear them first: songs, both eerie and beautiful, from across the waves. Dolphins breach in the distance, then closer. There are water plumes: from whales? All different sizes, species. They are the singers.

The water is alive with them all.

My tears are falling into the water as we walk in slowly.

'They – all the cetaceans – have come? Whales, too?' I say silently to Aslan.

Yes, they are kin.

The water is thick with them.

Behind on the shore, separate from us, the gasps of Jago and the others.

A dolphin comes close and I reach out my hand – a light touch. Then another and another comes close.

Then our rides are here – one hand to a dorsal fin – and we disappear deep into the sea.

77

Hayden

'Hi, it's me – Hayden Richards. I've been streaming these astonishing scenes to you from a beach near Boscastle in Cornwall.

'This girl – Tabby is her name – has this incredible connection to the sea, and whales and dolphins. She's been crying because of climate change; she's scared that no matter how much we try we won't have done enough to change things.

'But it's not too late – not if we all join together.

'Tomorrow, wherever you are – noon GMT – an hour of silence for the climate. Join us. Let's show governments everywhere that the climate must be their first priority.'

78

Denzi

We swim through the night. Sometimes I am here, full of joy and wonder to swim this far, this long, in the sea. And sometimes I'm not aware of where I am or what is happening – or even who I am.

I fear for Tabby. It's like she's given up. I'm not ready to do that and the rest of us will have to make her see that we still have hope, a chance to make things right.

Things fade in and out. I come back to myself when we surface once more to breathe – then dive down, down – deeper than I've been before. My eyes adjust slowly to the increasing darkness – there's an opening in an underwater cliff? Tabby leaves her dolphin and swims towards it; I follow.

When we're both inside, a door slowly closes; water starts to drain out, replaced by air. When it is gone she goes to a door, motions me to help her wind a wheel around and around until the door opens. We wait as pressure steps down and then go through another door.

Malina waits on the other side.

She holds out her hands to Tabby and pulls her into a hug. When she is released Malina turns to me.

'Denzi. Welcome to Undersea.'

We follow her down a passageway.

'How many of the Chosen have returned?' Tabby says.

'About half now. We'll have a full house by meeting time in two hours I should think. We've prepared a room for you, Denzi. Both of you go and shower, rest, until we call you again. There is food and drink in your rooms.'

We go through more passageways. I'm shown a door.

'Your room, Denzi,' Malina says.

I give Tabby a hug; she hugs back, tight. Then walks away with Malina.

79

Tabby

'Malina, do you know what definitive action means? It's something Phina said.'

'I've not heard those words said by her before, though just as the words mean – perhaps something done decisively, with authority?'

'Who has authority in The Circle?'

'Only the collective. In theory we are all equal. But Cassandra as our seer takes the lead in most things.'

'How does Phina fit in to that?'

'She challenged Cassandra some years ago. There was almost a split between us, until they agreed to disagree.'

'And made us.'

'Pretty much.'

We've reached my door now.

'Are you all right?' Malina says.

'No.'

'Can I help?'

'I don't think so. But thank you.'

'Don't worry about that which is yet to be. We will soon be meeting with all your sisters who love and cherish you. Together we will decide what is best for sun, sea, earth and sky. Right?'

'Right.'

'Go. Rest.'

Inside my room, door closed, I lean back against it. I'm tired in a way I haven't felt before and it's not from lack of sleep — Aslan was in charge most of the way back and filled my sleep with dreams of the sea. I'm tired in another way, one that comes from despair. It makes me want to curl up in a ball on the floor and wait for the end to find me.

But Malina was right. I'm not alone in this, am I?

Aslan showed me this too. He called the kin and they all came, their whale cousins too, and I've never seen or experienced anything like it. If it were a normal time it would have been a moment of extreme joy.

But it felt more like they came to say goodbye.

80

Hayden

It's only seconds until noon GMT.

Mum, Dad and I come out of the house, sit on the pavement. Around us – every neighbour, workmen on the extension opposite, every car on the road – all stop.

Every person is silent, sitting or standing where they are, not moving. There is a BBC camera crew with cameras trained on us and all around – and a reporter with a microphone. And they're still and silent too.

I'm focusing my thoughts, trying to be calm, to think about all the animals and plants that have become extinct that we are mourning now, and those on the brink. There are over forty thousand species at risk of extinction on the red list of the IUCN – the International Union for Conservation of Nature. Tigers, snow leopards, Asian elephants, species of turtles, gorillas, rhinoceros too – all are on a top ten list, so close to being gone for ever.

But it's hard to be mindfully present when I see what is happening here, on my own street. Is it the same everywhere – across London, the UK, the world? Little fizzes of apprehension and excitement inside of me keep drawing me away from what I'm trying to think about.

The minutes pass slowly.

We'd had every climate activist with a presence on social

media ready to take part, all around the world – we knew this. The thing we didn't know was how much everyone else would be involved. If our street is anything to go by? It's looking good. *Please* let this work.

There's no doubt that Tabby and the dolphins and whales, all seeming to cry with her for the planet, played a part. No one could watch that and not be both filled with wonder at these sea creatures coming together, and with sorrow that they could perish, disappear, along with so many more animals, plants. Even us.

But just where have Denzi and Tabby gone? All Tabby said was that they had to leave, nothing about where they were going. And when Denzi was leaving a message for his mum he said he was going away, wasn't sure if he'd be back. We waited on the beach for hours just in case they returned, but no.

None of us said this out loud but were they going *anywhere*? No matter how much the whales and dolphins seemed to be their friends, people can't live in the sea. Whales sometimes beach themselves to die. Was swimming out like that the human version of the same thing?

Jago stayed when Apple and me had to leave, to go back to London. The pain in Jago's eyes when Tabby disappeared in the sea with Denzi – he looked how I feel when I remember Eva. I bet he spends every minute he can there, staring at the waves. Hoping she comes back.

When the Silence for the Climate hour is up, everyone around us stands, starts applauding, cheering. And it feels like we've *done something* – something amazing.

The cameras and microphones are here now.

'Hayden, how did that feel?'

'Just brilliant.'

'I'm getting reports in from the studio. Scenes like this have been replicated everywhere, from London to Paris, Kyiv to Washington DC, Ottawa in Canada, Christchurch in New Zealand, Sydney in Australia. All over Indonesia, China, Japan, India and Pakistan. A report just in: Palestinians and Israelis have stood side by side and been silent together. Antagonists from around the world standing or sitting next to each other and being silent for the climate.'

Tears are rising in my eyes. Mum and Dad, on both sides of me, think that in front of rolling cameras is a good time for a family hug. But I go for it too.

'Well done you,' Mum whispers in my ear.

81

Denzi

There's a tap on my door.

'Yes?'

Tabby opens it.

'Isha has just given me a nudge via an ancestor. She wants a dreaming – now, before our meeting with all The Circle.'

'Any idea why?'

'Nothing bad, but apart from that I don't know. Ariel and a few of the others are racing around, finding as many of us as they can in a hurry. There's not much time until our meeting so we'll try it without the tea, which might not work for everyone.' She gives me some chocolate, eats a piece herself. 'Get settled, close your eyes and focus on the four. We'll see how many make it.'

We lie down facing each other like before. I'm not sleepy. I breathe the words close to her lips.

Sun . . . Sea . . . Earth . . . Sky

Sun . . . Sea . . . Earth . . . Sky

Sun . . . Sea . . . Earth . . . Sky

I can tell when Tabby is gone – wherever she goes. Her body goes limp and I'm still here.

I try again:

Sun . . . Sea . . . Earth . . . Sky

Sun . . . Sea . . . Earth . . . Sky

Although my eyes are closed, everything blurs around me as if I'm somewhere else, moving – it feels both intangible and transient.

'Denzi?' Tabby's voice. I concentrate on her and as I do things become clearer. 'Good, you made it.'

There are others around us, fading in and out a bit like a bad transmission. Tabby gathers them together and most stay, stronger now.

Isha is here and I can feel waves of excitement coming from her.

'Good news then?' Tabby says.

'You won't believe it. You have to see.'

She shares what she has seen and heard with her own eyes.

Silence for the Climate: in the UK, all around Europe, Near and Far East, Australasia, North and South America. Everywhere. The world stopped. An hour that changed history: that's what they're calling it. I feel shivery, feverish – goosebumps on skin that isn't here with me.

This is it; it really is.

And she shows what in part rallied so many around the world: Tabby and me going to the sea. The dolphins and whales all around us.

The UK Government has formed a coalition with the Greens, the only way they could stay in power with so many MPs defecting – to focus not just on reducing emissions and extraction but stopping them altogether. Similar moves have begun all around the world.

Tabby is crying. 'I thought I failed. This is really happening? Wait.' She fades out a moment. Returns with Cassandra, and

Isha relives it all for her too.

'Things are really going to change now. Aren't they?' Tabby says, almost like she's pleading for a gift she doesn't believe will ever be given.

82

Tabby

When we arrive at the meeting place my eyes widen. So many sisters are here – way more than were here when we've met before.

Every seat is taken – more stand at the back. The Chosen are waved down to a few rows saved together at the front.

Have they all come to Undersea – all The Circle from around the world?

What was it Malina said? That Cassandra asked us all to return. I'm uneasy: it's almost like they're evacuating every sister from whatever part of the world they lived in.

As we walk down the stairs I look around, curious, at all the faces I haven't seen in person before, even though I know them in dreaming. There are whispers and ripples of excitement everywhere: news of Silence for the Climate must have spread.

I settle in a seat between Denzi and Zara, look back as more and more come in, now taking seats on the stairs. Elodie comes in too – sees me and waves.

Then Cassandra and Phina appear through a door above and walk down to join us, and as they do the shuffling noises and chatter die away.

They stand together in the middle.

'Thank you all for joining together today,' Cassandra says.

'There are faces that I've only seen in dreaming for many years – welcome home. This is a moment of extreme crisis for sun, sea, earth and sky. Our decision is of such a degree of importance that any action taken' – she glances at Phina – 'must be unanimous, which is why, for the first time in millenia, all The Circle have gathered together from far and wide.'

'Who speaks for the Chosen?' Phina says.

Dimitra stands.

'Your decision in favour of a second chance for humanity was noted,' Phina says. 'Your method agreed. You have had a degree of success. Yet there has been no measurable deceleration to tipping points, let alone reversal.'

Dimitra is startled. 'It's only been a few days—'

'That's about all we have,' Cassandra says. 'Yet we also know that isn't all we have to consider.' She smiles. 'Isha has brought us news which I know most of us have now shared. This Silence for the Climate, started by an English schoolgirl, a friend of yours, I think?' – she nods at Denzi – 'that spread around the world.'

'There is no way governments can ignore the people this time,' Dimitra says. 'The old, the young, rich and poor, all social classes and races: all were together. And the things the Chosen have achieved are tying in with this historic event, making governments react and deal with the crisis.'

'Sisters. Can we take this risk?' Phina says. 'We've heard it all before. Will they do what they say they will, and if so, will it be enough to stop acceleration to climate tipping points that spell the end not just for endangered species, but for every living thing on this planet – including us? That is what we must decide today.'

'We, the Chosen, were created by The Circle to make this

decision,' Dimitra says. 'How can you take it away from us? It is ours to make.'

There is murmuring all around.

'We agreed unanimously before your arrival' – Phina gestures to the Chosen – 'that if reversal from tipping points wasn't clear, that we'd have no choice but to take definitive action. Unless another unanimous decision can replace this, that decision stands. Yet Dimitra is right. Any unanimous decision of the Chosen must still be paramount – this was also agreed.'

I'm surprised at Phina's words. She's bouncing this back to us? Many sisters around us are surprised too. Only Cassandra appears to have expected this – that, or she is better at hiding her reactions than the rest of us. But how can we do this without all the facts?

I'm on my feet without making the decision to stand. 'How can we decide without knowing what this definitive action is that you mean to take?' I say. 'You said before it wasn't the time or place to discuss it. We're all here now. Tell us.'

'Of course,' Phina says. 'It is the right time to set forth our options.'

'Proceed,' Cassandra says.

'As chief scientific advisor, I was tasked with finding a way to stop humanity harming the planet without damaging sun, sea, earth and sky and all the other living things that call our earth and seas home. Various projects were considered, investigated and most eliminated by my team, until we were left with one promising solution. This actually flowed on from my work with the Chosen. The changes needed to allow extended breath holding and survival with limited oxygen in the Chosen gave us the idea of investigating ways we could do the reverse.

'My team has engineered a protovirus. Essentially, it is a DNA sequence that, when exposed to the right stimulus, inserts itself into human DNA – and only human. It has no impact on even our closest primate relatives. It reduces binding affinity for oxygen in human blood to such a degree that human life cannot be sustained without reducing carbon in the atmosphere to pre-industrial levels. There will be no choice but to aggressively reduce carbon emissions and increase carbon uptake.'

There is quiet in the room as what she's said is taken in.

'Oh, well done, Phina,' one sister says.

'That's brilliant,' says another. A spontaneous sprinkling of applause begins, and grows.

Cassandra raises a hand and it dies away. 'But we may not need this . . . solution,' Cassandra says.

'Quite,' Phina says. 'It is time for the Chosen to decide on our next action.'

83

Hayden

This is just . . . insane.

Mum is going through my wardrobe and emerges with a dress she'd made me wear to a family wedding a few months ago. 'Yes. This is the one.'

'No way.'

She throws it at me. 'Put it on. It's not every day you are a special guest at an emergency climate summit and get to meet the Prime Minister.'

I roll my eyes but pull the dress over my head, unable to get the sick feeling of nerves inside under control.

'It'll be fine. You'll be fine. Just don't roll your eyes at the judge like I did my first time in court.'

My eyes widen. 'You didn't.'

'I did! Just remember that and you'll be fine.'

When we arrive, there are crowds of people all around and I'm scared to get out of the car, but they're not like mobs we've come across before; they're all cheering, wanting a photo with me, and it's trippy, like I've woken up as a different person – a rock star or an actor or something.

Once we get through security, much of what happens goes by in a blur. Lots of hand shaking, photographs. Denzi's dad is here too – he's part of this new climate coalition. I look and then look

353

again: he doesn't look well. Probably too many late nights working out all the details for today. Other activists I know online are here, and they all want to meet me in person before things begin.

We finally settle into our seats. It looks a little like the UN on TV: rows of raised benches with microphones, name plaques in front of each of us saying who we are. There are reporters and cameras too – it's going out live.

The Prime Minister begins.

'Welcome to everyone here today at this historic climate summit. An English school girl started something here in London. Something that captured hearts and imaginations around the world and galvinised all of us to tackle the climate crisis. Hayden Richards, the architect of Silence for the Climate, is here with us today. Hayden, would you like to say a few words?'

I swallow, mouth dry even though I've been practising this half the morning. 'We had our hour of silence. By being united and not saying a word, people around the world spoke louder than they ever have before. But while we sit here talking, more species are going extinct. This can't just be talk. Everyone around the world agrees: it is time to act.'

There is applause – which is nice, I guess – but I'm just relieved I got it out without stammering. Or rolling my eyes. And I'm struck again by how much I miss Bishan. He could have said more and said it better.

Others are called on to speak now, and the more I listen, the more I'm uneasy. There is no doubt that there will be people, powerful people, who don't agree with what must be done. You can't change everything and think no one will resist, but it's almost like they're keeping quiet while the world is listening. What are they planning behind the scenes?

For now it's all smiles and agreement.

The summit is nearing its end – the PM is just summing up proposed actions – when there is a disturbance in one of the rows behind her.

It's Denzi's dad.

He's pulling at his tie, loosening it, struggling to breathe. The Green leader next to him and an assistant from behind are there, and then people are standing in the way so I can't see – is he on the floor now? And an MP who is also a doctor is pushing her way towards them.

The Prime Minister takes the microphone. 'Everyone, please take your seats while we have an adjournment.'

Paramedics come and then he's on a stretcher. Soon the wail of an ambulance reaches our ears from outside.

84

Denzi

'Wait until you see it,' Zara says to me as we follow her to what I'm told is now the official place of Chosen decision making.

A door with a hatch is unwound and we step through into what is, at first, darkness. The door is closed as the last of us arrive and gradually my eyes adjust.

There is a huge dome over us, and above we can see the sea. Vague shapes in the water start to resolve. Fish and things with tendrils, and glimpses of silver that come closer now: dolphins.

We gradually settle, find a place to sit down. Tabby is next to me.

'Do you still want me to be the speaker?' Dimitra says, and there is a chorus of yeses. 'I don't know about you, but the – I don't know – poetic justice of this protovirus thing Phina has come up with? It's hard not to like it.'

Tabby waves a hand and Dimitra points to her.

'I get why you say that but the timing is all wrong.'

'How so?'

'If it was – I don't know – a hundred years ago? And we told everyone, stop industrialising and digging and burning or this will happen and you'll die. OK. But if this thing is released now, won't everyone who doesn't have a tank of oxygen die?'

'That isn't what we're deciding today, is it?' Ariel says. 'Not the details of if or how the protovirus can be used – it could just be a threat, say. That's all to be worked out. All we have to decide is whether we hang back and wait, see if humanity can sort themselves out and make a reversal of the rush to tipping points, or whether we need to give them more . . . incentive.'

'There's no point if that happens,' Tabby says. 'There was no point us going to our parents and trying to convince them, or in that whole silence for the climate – no point to any of it. If we go back to threats, they'll be backed into a corner and won't want to do what they're told. And we can't risk using this protovirus when we don't know the scale of it or what it will do. Governments and people everywhere need this chance to do the right thing, and for once it looks like that could really happen.'

Voices all around us murmuring. Agreeing with Tabby. Nodding.

'Let's take this to a vote and see where we're at,' Dimitra says. 'Who wants to wait, see what the human race can do, before considering using this protovirus thing as a threat or otherwise?'

Hands go up one by one all around the room.

Until all eyes are on Ariel.

She shakes her head. 'I don't agree.'

85

Tabby

The debate goes on and on, and still Ariel won't change her vote.

Finally Dimitra says we should take a break. Some leave, some stay and disperse in small groups. Everyone but Ariel, who is alone.

I tug Denzi's hand and we go to her.

'Ariel, what's going on?' Tabby says.

'I'm entitled to vote the way I think.'

'Is it really *you* who thinks like this, or is it Phina?'

Her lips are in a thin line. 'I don't do what Mummy tells me any more than you'd do what your dad tells you. Got it?'

'OK. Fair enough. But I don't understand.'

'I just happen to think the human race can't be trusted.'

'But think about what could happen with this protovirus. If it is activated and spreads, millions – *billions* – could die. Tanks of oxygen would be like gold and only the rich and powerful would have them. Until they run out that is.'

'She's right,' Denzi says. 'It would be Armageddon.'

Ariel shakes her head. 'Mum would never let it get to that point. Don't be ridiculous.'

'Then why do you think all of The Circle have been told to come back, to be here in Undersea?'

'To make these decisions. We all have to be here.'

'Or maybe it was to keep The Circle safe, hiding away from

this protovirus. How can you trust Phina?'

'You're on thin ice, Tabby.' Ariel's eyes are flashing. 'You don't know her like I do. Everything she does is for us – to save us, and not just us, every plant, animal and *person* on this planet. She'd never hurt anyone or anything unless she had to.'

She is wrong. Phina hurt me – many like me – without a care. She is dangerous. Even to her own kin.

I'm looking into Ariel's eyes and I can feel her belief, her certainty, even as everything inside me – as well as Aslan and my ancestors – tells me otherwise.

Aslan's words resonate: *dangerous to her own kin*. I have to tell Ariel what I saw at the swim school; there is no other choice.

'Ariel, there is something I haven't told you. I wasn't sure if I should. It's about swim school and the real reason I ran away from it.'

'Yeah?'

'It's what I found under the sports med building. Locked away in a cage, underwater. It was like a living experiment, one that had gone wrong. Sort of a half girl, half fish.'

'So? What are we after all? Half girl – or boy, Denzi – and half dolphin.'

'Ariel, that's not all. It – she – had your face. Blank eyes with no thought behind them, but they were *your* eyes. Everything about her face was exactly the same as yours.'

Her eyes widen. 'Get out.'

'I'm serious. She must have been your sister, a twin even. If Phina would lock your *sister* away alone underwater like that, how can you trust what she might do?'

'No way. I don't believe it.'

'Ariel, there's something my dad told me the last time I saw him,' Denzi says. 'It was being kept out of the news while it was investigated.'

'What next?'

'They found bodies buried under one of the Penrose Clinic research sites. He said they weren't people or animals – they were something no one had ever seen before.'

'It looks like Phina did more experiments when making us – ones that didn't work so well, maybe,' I say. 'Killed them and hid their bodies away. Like they could have done to us if they decided something wasn't quite right.'

'No. You're just making stuff up to try to make me change my mind.'

'It's true, Ariel. All of it.'

'I don't believe you and I don't want to talk to you any more. Just keep out of my face.'

She turns, walks away from us.

Dimitra is calling for attention. Everyone has wandered back and it's time to vote again.

The result is the same.

Part 9

@HaydenNoPlanetB

The biggest humanitarian crisis of all time is almost here. Seas rise, rains fail, whole nations of people are being displaced. A refugee crisis like no other has begun.

#NatureIsScreaming

86

Denzi

A meeting is called with all The Circle.

Dimitra stands. 'We have not reached a unanimous decision. We have tried to come together, but there is one of us who does not agree with the rest.'

'In the absence of a unanimous decision, we must revert to the previously agreed position,' Cassandra says.

Tabby stands up. 'What does this mean?'

Cassandra defers to Phina. 'We will proceed with disseminating and activating the protovirus.'

'Meeting adjourned,' Cassandra says.

'But—'

'Meeting adjourned.'

Everyone files out until only we are left – all the Chosen apart from Ariel.

What can we do? Many of them look to Tabby but she's shaking her head, darkness in her eyes.

87

Tabby

I'm not quite awake and not quite asleep, the events of the day going back and forth in my mind like a movie you don't want to watch stuck on endless replay. All of it is tinged by sadness so deep I can't move, frozen in place. Is there something I could have said or done to convince Ariel? Somewhere in the midst of analysing it all I must drift away.

Then I'm nudged awake by urgent whispering inside my mind: ancestors.

Isha needs you now.

Isha?

I open my eyes, find some chocolate root on the bedside table and swallow it down.

I focus on Isha – not her face but who she is inside. Find her circle and then she is there.

She's in pain, so much pain.

'What's wrong?'

'My parents. They . . . they both suddenly became ill, desperately ill.'

She shows me her memory. They collapsed, unable to breathe – as if they both had extreme asthma attacks but they don't have asthma. She called paramedics but they weren't in time to save her mum; she died. Her father is almost holding his own in the hospital on oxygen, and they can't work out why they became ill. What is wrong? And they won't let her see him until they work out if it is contagious.

'Oh, Isha. I wish I could be there for you,' I say, even as horror is dawning inside. Could it be?

'It was my choice to stay here, and you can't come. I get that. But it gets worse. I just thought this was some horrible random thing, but then – the news. There's more. It isn't just my parents. There's been reports of isolated cases all over the world. And one of them is the former Home Secretary, Denzi's dad – he's in hospital. I think all the others I've heard of that I can identify are parents of the Chosen.'

Fear and pain and horror: it must be, mustn't it? The protovirus – did we carry it? I explain what Phina told us earlier.

'It must be something they caught from us,' Isha says. 'What other explanation can there be? And your dad too. I'm sorry, but it was on the news just now. Your dad got sick too and . . . he's died.'

Ali? He's . . . died? The shock is so much I almost lose connection to the dream and to Isha.

I snuck away in the night. I didn't even say goodbye. And now . . . he's gone?

What Isha said gets through to me now: *people we've been close to*. Panic and fear twist my gut. I hugged Jago. Sascha too. Apple was there, and Hayden. She still did that Silence for the Climate thing and must have been OK then, but how long does it take?

'Isha – when? From when you first saw your parents until they became ill – how long was it?'

'I don't know . . . about two and a half days.'

And what about all the random other people on the train, and before that – in Brighton. In that café where we had breakfast when we first got there. The hotel too.

Phina must be behind this. Was it some sort of test of her protovirus? Did we carry it to our parents? Will it spread?

'Tabby? Are you still there?'

'Sorry. Yes. I'm going to find out what is going on. I'll let you know. Thank you – for telling me. First I'll gather the Chosen – can you tell them what you told me?'

'Of course.'

'Take care.'

We hug each other, a more complete hug than if she were physically in my arms. It is all of us – every thought and feeling laid bare, and there is so much pain.

I sit up, open my eyes.

Can Ali really be gone?

And what about Jago: is he all right? If he isn't, Phina must know what is wrong, and how to stop it or fix it.

She had better tell me.

I'm up and through my door before the thought has even formed.

Undersea is quiet – my sisters are sleeping – and with the quiet I can hear the throb of the sea and steady myself by feeling it with my hands trailing along the wall as I run. First, I wake Zara, Dimitra, a few others – tell them to gather everyone to dream with Isha.

Then I go to Denzi's door, tap on it.

He opens it, looks out with sleepy eyes. 'What's going on?'

'I need your help. I'll tell you on the way.'

Ancestors show me where to find Phina's rooms. Denzi follows and I tell him what Isha said as we run.

The shock and horror I feel are echoed in his eyes. 'My dad – he's in the hospital?'

'That's what Isha said. It was on the news. We're almost there – Phina's is the next door, around the corner.'

Take care, Aslan says.

'Yes. She is our enemy.'

Nothing is ever locked in Undersea. I don't knock, just barge into a sitting room. It's dark but lights come on automatically. It's empty, two doors leading off.

'Are you here?' I call out.

Faint sounds come from one of the adjoining rooms. The door opens and out steps Ariel half asleep, but her eyes open wide when she sees me standing there, Denzi just behind.

'What do you want?'

'To speak to Phina. Is that her room?'

'Don't wake her—'

But I'm across and open the door. Her bed is empty.

'Where is she?'

'I don't know. Probably in her lab – she works all hours a lot of the time. Why?'

I don't answer, go back out through her front door with Denzi, but now Ariel is following.

'Tell me what is going on,' she says.

'Our parents are dead or dying. From our visits.'

'What are you talking about?'

'Isha told me. Her mum has died. My dad too. Denzi's dad is in the hospital.'

'I'm so sorry if that's happened. But what has this got to do with my mum?'

'It has to be her, what else can it be? Somehow we must have been carrying this protovirus of hers and given it to our parents. She must be behind this.'

'I don't believe you. She wouldn't do that.'

I can see the panic on her face, the confusion – is she starting to question her loyalties?

'Let's ask her,' I say. 'And see what she says.'

When we get to the area where Phina's labs are located, the ancestors don't know how to get in but Ariel does. There's a keypad, a code.

'A locked door in Undersea?'

'For safety. Some things she's working on are dangerous.' Then, as if she realises what she's said, she flinches.

We walk down a dimly lit corridor, labs to the sides through windows, mostly darkened. We go to the door at the end.

Lights are on in this lab and we step through. There are all sorts of equipment, chemicals, benches, and that's as far as I can go in labelling what I can see. It's like a sci-fi movie gone mad. And there at the end is Phina, a series of computer screens in front of her.

'Ah, Ariel. And Tabby and Denzi too. Welcome to my lab.' She takes off her glasses. 'Is there something I can help you with?'

'My dad has died,' I say. 'Denzi's is in hospital. Do you know anything about that?'

'You know? Oh, from Isha, of course.'

Ariel is looking from Phina to me and back again. 'You're not surprised?' she says, uncertainty in her voice.

'No, I've been monitoring the news,' she says and glances at one of her screens – it's the BBC. 'Not everyone is like Cassandra who only trusts dreaming to find out things.'

I glance at the screen and my breath catches. He's there – Ali. Images of him from the geoengineering press conference. And even though Isha told me and I believed her, seeing him on the screen and the report that he's died? It's still a shock, as if some part of me was hoping it was all a mistake.

Phina follows my eyes to the screen. 'Few more deserving individuals could be found than this VP of Industria United, who launched geoengineering like it was a great accomplishment.' She's shaking her head. 'Though it was useful in the end.'

'He was my *father*.'

'I'm well aware of that – I picked out all your parents very carefully, after all.'

More things are slotting into place in my mind. 'You picked them out, but not just for genetic reasons – but also because of who they were or would be. You must have made sure they didn't have children in the usual way – what, did you drug them somehow? – and that they'd end up at the Penrose Clinic.'

'Yes, it all worked rather well.'

'And you always meant to kill our parents, didn't you? You selected them to murder them and did it in the worst way: using their children.'

She's amused. 'I haven't got a crystal ball. If you want to consult one of those, talk to Cassandra. It was merely an opportunity that arose.'

'You sent us to them carrying this protovirus. Didn't you?'

'Not exactly – it was activated by your phones.'

'What? The mobile phones you gave us?'

'Exactly.'

'How could you be sure who would get sick?' Denzi says. 'What about all the other innocent people we walked past or spoke to?'

'I was tracking your phones. I knew you'd have them close to you all the time after so long without. Once you were in proximity to your parents' phone, I initiated an update sequence on yours. This caused a small reaction in the circuits which created and then released activation factor. All you had to do then was give them a hug or hold their hand.'

'We didn't get sick,' I say.

'Of course not. The Chosen – with the altered oxygen binding in your blood – are immune. I'd tested that already.' She glances at Ariel. 'The Circle are not but have been made safe here until the protovirus degrades and becomes harmless in the atmosphere. Now, if you could please excuse me, I've got to get back to work.' She puts her glasses back on, turns to the screens.

Ariel has stood there, still, all this time, but now she stirs. 'I didn't believe you'd do this. And you're not even denying it, or explaining why? What about my dad? Did you do this to my phone – to kill him like that too?'

'Of course. Though I believe he made it to hospital in time. At least his demise hasn't been reported.'

Ariel – she's rigid, her arms wrapped around herself. 'You tested to make sure this thing wouldn't make the Chosen sick. You mean you tested it on me, don't you?'

'Indeed. I was sure you were immune but I am a scientist after all, and hypotheses must be tested.'

'And Tabby said I had a twin, that she saw her. Is that true?'

'Well, technically, no; we split the egg early to make two from one, before different DNA additions.'

'And she's in a cage underwater at swim school?'

'No, of course not; we wouldn't have left her there to starve after the place was destroyed in the hurricane. She's been euthanised. She wasn't a viable option.'

'That could have been me.'

'In a real way, it *was*. You're the lucky half. Now, if you could—'

Ariel screams and lunges at Phina, rakes her fingernails across her cheek. Denzi and I pull her back.

Four stripes of vivid red are welling up on Phina's face. She shakes her head, reaches for a tissue to dab it with. 'Ariel, dear. The animal side of you is getting stronger.'

Ariel is struggling against Denzi's hold. And I go to her, a hand on each shoulder in front of her until she looks at me. 'Let's leave her for now. We've got to get the Chosen together – go to Cassandra, tell her we all agree now, take it back—'

'It's too late,' Phina says.

'What do you mean?' I say.

'The update is scheduled to begin rolling out first thing tomorrow. It can't be stopped. And I'd said that your father's geoengineering turned out to be useful?' She nods at me. 'The one problem we had was distribution: how to get the protovirus everywhere around the world. That was solved quite easily in the end by surreptitiously adding our own contaminant in what they've been pumping out into the atmosphere.'

'But if you've already been doing this – you weren't waiting for our decision. It was always too late. Wasn't it?'

'Well, to be fair, without the activation factor, the protovirus is harmless and will degrade and disappear within days. But once my test of the system — using your parents — was successful, the programming for the updates was implemented.'

'You never meant to go by the decision of the Chosen unless it was what you wanted,' Denzi says.

'Not at all. I was just certain it wouldn't be unanimous.' She glances at Ariel who seems frozen in place, as if she can't take it in any more. 'And Tabby, before you think of running to your dear great-grandmother Cassandra for her help, know this: she's the one who had Cate killed.'

'What?'

'After Cate was arrested, Cassandra couldn't reach Cate by dreaming like she used to, unknown to most of us it must be said. Anyhow, as I'm the one with the right contacts on shore, she came to me for help. To get someone in to see Cate, find out what was wrong, and the order was given to end Cate's life if she could no longer be trusted to keep The Circle's secrets. They carried out this task.'

'I don't believe you!'

'The report back was that Cate didn't communicate in a meaningful way. The conclusion reached was that her mental stability was in question, and so the order to terminate was carried out.'

I'm staring back at her, appalled. Cate said she was a dead woman walking, her body without the rest of her. But somebody stabbed her. Cassandra didn't know then what Cate had done — that her essence was gone. Is this true?

Then Phina's eyes shift to focus behind us where the door is opening. It's Stacey and Elodie, and there in Stacey's hands – a gun.

'Enough chit-chat,' Phina says. 'Could you please see them out?'

Stacey gestures at us to go. They push us back out of the lab, down the hall and out through the door.

'Don't come back. The code has been changed,' Stacey says as it clicks locked behind us.

Ariel moves away from the door; she turns and runs.

'Ariel, wait,' I say. 'Where are you going?'

She doesn't answer.

She is kin.

'Can you reach her?'

She hears me but does not listen.

'Denzi? Can you try to help Ariel? I'm going to Cassandra. If anyone can stop Phina, it's her.'

As I race off, each foot that thuds down is like a heartbeat – Cate's.

Did Cassandra lie?

88

Denzi

Ariel has never run this fast. I keep her in sight but can't get closer. When we reach the winding passage, I know where she is going: the sea dome. Why?

When we get to the door with the winding hatch, it is already open.

We go through.

Many of the Chosen are here, but not as they have been before – there is something about their faces, the way they move. They are walking, circling around the dome. Ariel joins them.

I grab Zara's arm as she goes by. She turns to me, one eye open, one closed. Her face oddly blank.

'Zara!' I shake her and she tilts her head to one side, looks at me, both eyes open now. Puzzled.

'Denzi?' she says, then looks around, sees the others and their odd movements. 'What's happening? How did I get here?' Then, like she remembers, her face crumples. 'My mum and dad. And – oh. You don't know. Isha saw it on the news after Tabby was gone – I'm sorry, Denzi. It's your dad. He's died now too.'

It's a blow deep inside, as if I've been kicked in the gut. I'd convinced myself he'd be all right – he was taken to hospital, they'd look after him. He didn't always do the right thing – but just a short time ago he did, and he did it for me. I left without saying goodbye and he's . . . dead?

Fury rises up inside me, hot and red. Phina did this? I swore to protect my sisters in The Circle but the rage inside me isn't reason, it's reaction, and I can't handle the war between *protect* and *destroy* inside me, I can't . . .

Something in me is *changing* – I'm changing . . .

Before I can wonder what or how, I'm gone.

89

Tabby

I'm running to Cassandra's rooms. I ask my ancestors to tell her I'm coming.

There is puzzlement: they tell me she does not answer.

Something is wrong. Aslan.

'You can say that again.'

It's the kin. They are coming for the Chosen.

'What do you mean?'

The Chosen are kin now. All of them have changed even though they are not in the sea. They want to leave this place.

'Denzi, too?'

I said all.

'Where are they?'

The sea dome.

'Can you speak to them, the way you can speak to the kin?'

I'll try. There's a pause. *They circle, caged – asking for help from the kin. They do not understand where they are or how they got there. They're afraid.*

Do I go to them now? See if I can bring them back to themselves?

But I need Cassandra's help to stop Phina.

Is that the only reason I came here? Cate is gone – I can't bring her back – but I *have* to know if what Phina said is true.

I've reached Cassandra's door now and rip it open.

She's sitting on the floor, knees drawn against her. She looks up. 'Ah, Tabby, child. I knew you would come.' There are tears on her face but she's smiling.

I kneel down next to her. 'You have to help me. Phina has locked herself in her lab and is going to trigger activation of the protovirus, and something is wrong with the Chosen.'

She shakes her head. 'None of that will matter soon.' She's half laughing, half crying. 'The future voices – *our* voices – will be silenced. It was the only way.'

I frown. 'What do you mean?'

'The Circle will die so others may live.'

Tabby – the kin are here. All the kin.

90

Denzi

Fear, confusion – locked in this cave, but we don't know how we got here so don't know how to swim out. Above us we can see the sea but cannot reach it.

Help us!

Kin have come. All shapes, sizes; the deep gods – whales seldom seen above – too. They swim all around but can't find the way either, and our panic is rising.

The deep gods charge against the roof we can see through; again and again they strike, and strike against it hard and then harder while we watch, kin above and kin all around with me here also.

Again and again they strike.

91

Tabby

Aslan is showing me what the kin see – the water above the dome thick with so many of them, whales, too. And they are crashing into the dome? And then I can feel it too – the vibrations in the floor beneath my feet, in the walls around us.

Can they break it? If they do . . . *no*. The sea will rush in?

I begin to see what Cassandra has seen all along. She didn't tell all The Circle to return to keep them safe as Phina intended, not at all. She brought them here to die. I turn to her, shake her. 'You knew this would happen? And you just let it?'

She smiles, serene. 'Yes. It is the only way, Tabby. The future voices – our descendants – are silenced: we know this. I've seen it – I can see it on your face that you have too. We assumed this must mean the end for all of humanity on their poisoned planet. But I looked deeper: there is a real chance that we were wrong. Don't you see? For the future voices of our descendants to be silenced, it is us – The Circle – who must die. If humanity takes the right path with the climate, there is still a chance that this planet will survive. We must die so they may go on.'

'No, you're wrong! You have to help me stop Phina!'

'She will die with the rest of us. It doesn't matter.'

'You don't understand. Phina says the protovirus has already been dispersed around the world, that she's set up automatic updates to mobile phones to activate it.'

She frowns. 'That can't be right. I worked it all out – The Circle will be destroyed to save the rest of humanity.'

'Not unless we can stop Phina's updates, and she's locked herself in – we can't get to her.'

'It doesn't matter. They'll die. The sea will claim them with the rest of us.'

'But will that stop her computers triggering the updates?'

No. It won't. They will automatically back up online if there is any disruption or problem with her systems.

An ancestor – a voice I recognise. Yvonne?

I used to work with Phina. I know her fail-safes. I can sabotage them.

Thud, thud. The noise – the vibrations – increasing. I have to go there before it is too late.

But with everything else there is one thing I want – *need* – to know above all others.

'Phina told me it was you who gave the order to have Cate killed. Is it true?'

'It was only her body. When you couldn't hear us, she spoke to me – I told her. She forgave me.'

Only Cate's body: her arms that held me. Her lips that kissed my cheek. Her hands that held mine.

Cassandra's hand grabs my wrist. 'It's time. Take the knife.' She gestures – the cloth on a table, the circular knife within. She wants me to harvest her – the blood ritual. The way she harvested Alicia when she was a child. But if I do, Cassandra and her memories will always be inside me.

I shake my head, pull away. No, never. Not after what she's done. She can die and be gone for ever, like Cate.

We have to go now! Yvonne.

I turn and run as fast as I can back to the door to Phina's labs. Yvonne says the door code is changed using a regular mathematical sequence. She gives me different sequences to try – the first doesn't work. The second doesn't either. But on the third try the lock clicks and I push the door open.

Stacey stands there – a gun in her hand still, but not held up. She's scared. There is another *thud*, *thud*, and she flinches.

'What is that noise?'

'Whales and dolphins are attacking the sea dome,' I say. 'Soon it will be breached.'

'My sisters.' She pushes past us and runs through the door, her gun clattering on the floor.

I run for the lab.

Wait. I need to take control of you to do this.

I shield my thoughts. Yvonne wants me to let her take over my body, like I let Cate do once. Cassandra warned me to never do that again, that it was dangerous – I wouldn't be able to get back in control unless the ancestor I'd let in allowed it. Cassandra, who lied about Cate, but I've no reason to think she lied about that. And it's Yvonne, an ancestor Cate told me not to trust.

The only way I can reprogram the system fast enough is if I do it – it takes too long if I have to tell you each keystroke. I have to finish before the system is flooded.

I relay to Aslan what she has asked me to do.

This is dangerous?

'Yes.'

But hold on to me and I'll hold on to you. The silver rope, knotted to my virtual hand, in his teeth. *I'll keep you safe.*

I relinquish. Yvonne fills me inside, tries me on. Pushes me away to a corner inside, but not so far away that I can't see and hear what happens around her.

She walks back, reaches for Stacey's gun left abandoned on the floor. Holds it in her hand and goes to the lab at the end.

Elodie and Phina are both there in such worried, focused conversation that they don't see Yvonne through the glass in their door.

She pulls it open and they turn.

Phina frowns. 'Put that gun down, Tabby. You know you'd never be able to use it.'

Yvonne smiles. Pulls the trigger and Phina falls back, stunned, holding her stomach – there's blood and the shock of it makes me retreat even more.

'Tabby?' Elodie says. 'This isn't you. Who is there?'

Yvonne gestures with the gun at Elodie. 'Go. Over there on the floor. Next to Phina.' She smiles. 'I'm Yvonne. Do you remember me, Phina? Your trusted co-worker? The one you killed when you did the first test of your protovirus? I was gasping for air, begging for help. I have allergies and I thought – everyone thought – that that was what killed me. But it wasn't, was it?'

'You worked that out, did you? Well done,' Phina says. 'And you've stolen this poor girl's body, too. Why?'

'I've got what I wanted. Watching you die, like you watched me.'

'Let Tabby come back. Please,' Elodie says.

'Be quiet!'

I can hear but not feel the vibrations – the sounds are increasing. 'What is happening?' Elodie says.

382

'I thought I told you to be quiet? According to Cassandra, we're all about to drown. Well, I won't but you will. I don't think it'll be much longer.'

Do what you said you would do! I'm shouting inside to Yvonne and feel her – me? – shake her head as if an annoying fly is buzzing around.

'Well yes, all right. But only because that'll upset Phina more than dying: knowing her glorious weapon misfired before she died. Speaking of weapons, *Don't* move,' she says to Elodie. 'Or you will join Phina sooner rather than later.'

Yvonne turns a chair and monitor so she is facing the two of them. Lays the gun between her and them, and then her fingers are on the keyboard.

Password incorrect.

Again.

Password incorrect.

Again and again and again. And then, finally, it works. 'Phina, for such a smart woman, your prime sequence passwords are *so* predictable.'

I can't feel Yvonne's hands on the keyboard or know her thoughts. But I watch in awe as her fingers fly across the keyboard. As far as I understand, she seems to be searching files for something, then logging into something else. Can she do what she said she could – can she stop the updates going out?

She's cursing under her breath, trying another way . . . then, triumph!

'OK, got it!' she says. 'There, Phina. Your automatic backup is disabled.'

Phina has pulled herself half up. She's laughing and gurgling on blood. 'Doesn't matter. There is also a backup to the backup system you don't know about. It's in a submersible in a cave you'll never find. The updates will be triggered in a few hours now.'

What about the internet? Can we cut it off – would that do anything? I shout inside.

'Hmmm. It might?' Yvonne thinks to me. 'But it's protected – there isn't just an on-off switch. It's spliced from the main ocean cable not far from here.'

Let me back in! I can find this cable in the sea, destroy it.

'No. Never!'

You'll die if I don't help you.

'This body is made to survive in the sea.' But even as she says it her fear is growing.

Then, confusion. There is something she doesn't understand? Then things shift, change. It's Aslan – he's taking over, forcing her aside and she's panicking. He's pulling hard on something . . . it's silver. Gradually I feel it wrapped around my hand: my silver rope – and it feels as if it is pulling me back into my body. Where I belong.

I didn't like her, Aslan says.

'I didn't much, either. Thank you.'

Is she gone?

'I don't know. Yvonne?'

What happened? How did you do that? Confusion, fear, but most of all *rage* at what she has been deprived of – another life, my body.

'None of your business.' I push her back with the rest of my ancestors, tune them out.

She's back inside me where she belongs.

The sea dome. Aslan shows me as it cracks. Breaks. There is an almost instant change in air pressure – rapid, intense, and Elodie cries out. Screams of terror sound all around us.

Despite what Elodie has been, what she may have done, I would save her life if I could.

I cannot.

92

Denzi

At last: what is above us, keeping us from the kin, has broken.

The sea rushes in to claim this place back, to join us. Where it was always meant to be.

Water rushes in and through, taking us with it at first. Once it has begun to fill the space, we make our way back and out – and finally join our kin in the sea.

Free at last.

93

Tabby

With the pressure of all the sea above us, once water has found an opening it hurtles through Undersea.

The labs at the centre are amongst the last to flood.

My arms are wrapped around my head, but sounds bore into me with the rushing of my blood through my body: the screams of my sisters, all around, their terror, agony, last thoughts. I share ancestors with so many that I'm seeing and feeling it all through them and can't blank it out no matter how hard I try. The weakest go before the water, the extreme pressure crushing breath from lungs. Others are thrown against walls, bones broken, skulls crushed, drowned if any life remains.

I'm the last seer. I could dream, find their circles, keep them inside me with my ancestors.

Be more and more crowded out until I can't even think as myself.

But there's no time, no chance – if I stopped to dream, I'd drown. I need to get out, find the cables. Stop the signal.

The lights go out. When the water finally rushes in, taking me in a dark, cold embrace, Elodie is already gone. Her heart? The pressure? I don't know.

Once it has equalised enough that I can move without being pinned back, I feel my way to the door and swim through to make for the broken sea dome – the way out.

Belongings – furniture – bodies. All float in the dark water unseen, and the horror makes it hard to go on. Sometimes I have to move them to make way.

I have to get out and to the surface before I run out of oxygen, and can feel its debt already.

It'd be easy to give up.

Let me take over, Aslan says.

I close my eyes, pretend I am somewhere and someone else until everything fades away.

I wake when we surface and breathe in deep. It's not much lighter than it was far below – night-time, no stars, only a faint glow where the moon may be under a sky full of chemicals.

A sky full of protovirus.

I can't process – even begin to understand – what has happened. What Cassandra knew was coming and didn't try to stop.

Phina: we have to find a way to cut off her backup signal.

A submersible hidden in a cave, she said – that sounds like it would be hard to find. But what of the cable in the sea?

'Aslan, can we find the cable she has spliced on to for the internet? If we can destroy it, maybe we can stop the signal. Do the kin know where this is?'

There is a pause. Then: *They say there is a dead snake as long as the sea not far from here.*

388

94

Denzi

There is an endless snake that runs along the bottom of the sea: it threatens the kin. It must be destroyed. These thoughts are shared by all the kin and we leave our games, swim back down, deep, deep, to the very bottom of the sea.

It lies there, dull and still, stretching on as far as sight in both directions. Surely it is dead already?

No, there is life inside, hidden away. We must destroy it.

This is the realm of the deep gods and they, the strongest of us all, take charge. They ram into the snake again and again. It does not strike back but neither is it broken.

Kin say there may be another way if we can find it. A place where another snake joins to this one?

We separate and search all along the snake, wary in case it should strike. We do not find another like it, but then I see there is something else – more a worm than a snake.

The kin come to see. It is thinner than the long snake, but yes, this is what we seek.

The deep gods smash into it again and again.

Finally something gives. There is a dazzling flash in the water; I fear for the kin, but it is soon gone and they swim on unharmed. It breaks away, a dead worm from the snake.

We thank the deep gods and surface together to breathe. We are hungry; there are fish to chase. We will dive now, but there is a sound. One I know but don't know, and puzzled, I turn.

A two legs with the kin – her mouth is moving and then there is the sound again. And the kin tell me to listen, to focus on the sounds she makes.

Everything shifts, *changes*. The world around me and inside me also.

I was in the dome, and now I'm in the sea? At the surface. Dolphins and the Chosen all around us.

'Denzi?'

It's Tabby next to me, concern in her eyes. My name: that was the sound I heard – Tabby saying my name.

'What's happened? Why are we here?'

'Do you remember anything?'

I frown, trying to go back. 'I was in the dome. Zara . . . she said . . . my dad: that he died?' And *fury*, and something shifted and changed inside of me. Then a flash of images almost too fast to follow runs through me and I gasp. 'The kin, our kin. Deep gods – what are they? Some kind of whale?'

And what we did.

I'm taken over by *horror* and want to get away from myself again—

'Denzi? Please. Stay.' Tabby's hand on my shoulder.

'We destroyed Undersea?'

'The kin did. The Chosen called them and they destroyed it.'

'All our sisters? What happened to them?'

She shakes her head, tears in her eyes. 'Only the Chosen have survived.'

'I swore to protect them and this is what I've done.'

'It's you, but not you. Another part of you inside. You were frightened, felt threatened and asked for help. That is all you did.'

'What about Phina and her updates?'

'We managed to disable her backups before the labs were flooded and her computers destroyed. But she said she had another backup hidden in a submersible in a cave we'd never be able to find. We found her link to the internet cable on the ocean floor. Smashed it. I don't know if that will stop the updates or not.'

That sinks in.

'How long until we know?'

'Isha said it was two and a half days from when she saw her parents until they became ill. I'm going home. I have to know . . . if my friends were infected too. I have to go, even if just to say goodbye.'

My eyes focus on Tabby's. I hold her hand to my face, and if we were the only boy and girl left in the world, I'd never let her go. But all around us the Chosen, the kin, splash and swim.

'The sea is our home. We are your pod. Stay.'

She shakes her head, takes her hand away. 'I can't.'

'Do you want me to go with you?'

She hesitates. 'I want you to do what is right for you,' she says, and looking into her eyes I know it is right to be with her.

But I'm not free.

'I can't leave the Chosen and fail at my promise again; they are all the sisters left. I have to protect them.'

Eyes I thought I could drown in for ever are full of sadness. And understanding. 'It's OK. I get you, why you have to be here for them.'

'Will you come back to us?'

'Maybe, one day. But even if we succeeded in stopping Phina I still need to be there. To do everything I can to make sure all the gains that were made against climate change aren't forgotten. I have to hold them to it, make things change. But you could come to me. To Hastings. Remember our place? Where we promised on the beach? I'll go there at the summer solstice every year. You can find me there.' Tears spill down her face. 'I have to go now – I just have to.'

Then she's in my arms, trembling and holding on like she'll never let go.

But she does.

'Goodbye, Denzi.'

95

Tabby

'Aslan? Take me to Jago.'

Now that Aslan is in charge, I'm free to go to the dreaming. To try to cherish some of the dead the way I saved Con. It scares me to think of so many more voices inside me at once. But they're my sisters: I have to try.

But when I close my eyes and reach for them inside, it's too late. Their circles aren't just dim, like Con's was after he died, they're gone. I'm caught in grief. The loss of so many, those I loved and knew intimately – I can't begin to understand how I'll ever be able to live and breathe without pain again.

I focus: on here, now. The sea and the kin. I have to go to Jago; I have to know if he is lost to me like so many others.

Aslan has first one kin and then, when that one tires, another take us speeding through the sea to get to Cornwall as soon as we can.

It's late morning when the kin take their leave near the shore, and I swim in until my feet can finally touch rocks and sand underneath. I'm walking the last steps to the beach, gathering energy, ready to run to Jago's house. But when I step out of the sea, he's there.

'Tabby?'

Now we both run – to each other. He holds me close a moment, but then I push him away to arm's length to study him.

It's been over three days since I last saw him; Isha said her parents were ill two and a half days after she went to them.

'Are you well?' I say, finally. 'No breathing problems or anything?'

'Do you mean, like Denzi's dad?' he says, hesitates. 'And yours . . . do you know?'

I nod. Tears in my eyes now. 'We carried something to them that made them sick – something The Circle made. We didn't know – they used us. I was so afraid you'd get ill too.'

'Nothing wrong with me. Bit tired from camping out at the beach all hours, waiting to see if you'd come back. And you did.'

There are tears in his eyes now too. He's well, so if the timing is what Isha said, maybe he hasn't caught it. But what if destroying Phina's internet cable didn't stop activation of the protovirus?

I was so focused on getting here, getting to Jago, that everything else was held away. Now it's rushing back: the pain of what happened to my sisters, the terror of what may still come. And I'm shaking, overcome, my whole body wracked with sobs that I can't control.

Jago just holds me until finally I can't cry any more.

He pulls me down to sit next to him on the beach and takes my hand. 'Tell me what you can,' he says.

This time I don't hold anything back. I tell him how and why the Chosen were created, and what we are; how we destroyed Undersea. How the rest of my sisters died. About the protovirus and not knowing if what we did stopped it from being activated. And how – and why – I survived; Denzi and the rest of the Chosen too. That they went off to live in the sea.

'But you came back.'

'I couldn't hide away. I had to know if you were OK. If we stopped the activation of the protovirus. If we didn't, there's maybe only a few days before everyone starts to die. And if we did stop it, this is only the beginning of the fight to save sun, sea, earth and sky. I have to be part of it.'

He nods, eyes on mine, serious. 'You're amazing, you know that?'

'An amazing freak, you mean.'

He shakes his head. 'I'll tell you what you are – my friend. And we'll get through this, together.'

'What now?' I say. 'I mean, do we tell people – authorities, at least – what might be coming?'

'Have I got this straight? If the signal didn't go out, this protovirus thing is harmless and will degrade, disappear. If the signal wasn't stopped it will already have gone out, and there's nothing that can be done to stop it.'

'That's right.'

'So, if we tell everyone, all they'll do is freak out and panic, maybe for nothing.'

'Yeah. When you put it that way, I guess we say nothing. We wait.'

I'm in Cornwall at Jago's for almost a week before I let myself believe. We stopped it, didn't we? What Denzi had said could be Armageddon: the end of the world. People are living and breathing, talking and arguing like they always have done, good and bad. And there is a story in the news that one of the main cornerstones of smart-phone operating systems failed when a needed, scheduled update never came.

I'm still scared that somehow the update will come, activate the protovirus. Yet now I greet every day with hope, not despair, as another day that it hasn't happened; every day means it is less likely to do so.

And we're beginning to look ahead, getting ready for the next steps in the climate war. We're going to London to meet up with Hayden and some other activists – Isha, too – to see what we can do to help.

Yet the agony of losing my sisters will never leave me.

All those years ago, when Cassandra saw the future, she saw humans destroying the planet and then the future voices silenced. Everyone thought this meant everyone and everything died.

All of Phina's plans were an attempt to change the future and stop this from happening. No matter how twisted her methods, there is a logic to what she wanted to do.

But somewhere along the way, Cassandra realised that just because our descendants disappeared, it didn't have to follow that all of humanity was gone too: our future voices are only *our* descendants after all.

Yet I'm not convinced it had to happen this way. Cassandra was blind to other possibilities because she saw things a certain way. She was bound to one possible future, and that binding is what made it inevitable. Cate and the entire Circle got caught up with it, just like I did.

Cate sacrificed her life to help me. Didn't she? I know who Cate was inside, that the core of her wasn't there when her body was stabbed and died. But that isn't how it *feels* in my gut. Cassandra said Cate had forgiven her – she might have been telling the truth. If Cate did, was it right for me to still hold this anger against her?

Maybe not. But I wanted someone else to blame for Cate's death – someone other than Cate, or me. Jago says I can't take the blame for what somebody else chooses to do, and logically I get what he means. But it's hard not to feel like it's all my fault, or Cate's, and I don't know which is worse.

Cassandra – for all her years as a seer – didn't seem to understand that time is in flux: always. Backwards and forwards. The only certain point in time is the one I'm living right *now* – this exact second. Sharing memories with my ancestors has shown me that the past will always be coloured by who remembers it. And the future depends on every step taken by me, by you, and everyone else – human, animal, bird, fish, insect, plant – towards it.

But it is best not to look so far ahead that *now* is forgotten.

Aslan was right. It is always better to chase the fish.

Epilogue

Hastings, Summer Solstice

Five Years Later

Tabby

I stand in the sea.

The tide is coming in. It's gone from only just reaching my feet and falling back, to finding my knees at the highpoint of the waves. Cool water teases, tempts, but there is something I have to do before giving in to its call.

The sun will set soon. I can't wait much longer. Denzi isn't coming, is he? My fifth year coming here alone, and my last. It is time to say goodbye.

I breathe in, out, in, out, and ready myself for the promise . . .

The kin approach, Aslan says.

I scan the sea. They breach the water as one: a pod of dolphins and – there he is, Denzi. Holding on for a ride. And I catch a glimpse of another behind him – a flash of long hair. Someone comes with him?

When the dolphins breach again, their passengers are gone.

I see ripples in the water getting closer. A splash kick. They surface together, waist deep.

Denzi. Ariel. I know them both so well with all we went through together, but they have changed – in both subtle and not so subtle ways. More muscled, stockier – to keep warm in the sea? Denzi's hair is long and wild, Ariel's even more so. Clothing must be optional on a warm night like this.

And the biggest change of all: Ariel holds a small child.

I smile. Happy, relieved, that they're OK, that they came. 'Hi. It's good to see you. And who is this?'

My words seem to startle them. They are wary, like they might disappear back into the sea.

They remember but don't remember. It is hard to return.

'Denzi? Ariel? You remember me, don't you? I'm Tabby.' I say the words slowly.

After a moment, Denzi nods. Licks his lips. 'Yes. Tabby,' he says and his voice is odd, like an instrument he used to play and isn't sure of now.

'Is that your son? He's beautiful.'

They both smile now and Ariel looks at her child, then to Denzi, and the look is so tender, so real. At least part of Phina's plan has worked: a new generation can arise, one that can live in the sea. Though with Undersea destroyed – and all their supplies for IVF – the only male of the Chosen who has survived is Denzi. I'm guessing with that limitation, repopulating the world can't happen. Anyhow, with the future voices silenced, this must mean that this child or any others they may have cannot go on to be part of The Circle.

Their calf is kin. He does not understand your words.

There is a pause, as if some unheard conversation is taking place between Denzi and Ariel. Then they walk towards me in the water, come up to me. Shyly show me their son who smiles a gap-toothed grin and wriggles until Ariel puts him down and he splashes on the shore.

I tell them everything. The clear skies they can see. Geoengineering had to be phased out, not stopped all at once or the rebound effects would have caused too much harm, but the last of it is gone from the skies now. And I've been working with Jago, Isha and Hayden, and Apple too, now back home in the States, along with others around the world – making sure no one forgets our governments' promises. Hayden's mum and Bishan's dad, both lawyers, have joined forces to pursue international claims and compensation from the biggest companies and governments on behalf of children everywhere; I've helped finance that. I didn't want to take the money I inherited from Ali, knowing it came from an industry I hate. But Jago made me see that I could take it and use it where it was needed.

Overall, there have been hard-fought gains around the world. Not quite carbon neutral as a planet, but getting there.

And there is reason to hope: that humans have finally got it, finally understand, that if you destroy your home you'll have nowhere to live, nothing to eat. No place to raise your children.

'Are you all right? Alone,' Denzi says. He worries about me still. 'Come with us.'

Ariel tentatively takes my hand. Gives it a tug. 'We are kin,' she says – the first words she's spoken.

I shake my head. 'My place is here for now.'

We promise together as the sun sets. It's glorious but doesn't burn across the sky – a beautiful and totally normal sunset.

The night passes like a dream: swimming, together. With my kin: Denzi, Ariel. The dolphins too, and Aslan inside.

And then we say goodbye.

I'm sitting on the beach on my own when Jago comes with the sunrise, like I asked him to.

He sits next to me.

'They came this time.'

'They?'

'Denzi and Ariel. They have a son.'

'Are you OK?'

'Yes. Completely. They are so happy together: it must be right.' I hesitate. 'They asked me to go with them.'

'And you stayed.'

I nod. 'We said goodbye. I don't think I'll see them again.'

My tears come now and Jago's arms are around me. He gives me a kiss that is perfect, just like how we are together. It took a long while for me to work it out. To stop missing Denzi and to see Jago, my friend, for what he was to me, what he could be. We may be different, but we're two pieces of a puzzle that only fit together.

He kisses me again and the world disappears. The voices too. My ancestors know to keep quiet now unless I need them.

'It's time to go,' I say.

We get up, brush off sand. I look back, and the longing is still there inside me.

The sea calls me; it always will. One day I could walk into the waves and disappear. Just knowing this is somehow enough.

Denzi and the Chosen are out there, somewhere. Living as they want. Changing more and more. Having children that maybe, one day, will choose to walk from the sea and back to the land. What will they find?

That is up to us. All of us.

photo by Debra Hurford Brown

TERI TERRY

is the bestselling author of the *Slated* trilogy and
prequel, *Fated*, the *Dark Matter* trilogy, and of
Mind Games, *Dangerous Games* and *Book of Lies*.
Her most recent work is *Black Night Falling*, which
is the last title in *The Circle* trilogy. Her books have
been translated into seventeen languages and
won prizes at home and abroad.

Teri hates broccoli, loves all animals — especially
her dog, Scooby — and has finally worked out
what she wants to do when she grows up.

'Teri Terry is a master of the thriller'
Scotsman

THE *DARK MATTER* TRILOGY

AVAILABLE IN PAPERBACK, EBOOK AND AUDIO